I0586164

The LOST STORIES *of*

LUCY MEREDITH CARTER

LINDA RUTH BROOKS

GUM TREE
press

Copyright © Linda Brooks 2024

The right of Linda Ruth Brooks to be identified as the author of this Work has been asserted by her in accordance with the Copyright, Designs and Patents Act 1988.

ALL RIGHTS RESERVED. No part of this publication may be reproduced, stored in a retrieval system or transmitted in any form by any means, electronic, mechanical, photocopying, recording or otherwise, without the prior consent of the author.

A catalogue record for this

 book is available from the National Library of Australia

NATIONAL
LIBRARY OF AUSTRALIA   Fiction/social issues/contemporary romance

Cover, text design, typesetting & interior design by *Linda Ruth Brooks*
Photo artwork: *Linda Ruth Brooks*

ISBN: 978-0-6455650-3-4

Fiction/juvenile/military history/family

The Lost Stories of Lucy Meredith Carter is a work of fiction. This book, and others by Linda Ruth Brooks, can be purchased through online bookstores, retail outlets.

What if you slept ...

What if you slept
And what if
In your sleep
You dreamed
And what if
In your dream
You went to heaven
And there plucked a strange and beautiful flower
And what if
When you awoke
You had that flower in your hand
Ah, what then?

Samuel Taylor Coleridge

AUTHOr

Linda Brooks lives in Adelaide. She writes nonfiction, poetry, fiction and short stories. She has published and illustrated children's books. She completed a BA Hons in Creative Writing from Southern Cross University (2019). She gained a publisher for her childhood memoir *A Curious & Inelegant Childhood*. She has written a nonfiction book on living with Asperger's Syndrome (autism spectrum) *I'm not broken, I'm just different* and the children's book *Callan the Chameleon* with contributions from Professor Tony Attwood.

Published in anthologies: *Coastlines 5, 6, 7 & 8* by Southern Cross University; *Wood, Bricks & Stone*, Catchfire Press; *Grieve*, Newcastle Writers Centre; *Third Wednesday Poets*; *Seeking the Sun*, Central Coast Poets; *Times Past* Stringybark Press and *Longing for Solitude*. Awards: Rebecca Coyle Scholarship for Hons; first prize for The Legacy University Level Creative Writing Award; first prize in the Gabe Reynaud Creative Writing Award and the Mater Misericordiae Grieve Writing Award.

A registered nurse and advocate for disability in a previous life, Linda has a rich background in listening to the stories of others, never shying away from the darker, gritty tales. And yet, humour is never far away. Linda enjoys hearing from her readers (even if they've found typos): lindaruthbrooks@bigpond.com

AUTHOR TITLES

Nonfiction:
I'm not broken, I'm just different
(on Asperger's with Professor Tony Attwood)
A Curious and Inelegant Childhood

Adult fiction:
Behind Whispering Hands
The Unprize
A broken hallelujah
Scarlett doesn't live here anymore
Under the Bracken Fern

Children's books:
A Tabby Never Forgets
Callan the Chameleon (Asperger's Syndrome)
Dusty Bunny's Very Important Job
Izzy & Pudding the Cat
I want a monkey!
Madam Iris Bigglesworth
The Banyula Tales - 6 stories
Who Stole Christmas?

Publisher of the anthologies:
We are Australian'
The Great Australian Shed
Waltzing Matilda

Contents

PROLOGUE

This story was inspired by a man I never met. Harry Daniels. My uncle. The soldier husband of my aunt, Hazel Stockdale. My interest in the life of Harry Daniels was triggered by the close relationship I had with another uncle, Gordon William Stockdale, my mother's brother, who served with Harry, and who shared my birthday and my life journey after the Second World War. Uncle Gordon was a Lance Corporal in the 4th Field Ambulance (stretcher bearers) in Papua New Guinea.

Some time before he died, Uncle Gordon entrusted me with his war medals as well as those of Uncle Harry.

Harry Daniels & Hazel Anne Stockdale

Harry Daniels was a Private in the 2/17th Battalion, AIF. He was killed in the fiercest day of fighting in 1943 at Finschhafen in PNG. He had married my aunt, Hazel in April of 1943. She was a registered nurse—elegant and quick-witted. I nursed Aunt Hazel in the last two years of her life in the Charles Harrison Memorial Home. I grew up knowing very little about Uncle Harry. He was the silent tear in my aunt's eyes, remembered as the love of her life.

Apart from those medals, Harry Daniels had all but disappeared. It took me a long time to trace his war records and found nothing while searching family tree records. I held his medals and yet, what had he left behind? I grieved for all the things he never had—a life with his new wife, children, a modest home, a war loan.

When I acquired Harry's war records I was thrilled to make a rare find; a photograph of a man full of life and fun. He was a man without a story, so I gave him one, here. I followed his trail by reading the book, *What We Have, We Hold*, which narrates the army life and battles of the 2/17 AIF Battalion.

Unlike Harry, Uncle Gordon came home from the war. He shared some of his stories with family. He had been at his sister, Hazel's wedding to Harry and was with Harry when he died in New Guinea, an event that haunted him.

Gordon William Stockdale in his later years with wife Alice

Stretcher bearers in PNG

The LOST STORIES of

LUCY MEREDITH CARTER

LINDA RUTH BROOKS

GUM TREE press

A Dark, Forbidding Day

The Ennis family home, Henry Street, Quirindi, 1951

THERE was a crowd of people at 84 Henry Street, Quirindi, a two-storey Old Colonial, once the grandest domicile in the street, but more lately a boarding house, presided over by the widowed Ethel Ennis, a stout woman with firm jaw and fine white hair, restrained with meticulous care in a bun at the back of her head.

Negligent clouds crept across the sun, then continued on their way in a sullen sky. Light filtered through cast-iron lacework, mottling the front verandah of the old house in a parade of shifting shadows that flashed and leapt like dark, slender ghosts.

Heavy velvet drapes, pushed aside partway, allowed pale autumn sunlight but faint presence in the front room—a former reception area, filled with guests, dark-clad and solemn, whose stilted conversation, constant checking of timepieces, and glances at the front door suggested a desire to be elsewhere. An obligation to their hostess, implied by a table laden with food held them captive as they murmured softly phrased condolences, touching each other with light fingers of grief.

Huddled in a dim corner sat a small girl, the granddaughter of Ethel, Lucy, whose copper-red hair provided the only colour in the dull room. She tugged at a dark, oversized dress that hung to her ankles, chafing at the heavy fabric. The dress, borrowed from a distant cousin, never met, had been handed to her that morning

1

by her bustling grandmother, Ethel, who reigned with stoic dignity over a wake for her daughter, Sylvia, the child's mother. Ethel's eldest daughter, Fliss, disabled and mute after a stroke, sat in a dark corner of an adjoining room, tapping a foot on the floor.

Lucy stared at a faded Persian rug, shrinking from her grandmother's pleas to eat or drink. She looked pale and tired in the heavy black dress, her large green eyes dull with sadness and confusion. She moved through the adults, slipping between them, looking for solace. Her father struggled to concentrate on the words of condolence from the mourners as his eyes followed the child. At times he broke free to move towards her, patting her head or resting a hand on her shoulder. Visitors petted and stroked the child's face, offering the usual grownup platitudes, those empty pious words that hold so little comfort for a grieving child.

When large tears fell down her cheeks Lucy retreated to a corner of the room, afraid of attracting more solicitude, more pity. Then, quickly and quietly she ran out the back door and down the thick timber steps to the yard. Throwing herself on a hay bale beside the hut, she lay with her arms covering her face and sobbed with jerking gulps.

A large white hen wandered nearby, stopped and stared, then hopped onto the bale. Neck tilted, one sharp black eye fixed on the girl, it pranced closer. Lucy sat up and took the bird onto her lap, soothing and petting it. Her tearful sobs became hiccups. The chook's head bobbed happily as Lucy stroked its feathers. Curving the hen into her arms Lucy drifted off to sleep. Unfazed by Lucy's twitching dreams, the hen tucked its head under a wing.

A SOLDIER sat on the bottom rung of thick timber steps overlooking the back yard, whittling a stick he found lying around. His digger's hat was pushed back revealing tamed and slicked hair.

When the child woke, she rubbed swollen, sleepy eyes, then, still cradling the hen she wandered over to the soldier.

'Hello,' she said. 'You must be a new boarder.'

'Hello, little one. I'm Harry.' The soldier paused to flick wood shavings from his knee.

'I'm Lucy. Can I call you Uncle Harry?'

She shifted the hen higher in her arms. 'Nanna says it's polite to call grownups that.'

'Sure. That'll be just fine.'

'This is my Nanna's boarding house.' The child waved an outstretched arm, as if to include the known universe, then kissed the tolerant bird on the head. 'Nanna's a bit bossy, but I 'spec you're used to that, being in the army and all.'

'I'm sure I'll manage, child.'

'I'm six years old.' Lucy held up six fingers, a feat made difficult by the wriggling hen under her arm. 'This is my chook, *she's magic.*'

Lucy gnawed her bottom lip with tiny white teeth. 'I'll have to give her a name. Hmm. Do you know any good names, Uncle Harry? I bet you've read a bunch of books. Old people usually have.'

The hen stared at the digger as if she too was waiting.

'What about Esmeralda?' Harry said.

'Ooh, I like that. It's a lovely name. Where's it from?'

'A very old book—*The Hunchback of Notre Dame* ... erm, Esmeralda was a gypsy who lived in Paris a long time ago. She rescued a poor misshapen man.'

A frown wrinkled Lucy's forehead. 'What's misshapen?'

'Well. Er ... crippled, sort of.'

'Oh. My aunt, Fliss is sort of crippled.'

Harry flinched.

3

THERE was a rumble of noise from the house. Lucy glanced up. 'There's lots of people here today. My Mum died. That's why they're here,' she said, with that blunt manner of a child who hasn't yet learned the tight rules of correct conversation.

'I'm sorry, pet. I lost my father when I was about your age.'

'Lucy!' Her father stood at the top of the stairs, eyes taut with worry.

Tucking the hen under her chin Lucy ran lightly up the wooden stairs and slipped her hand into her father's. 'I'm here, Dad.'

She lifted the hen with pleading eyes. 'This is my new pet chook, Dad. Her name's Esmeralda and she's magic. She's helping me to be brave.' The bird clucked with indignation at the movement.

George's answer was a soft low murmur as he nodded.

Lucy listened with a tired smile then rested a cheek on his hand, looking up at him with such tender admiration that Harry's heart tripped.

It was an image that reminded him of his own mother's fear in those fatherless days in London during the Great War.

ZEPPELINS

Ennis Family Home, Henry Street, Quirindi, 1955

THE VEGETABLE truck lurches to a stop on the kerb outside 84 Henry Street, Quirindi. The driver parps the horn three times, leaps out and throws the canvas flaps back. Inside the house, Ethel is listening to ABC radio and shouts 'Bravo!' at the news that mass immunisation for polio will begin. Not in time for her sister Bea's dragging leg but good news for others nonetheless.

Ethel's granddaughter, nine-year-old Lucy, sits on the front verandah, toes pressed together, pink ballet shoes tapping an impatient rhythm. When her grandmother fails to respond to the lure of the vegetable truck, she calls through the open kitchen window. 'Nanna! It's Mr Evans. Come get strawberries!'

The vegetable truck moves on. Lucy sighs and wriggles back in the seat. There's no use nagging Nanna Ennis for anything.

Clouds puff across the sky. Spring rain falls in soft warm splatters, trembling on amber-spiked florets of the grevilleas that edge the house.

Lucy shivers, causing a braid of copper-red hair to loosen its spiralled confinement. 'Bother,' she says, smoothing the tangle, 'Dad took ages platting my hair.'

An open magazine flutters in the breeze, its pages displaying a range of birthday cakes.

A large white hen is perched on the child's lap, as composed as any queen on a throne. 'I'll be ten-years-old soon, Esmeralda.' Lucy whispers, as if birthdays are secrets, kept only by regal white hens with magic powers, or if speaking aloud about birthdays will somehow lead to their disappearance.

Nine-year-old Lucy Meredith Carter is acquainted with acts of disappearance. Leaving her seat, Lucy wanders to the back yard, hoping to find Harry, who is always there and ready for a chat.

She drags her feet on the dusty path to Harry's hut.

'Hey, little Lucy. What's with the frowny face?'

Lucy presses a hand to her forehead.

'Grownups don't tell kids anything.' She quickly flicks the pages of her notebook demonstrating the dearth of suitable information.

'Do you remember being a kid, Uncle Harry?'

'I do. We lived in London when big, silver Zeppelins flew over dropping bombs.'

Lucy crosses her legs, plops to the ground and begs to be told the story. Harry flicks open a slatted, foldup chair and sits down.

Ellington Street, London 1916

THE AIR-RAID siren sounded late at night.

'I need you to be brave, Harry,' Mum said.

Words were coming out of Mum's mouth but she wasn't moving. When the air-raid siren had first gone off, she'd run into her bedroom and put a thick coat over her nightie, then dashed back into the living room, but she seemed stuck there, as if her head had run out of thoughts.

She stared at the red coals in the fireplace as though she was waiting for them to do something. When she threw open the front door there was smoke everywhere. Searchlights sliced up the sky until they caught on a Zepp, a terrific sight for a boy to see, all silvery-grey and shiny. For a minute I forgot it was there to drop bombs.

Next door, Mr Penshurst ran out his door.

'Too late for the shelter, Missus,' he yelled at Mum. 'You'd better come to ours. We've got a cellar.'

Mrs Penshurst carried a baby and was dragging their youngest boy, who stared upwards— 'Mummy, there's a big grey whale in the sky. Look!'

I thought cellars were rooms for vegetables, salted meat and bottled fruit. I didn't know the neighbours even had one, much less used it as a shelter during air raids. The butcher had a big family. How would we all fit?

Mum didn't move. Maybe she wasn't sure about the place either. Then she jerked forward, grabbed my hand and followed him.

Mr Penshurst ushered us inside. 'The Huns won't be happy till they've flattened every bloomin' building,' he said.

The room wasn't as small as I thought.

It had rough wooden benches, just wide enough to sit on. There were high shelves with boxes and grey blankets. There was a soot-blackened lantern, a pile of newspapers and a wooden orange crate with crayons, paper, ink and stamps. The room smelled of damp wool and kerosene. I gagged.

As he shut the door I panicked at the sudden darkness, gripping my mother's hand. A hissing match dispelled the thick blackness as the man lit a candle and set it on a small table. His wife soothed the whimpering baby and chided the small boy who'd been staring at the Zeppelin in the street.

Billy Penshurst came and sat beside me. We were in the same class at school. He took out a bag of marbles. I was itching to see them. He owed me a tiger's eye from our last game.

The fat candle looked like an old tree trunk, with slow yellow vines snaking down. Hot wax pooled on the table, wet and sluggish, turning white at the edges. Our candles at home sat in clear glass lanterns with shiny brass bases.

Mr Penshurst leaned over to Mum. 'Where's y'girl, Missus?' His voice was loud and strange in the small room.

Mum didn't answer so I tugged on her sleeve.

'School.' Mum pulled me closer.

'Husband overseas? In the infantry?'

Mum gripped her purse. 'Killed. Canada.'

'Canada?' Red shadows from the blinking candle wobbled across his face. The hair on his ears seemed on fire.

'Are the bloody Huns bombing the hell out of Canada too?' Billy asked, earning a jab in the ribs from an older sister.

Mum let out a long slow sigh, like the air on my bike when I had a puncture.

'He … left years ago. Went to find gold. Joined his brother in Canada. Enlisted. Killed on the continent somewhere.'

The butcher shook his head. His neck wobbled like white pudding.

'There'll never be an end to it,' Mum said, 'never.'

She sounded odd. I tapped her arm. She'd never talked about our father. She was using her official voice, like when she taught girls how to sew in our sunroom so they could get jobs in the workroom at Knightsbridge, making clothes for the Red Cross.

She was a dressmaker. 'It's my bit for the war effort,' Mum had said, when I'd intruded into the sunroom begging for biscuits and milk. The sewing machines made a dreadful din. I had to yell to be heard. I hated that there were giggling girls coming and going with their perfume and cigarettes, dropping wet umbrellas in the hall.

'Off you go, Harry.' Mum flicked my ear.

8

Clarissa pinched me. 'Mum's getting paid milk money for teaching them. If you didn't want to have dry porridge you'd better lay off grizzling.'

Clarissa was ten years older than me. She hated sewing. Mum had been at her for years, but she wouldn't touch the machines. Mum worried about her. 'If you don't persevere and learn to sew, Clarissa, you'll be sent to the munitions factory to make bombs all hours of the day and night as soon as you've finished school. God-only-knows how awful that will be.'

I said it sounded like a marvellous place and begged to be taken there one day. Clarissa slapped the back of my head and told me not to be a complete idiot. Mum had gone really still. 'You don't know what you're talking about, Harry.'

ON THE HARD bench of Mr Penshurst's cellar Mum's hand squeezed mine so tight I tried to pull away. She stared hard at the butcher, sucked in a deep breath and said, 'It's not safe anywhere anymore. Our children—what are we to do with our children? How do we keep our them safe do you think?'

'Can't,' said the man. 'Not possible. Can't leave the little blighters underground all the time.' He laughed, a low rumble that filled the room. 'We've just got to get on with life, Missus. There's no safe place. Not in this part o' the world.' He took the sleeping baby from his wife's arms, holding it the way he cradled Christmas hams in the butcher shop. 'Not unless you get on a ship to the North Pole.' He snorted. 'Or Australia.'

Mum's voice rose. 'Australia? Do you think we could, Mr Penshurst? Get on a ship to Australia?'

The butcher's mouth fell open. He rubbed a large square hand over his forehead. 'Incredible.'

That was a new word for me.

THE NEXT DAY, Mum was a volunteer at the train station, pinning names on children going to the country to escape the bombings, away from the city, and family. When she came home, she asked for a cup of tea and said, 'I can't take any more.'

THREE MONTHS later we left for Sydney.

I said my new word to everyone I met on the ship. 'We're going to Australia. Isn't that incredible!'

When we docked Mum waved a lace handkerchief frantically so her friend Miriam could see us.

'I knew her in my salad days,' Mum said.

A CHAIR SCRAPES, jolting Harry.

'That's a great story, Uncle Harry. Did you ever get your special marble back?' Lucy clambers to her feet.

'Can't rightly say I remember.' Harry frowned.

'What did y'mum couldn't take any more of?'

'War.'

LOST STORIES

Lucy Meredith Carter, *Book Of Known Facts*, Quirindi, 1955

I don't have being-born stories or stuff like other kids.

Other kids have interesting stuff to bring to Show and Tell, like christening dresses and silver rattles.

Other kids have exciting stories about being born, like my best friend Jenny who was born in a barn.

I wish I had a story like that, instead of being tied to a war that was over before I began.

A war people talk about winning, as if it was a game of rounders, or tennis. A game that boys at school play in recess and lunchtime, whenever they can.

MY NAME IS Lucy Meredith Carter, but everyone calls me Lucy. I was born on the day the war ended, the 15th of August 1945. It was the day people danced in the streets of Sydney. It was a Wednesday, at half past nine in the morning. Nanna Ennis, Ethel tells me over and over that I interrupted the Prime Minister's speech on the radio about Japan's surrender. She said no one heard me cry because everyone in the whole hospital was making a dreadful racket.

My father, George Carter, was born at Black Mountain, in bushranger country. He has three sisters. Nanna says, 'You can tell your father grew up with a houseful of women.'

11

Dad didn't go off to war, but men in Nanna's family went and died or had wounds from the fighting. Nanna lost a husband from the first war and a son in the second. Mum used to say that was why the war was stuck in Nanna's head because she talks about the war as if it is tacked on to everything that ever happened. When we get a tray of peaches Nanna says, 'We couldn't get that many in the war'. Worst of all, Nanna measures me by the war. If anyone asks about me. Nanna says, 'Lucy was born the day the war ended', making me stuck to a date in history, not a normal birthday. I ask her if she lost my stories, but she growls and says, 'don't be silly, Lucy.'

Nanna doesn't understand about lost stories.

Nanna Ennis' house is on Henry Street, the same street as our cottage. Her house is huge with bedrooms upstairs and downstairs and verandahs all around. Ennises have lived on Henry Street for generations. Nanna grew up in that house with her sisters and brothers. Henry Street is a long street that begins and ends near a bend in Quirindi Creek as it curves around the town. Nanna's end of Henry Street had bad floods in 1949. I was only four then, but I remember people sandbagging near the creek to save their houses.

Nanna takes in boarders, but she doesn't like anyone calling her house a boarding house. The boarders come and go. Some don't stay long. She usually has two or three. There are two girls sharing the upstairs bedroom. They work at the local factory on a food production line so I call them "the factory girls". They give me sweets sometimes. and Uncle Harry always has lots of time to chat and tell stories. There's a young bloke in a small room that used to be a storeroom near the side garden where the wisteria grows. He plays the ukulele and studies something complicated at the local tech. 'He never forgets to turn up when there's food about,' Nanna says. I call him Uncle Garnett even though he's not a relative. Uncle Garnett taught me to whistle. But my favourite boarder is Uncle Harry. He always has time for a kid with too many questions and a bad habit of writing stuff down when people are talking.

Along with looking after boarders Nanna takes in ironing. Townspeople come and drop off baskets of crumpled clean clothes for her to turn into what she calls 'crease-free perfection'. She hangs them on a big rack in the guest room, with the hook part pointing in. She ties the hangers with white tape. Then she pins a label with the person's name in careful cursive and the amount they owe for her hard work.

Dad made a clothes rail for Nanna, low enough for her to reach. Nanna makes lists of things she wants Dad to fix. Dad does lots for Nanna but she is picky about nearly everything he does, especially about looking after me since Mum died. Nanna When I tell her off about that she says, 'I wasn't raised to flummery up to people.'

WHEN my mum died I cried so much it was hard to breathe. Before Mum died she went away a lot. I don't know where she went. No one wants to talk about that. If I ask questions, Nanna rambles about "the can't be said", and "the shouldn't be said".

Someday I'll get things figured out. So many people have lost their stories. I imagine them drifting through the air like cloud words where a sad story might bump into a celebration story and say, 'I do beg your pardon, I'm not quite myself at the moment.'

The war must have made a lot of lost stories. The air in some places must be crowded with them. I write things in my notebook. If I keep track of facts they might fit into my story. My special book used to belong to Mum. It's covered with silk-embroidered peacocks. It had wildflowers inside, pressed and dried, their petals as dainty as insect wings.

Dad carefully brushed the flowers into a shoe box for safekeeping. Inside the cover, under Mum's name, I wrote: *Lucy Meredith Carter—Book Of Known Facts.*

APART from Dad, my aunt Fliss is my favourite grownup. She lives in a convalescent home called Montview.

Fliss had a thing called a stroke and lost all her words. She didn't get any of them back, not a single one. She can make sounds, like *tsk, tsk,* and hum along to music. She has word cards, but she can't make a proper sentence. She just jumbles them up, then she might laugh, or cry. You never know which. Her right leg is stumbly and slow. Her right hand is twisted and curved. She can't do buttons up and she can't write stuff down anymore.

All of Fliss' stories are lost.

Born on the Same Day

Montview Lodge, George Street, Quirindi, 1955

FLISS sits in a wrought-iron chair on the stone-paved courtyard of Montview Hostel & Convalescent Home more commonly known by the locals as Montview Lodge, or just Montview. Curled at her feet, Ramius, the resident cat, sleeps, whiskery eyebrows twitching as he dreams.

Not yet thirty-five, Fliss isn't the youngest patient at Montview. Two wounded diggers, amputees, sprawl on dull grey blankets near the vegetable patch, coaching the Barashev gardener in the fine art of Australian swear words, gravely offending an ancient school headmistress on her creaking daily meander who calls to them to cut it out!

Fliss envies them all, their nonchalant ease to speak freely.

MONTVIEW was once a thriving farm with a rambling farmhouse but rooms are now filled with the broken, the despairing, the elderly and infirm. The place is owned by the Barashev family, Russian Jews, forced to escape tyranny, homeland and Europe before the war.

The sadness of their past lives has filtered down, becoming weaker as it reaches the younger children who were born in Australia.

The Barashevs left their country with one old, tired horse, a rattling wagon piled high with what they could take, and each other.

Fliss knows this—she understands their words even though she can't produce any of her own. Fliss had so much to tell, so much to keep secret, so much she wanted to say. So much that needed the right words. Always looking for the right time.

Until it was too late; with all the words locked within.

She sighs—If I had words, where would I begin?

AS FOR LUCY, if she had the whole history of the world, she would still want to know more. And there's no subject for which she has greater curiosity than the past, and her family.

'Guess what Fliss!' Lucy flops into a chair beside Fliss, flicks her book open and waits… Fliss throws her hands up with the desired measure of anticipation.

'Our new teacher has the same birthday as you and Dad. Fancy that, three people I know with exactly the same birthday.'

She snaps the book shut. 'Imagine, Fliss. It would be so much better to share a birthday with a person you know than … than the date some crummy old war ended.'

A wintry night, Quirindi and Black Mountain, 1916

IN THE YEAR of Our Lord, 1916 AD, in spite of the Great War raging all over Europe, or, perhaps because of it, two babies were born on the same stormy winter's night, in the state of New South Wales, Diocese of Quirindi. Both babes were born to humble, working class parents.

Flooded roads, hail and killing winds prevented the local doctor from leaving his abode to attend either birth. In a weathered cottage on Black Mountain, Jim Carter, gifted toolmaker and indifferent farmer, fretted over his pregnant wife, a sweet natured girl, whose health had long worried the family.

Only the calm presence of his wife's mother, a seasoned midwife, who had travelled from distant parts for her daughter's confinement, allayed Jim Carter's fears.

A lusty cry announced the arrival of the couple's third child, a son. Permitted entrance to the bedroom, the babe's two older sisters were introduced to George Charles Carter.

'He's a wee skinny monkey,' remarked the babe's maternal grandmother, a précis not easily forgiven by her daughter, but blithely overlooked by the relieved father.

'He'll thrive.' Jim was grateful on that stormy night for his mother-in-law's midwifery, along with the unexpected favour of the gods for a delivery free of complication.

THE SAME could not be said of Ethel Ennis, at Henry Street in the centre of town. After a protracted labour, Ethel gave birth to her firstborn, a girl, with only her devoted sister, Bea, in attendance.

Ethel's husband, Bill Ennis had enlisted as soon as The Great War began, cheered on by his drinking mates at the Imperial Hotel on Henry Street, a short stumble from home.

Ethel waved a limp arm in the direction of the infant, and dictated the babe's name, Felicity Anne Ennis, Ethel's mother's name, an appellation scorned by the absent father on his departure to foreign lands and glorious adventure.

Swaddling the infant, Bea, unable to bear children of her own, remarked, 'What a shame poor old Bill missed the arrival of his firstborn. How he must be suffering, in those foul trenches.'

Ethel sighed, accepted the babe, and wondered if in fact, poor old Bill was in the trenches, or at a bordello, or perhaps a bar, as was his wont before the damn war.

The babe didn't cry, but began immediately to make herself

appealing, to earn her mother's love, with soft sounds and pink, seeking lips.

DESPITE worries about the future for their children, neither family wonders if their offspring will meet. Have their lives intertwined. And when they do meet it's on an ordinary day, bitter with winter's chill.

The milk run, Quirindi, 1934

SITTING on the back of the milk cart, George Carter shivered in the early morning chill. At 5am, the sun was beginning to peep over the horizon. Mr O'Neill, the local milkman, slowed the horse with caressing hands. George leapt out and fetched a billy from the doorstep at Montview. Ladling milk into the pail, he delivered it to the door.

Mrs Barashev was waiting inside the kitchen door. 'I need an extra pail today, young George Carter,' she said with the crisp roll of a Russian accent. She was usually the only one up at this hour, dressed and groomed, waiting for the milk to be delivered. George smiled as he thought of the women who twitched curtains and only emerged with hair curlers and faded dressing gowns to collect their milk when the cart was gone.

'Thank you, young George.' The woman reached in an apron pocket for the change, counting it out carefully in Russian. Smoke curled out the door. Mrs Barashev had the stove ready to separate the cream. There was a spicy aroma of vegetables and beef wafting out the door. George's stomach rumbled.

A small dark-eyed girl peeked around Mrs Barashev's long skirt.

'Wait a minute, young George.' The woman returned to the

warmth of the kitchen.

George blew on his hands. The little girl giggled and blew on her hands. 'I'm Katya.'

Mrs Barashev appeared at the door. 'Here you are George, have some *pryaniki*.' She handed him a paper bag of honeyed biscuits. 'Share them, won't you.'

'Thanks Mrs Barashev.' George crammed the warm package into his coat pocket, his mouth watering at the thought of the spicy crescent shaped treats.

The girl released her mother's skirt as Mrs Barashev wandered back to the stove. Regarding George with huge coal black eyes, she tilted her dark head.

George quickly handed the child a biscuit and held a silencing finger to his lips. The tiny girl accepted the treat without taking her eyes off George. 'Mama, can I go with the milk cart and the milk horse, and George Carter?'

Maria Barashev sighed. 'George doesn't have time…'

'I don't mind Mrs Barashev, really. I've three sisters.'

The woman relented, found coat and mittens. The tiny girl skipped to the cart where George hoisted her up.

THE QUIET street came to life slowly as the sun crept higher. The sound of music, children and early morning chaos reached George as he went from door to door, struggling to keep a grip on the clanging milk cans as a docile draught horse slowed, reins lightly held by Mr O'Neill.

He ran from door to door, collecting coins under pails, carrying billies, empty then full, covering the billy with whatever was left, a lid, a wooden cutting board. Sometimes he rang a doorbell, or knocked, to let the owner know their milk had arrived.

Near the end of the run there was no billy at the Ennis house.

George hesitated on the stoop. Mrs Ennis wouldn't be pleased to miss out on milk.

From the kitchen window Fliss watched George rub his hands together and blow on them. A serious boy, his brow was furrowed with concentration. His face was flushed as he struggled to keep a grip on the large metal milk cans.

Sylvia flung the door open. 'Hello,' she said. 'Who are you?'

'The milkman ... I mean ... I'm helping Mr O'Neill.' George stumbled back down a step.

'Are you then?' Sylvia said.

George's face reddened. 'You left the ... there isn't a billy for the milk.'

'Darn, that's brothers for you. David!' Sylvia shouted into the house, then folded her arms with a sly smile and added. 'I'm Sylvia Ennis. Have I seen you at school?'

'Ah, no. I'm at the tech college.'

Ethel Ennis stepped onto the stoop. Smoke curled out the door. 'How's the family up at Black Mountain, George? How's your mother?'

'Well as can be expected, Mrs Ennis.' George rubbed red blistered hands together. Ethel winced. 'Why don't you wear gloves, George? The cold is frightful at this hour.'

'Makes it harder to carry the pails. They slip around a bit.' George worried his bottom lip with his teeth and looked back to the cart.

Ethel stared past the milkman's cart to the hills that were pinking with life then called back into the house. 'Where's David, Felicity? I need that billy.'

Fliss fetched the billy and headed to the door but Sylvia snatched it and stepped onto the top step. 'That's our Felicity,' Sylvia waved an arm towards Fliss. 'Otherwise known as Flliss. She's off to become a nurse in the city. She's seventeen.'

'Sylvia!' Fliss jabbed her, hard.

A SMALL dark-eyed girl peeked out from the milk cart.

'Good heavens,' said Sylvia. 'Who's that kid?'

'Oh, her? That's Katya, the Barashev kid. Her mother lets her tag along for a few streets. Reckons she never sits still at home so…'

The child heard her name and ran to George's side. 'I'm a milk girl,' she said, with a gap-toothed smile. Her ruby lips pursed to let out icy vapour.

'Bye, then.' Picking the child up George loped to the cart where the horse was protesting the delay, raising impatient hooves. George lifted the child into the back of the wagon.

'I love you milkboy,' she said.

'Good grief,' muttered Sylvia. 'What a precocious brat!'

'Well, that's the pot calling the kettle black!' Fliss said, hauling on Sylvia's sleeve.

ETHEL started boiling the milk on the stove to separate the cream. 'Watch that will you Felicity.'

Fliss stirred the bubbling milk and watched the cart disappear as the sun rose over the street accompanied by the sound of music, children and early morning chaos.

'Mum…' said Sylvia, 'Who's the new fella helping Mr O'Neil with the milk run?'

'George Carter. Bill Carter's son. Sad story. The mother's ill, some horrible muscle-wasting disease. Bill's struggling with the farm. George got a scholarship at school and he's an apprentice draftsman with a company in town. Bill says he's not cut out for farming, anyway he wants something better for the boy, and George sends money home to the family.'

Ethel scooped the clotted cream from the top of the saucepan and poured the milk into metal jugs before placing them in the big beige enamel fridge.

GEORGE'S arm tingled on the long drive back to the dairy, and then on his bike ride home, remembering Sylia's touch.

THE WHOLE MRS KINGSTON BUSINESS

Lucy Meredith Carter, Book Of Known Facts, Quirindi, 1955

SOMETHING is up with our neighbour, Mrs Kingston.
She is forever coming over here and taking over.
It's getting annoying.

ACROSS the road, at Number 4, Mrs Kingston watches me sweep our paths. I flick dirt everywhere, to let her know I can take care of things. She's always popping over to our house: to drop off tuna casseroles, to see if we need any domestic help or ask dad's advice.

Here she comes, with short, half-running steps as if she's trying to catch up with something, but worries she never will.

'Yoo hoo!' She walks down the path a few steps, then whispers loudly. 'Lucy, can you tell your dad I have a parcel for him.'

'Sure Mrs Kingston.' I wonder if the parcel is for my birthday.

'Righto then.' She walks further down our front path, looks up and down the street then tilts her head. 'Um. The Post Master died. Apoplexy. Quite sudden, you see.'

'Oh?' I don't know why she's telling me but it seems important.

Mrs Kingston fluffs her hair. 'Anyway, that's why I have the parcel. Goodness knows when they'll sort the deliveries… Only the Quirindi mail is affected though, not Wallabadah.'

'I see,' I say. Mrs Kingston works at the post office three mornings a week. Apparently it's a government department. She

23

often talks about "legal responsibilities for mail". I'm not sure whether she has more to say so I wait.

She stands there, as if there's something else on her mind. 'I…er, um, and tell Geor…your father that tomorrow will be fine for him to trim the roses. He asked me to let him know…' She smiles as if she's finished what she had to say and is pleased that she got it out.

'Thank you,' I say.

She wanders back across the road, stopping to brush something off the letterbox with an apron corner.

MRS KINGSTON is a widow. She has fifteen-year-old twins, Ewan and Billy. Dad reckons she has her hands full with them. She tries very hard to be fussy about the house. With boys like Ewan and Billy that isn't easy. The house seems to droop. The gutters sag and leak. There are so many things that need repairing. Dad tinkers around over there. The garden tap is bent, probably from the twin's rough games of cricket.

Nanna Ennis says that they're great gawping boys, big as grown men. They look as if they should be really useful, but they break things and leave stuff lying around.

Any old time of the day or night Mrs Kingston can be heard calling to them to *come* or *go,* to *bring* or *take.* 'I despair if they'll ever be any use to man or beast,' I heard her say to Nanna Ennis.

Mrs Kingston was a good friend with Mum. She brings us casseroles and offers to do stuff, "woman's work", she calls it. Dad and I don't really need her to help. Nanna Ennis said, 'I think Marj is sweet on your father, but I don't think he's interested in that kind of petticoat government.' Nanna usually makes sense of things, but I didn't understand that at all. And for once I just shrugged instead of asking a whole bunch of questions.

Standing on her front lawn Mrs Kingston shields her eyes from the afternoon sun and glares at a torn window awning, one that makes the house look as if it's winking when the lights come on at night.

IN THE MORNING over breakfast I decide to talk to Dad about Mrs Kingston.

'I quite like Marj,' I say, dipping a toast soldier into the gooey egg.

'These are yum, Dad. You're getting better at making breakfast.'

'Excuse me?' Dad stops his glasses from slipping down his nose.

'The eggy soldiers are yum.' I say the words precisely. Dad seems a bit distracted this morning.

Dad looks up from his plate. 'Not that. The other thing...'

'Oh, about Marj? … I mean Mrs Kingston. I said I quite like her.'

'You do? That's nice.' Dad wipes egg from his chin with a tea towel.

'Dad, don't use a tea towel to wipe your face. You've got a lovely handkerchief I ironed for you. Why don't you use that?'

'I'm, er, saving you ironing?'

'You're not really. Tea towels are bigger to iron.'

'Crikey! You don't iron tea-towels do you?'

'Of course!' I say. 'Nanna does.'

'That shouldn't surprise me.' Dad sips his tea. 'Your grandmother probably irons cleaning rags.'

'Don't be silly, Dad. Now, about Mrs…'

There's a rap on the screen door. It's Ewan, one of the Kingston twins.

'Come in Ewan.' Dad waved to Ewan to come inside.

'Can't. Got m'boots on, Mr Carter. Just returnin' y'grass

clippers. Mum says thanks.'

Ewan yanks the screen door open, leans in and hands Dad the gardening shears. 'Small kitchen, aint it.'

'Thanks,' Dad scrapes the chair to stand but Ewan's gone, leaving the screen door banging.

'Ewan should work for the post office.' I tell Dad. 'Writing telegrams.'

Dad laughs.

I don't think Dad is catching on, so I start again. 'Dad, I think Mrs Kingston wants to be your girlfriend.'

He splutters, spitting some of the tea. 'That's silly, Lucy.' He tries to mop up the tea. 'Marj doesn't want any such thing.'

'But Dad. I think it's why she helps us and does all that cooking for us.'

'Really Lucy, you've got the wrong end of the stick.' Dad has gone all red in the face. 'Who've you been talking to?'

'Of course, we'd have to live there. Their house is bigger. The twins must take up an awful lot of room. I'm not sure I'd like two brothers. Ewan is shy, and Billy, he just stays in the shed. It would be terribly hard to get used to, but if you, well, *liked* her.'

'Lucy stop! In the space of five minutes you've had me married, shifting house and becoming stepfather to two teenage boys. What else? Would you like to plan my funeral while you're at it? This is nonsense. Truly. If I ever do remarry, it won't be to Marj Kingston. She's a very nice woman … a friend and neighbour. And don't go writing that down in your precious notebook. And whatever you do, don't go blabbing to Mar … Mrs Kingston.'

Dad jumps to his feet and clatters his plate into the sink, flicks the plug in and turns the taps on.

'Oh Dad, I'm sorry. 'I'm only trying…' I start to sob.

'Don't cry, Buttons. We're okay aren't we? The two of us?'

I SIT with Dad while he works with plans and drawings. I like the *scratch scratch* of the pencil as he shades in the trees and shrubs for the council plan he's working on. His office has been at home since Mum died.

Esmeralda pecks on the floor in the wood shavings from Dad's thick pencils while I sit on a pillow and dress my dolls.

I'm glad Dad thinks we're doing okay. I hum a funny little song I made up. 'I'm sorry about Mrs Kingston, Dad.'

He turns from his work. 'Lucy, Mrs Kingston misses her husband. It was a terrible tragedy. She never got over it.'

'Oh, I didn't know that,' I say. This is more than Dad usually tells me about anyone.

'Was it in the war?' I ask.

'No, after he came home.'

'Will you tell me the story?'

Nessa dorma, Quirindi, 1947

ERROL KINGSTON, courier for Quirindi, Wallabadah and surrounds, sang as he drove the van, an aria, a ballad, a ditty, a hymn, right arm resting out the window, or waved about theatrically.

Until Marj gave birth to fractious twin boys and Errol's singing set them off. He stopped singing on family outings or trips to church, but on longer trips, those pink-dawn collections or deliveries, Errol Kingston sang with gusto, resting an arm out the window, or waving it about, for Nessa Dorma, or an aria.

Until one dark Wednesday, a long-haul eight-wheeler came too close, ripped his arm off, clean taken away.

He crawled from the van, lying on the road, that lonely road where no early morning cars traversed.

No farmer or housewife heard his cries or moans.

LATER, much later, in the sultry afternoon, when heat rippled from tar on the road, Marj Kingston snapped crisp white sheets off the rope clothesline, pressed them to her face to smell the sunshine as she hummed Nessa Dorma, or an aria.

Two solemn policemen approached, took off their caps, placed them under their arms and spoke in low murmurs.

Marj fell to her knees, spilling clean washing onto the ground.

Past Love

Montview Lodge, 1955

THE PHOTOS on the narrow mantel in Fliss' room mock her. Ethel, dominating the picture although she is standing at the side, shorter than the others. Sylvia with her bright smile. David, grinning broadly in a new suit.

Over a decade has passed. The siblings with their new adult status and optimistic hopes for life, the ideal bliss of it all. Sylvia had teased Fliss to wear her Sister's veil and Fliss had slapped her playfully. Sylvia was still deluded by the romantic notions of nursing. Gliding down pristine corridors, wiping the brows of handsome doctors, attending to young flirting soldiers. It didn't matter how often Fliss told her that short visits to the lounge area on the ward was different from the reality of the wards.

For Fliss it's still hard to believe they are both gone, Sylvia to the horror of cancer and David to the killing fields of war. Only Fliss remains of the three children. The weakest.

The door swings open. 'What are you doing, Miss Felicity? Daydreaming again? You won't be ready for Lucy's visit if you don't hurry up.' Sacha grabs a white towel and dries Fliss' hair vigorously.

'Yi,' Fliss has sounds, not whole words. Pieces of a puzzle.

Sacha stands back, her lips pursed, deciding what to do with Fliss' unruly curls. 'You have no photos of your fiancé,' she says, as she reaches for the wide-toothed comb. 'Such a shame.' She flicks Fliss' hair with the comb, then arranges it with her slender fingers. 'Was he handsome?'

Fliss smiles, then laughs.

'Ah, verrry handsome. I see.' Sacha places the towel around Fliss' neck so wet hair doesn't dampen her dress. 'Well, Miss Felicity, your niece will be here soon. Let's get your shoes on.'

Care packages, Presbyterian Church, Leichardt, 1940

THE CHURCH hall was smaller than Fliss imagined. Her hopes of slipping in the side door, leaving the knitted socks, then leaving quickly faded. She was met at the drop-off table by an earnest middle-aged man, hungry for conversation and full of good cheer. Fliss was reminded of the times she enjoyed attending church, long ago now.

Women were busy organising care packages.

Music started up, a piano and a violin. Fliss was a long way from the door so she took the nearest seat, a chrome seat crammed against the faux timber wall. Fliss had left the things Sylvia made, but wished that her sister had come along with her. Sixteen was too young to be out on the town with friends, but the Saturday night church social was underway and Fliss was trapped.

It was coming up for Christmas 1943. There was talk that the war was winding up in Europe and there was an air of optimism in the hall, or perhaps it was the necessary bravado of wartime.

A woman in the row in front of Fliss turned and smiled warmly. Fliss smiled in return. The woman was dressed in a stylish sage-green dress and smelled of roses. She was about Fliss' mother's age, but her hands were pale and soft. She turned to talk to the man beside her and her voice was lilting. The man's head leaned towards her, one hand resting on her back. Fliss leaned forward and noticed the man was wearing a uniform. He was a digger, a recruit by the look of him, although he wasn't as young as many of them. There was something formed about him, something strong and protective as he bent towards the woman.

When the music was over, everyone stood. Fliss moved towards the door, bumping and apologising, making slow progress. She heard the man introduce the woman as his mother. Fliss couldn't move around them, so she waited, wishing to be invisible, or better still back in the flat with Sylvia. Looking at her watch she realised that Sylvia had probably given up and gone out. It was her first stay in the city, a celebration for topping the class in the stenographer's course. Sydney was a long way from Quirindi and country life, but Sylvia had wasted no time making friends.

The digger was in no hurry. There were many seeking his time, but he didn't move from his mother. Perhaps it was the end of his leave. Fliss avoided soldiers. There were some on the rehabilitation ward, brash young men or teenagers wearied from battle or having spent months in tent hospitals. Fliss thought of all the diggers out celebrating their last leave, some with sweethearts, family, or mates at the pub trying to get as drunk as they could before returning to barracks.

The man saw Fliss and smiled, a larrikin grin, his eyes lingering. With a gentle hand on his mother's arm, he moved around her and came towards Fliss.

'I haven't seen you here before,' he said.

'I only came to deliver some things. For a friend.'

'Ah, my mother will be pleased. She is collecting for comfort packages for the overseas lot.' The crush of the crowd brought him closer. He smelled of soap and lemons.

'Was that your mother sitting next to you?' Fliss asked, then blushed, not wanting him to know she had noticed him. She tilted her chin and added, 'she looks too young and lovely to be anyone's mother.'

'Ah,' he said, the sound a low vibration, 'good looks run in the family.'

Fliss laughed. 'So, you look like your father?'

He surprised her with a deep rumbling chuckle. 'May I walk you home?'

'What makes you think I'm going now?'

'You've been edging towards the door since you came.'

'Oh dear. I thought I was being subtle. But ... are you ready to leave?' Fliss' words stumbled between them, an affliction he didn't appear to suffer. She suspected he was enjoying it.

'For you I'm ready.' A simple statement delivered with clear-eyed candour.

He talked nonstop, regaling Fliss with stories of his mates and tales of his mother and sister. He said nothing of war, of enlisting, of battle. That night, he was just another guy walking a girl home. His quiet conversation was disarming; however it was the memory of his tender regard for his mother that lingered long after they said goodnight at the big brass door to the nurses' home.

WHEN SYLVIA arrived back at the flat the sisters shared, she was full of good cheer and chatter Fliss resolved not to mention the soldier no matter how much Sylvia teased her about failing to come back in time to go out. However, Fliss needn't have bothered, Sylvia glowed with post dancing bliss and her surprising news.

'Felicity,' she crowed as the spun around the room, falling onto the camp bed Fliss had put up for her visit. 'I've got a job. Here in the city. What do you think of that?'

'This was supposed to be a weekend visit.' Fliss slumped onto the narrow bed. 'Mum will put the kibosh on that idea.'

'No she won't. Not if I live with you.'

'Don't be daft, Syl. You can't live in the nurses' home. It's not allowed.'

'I know that, silly. We'll get a flat together. You're allowed to move out now that you're a Sister.'

Fliss moaned theatrically and rolled around on the bed. Sylvia joined her and tickled her mercilessly until their squeals earned a sharp rap on the wall. 'Mum's going to kill me,' Fliss said.

'No she won't. I left a note.'

'FELICITY, listen to this!' Sylvia snapped the newspaper onto the tiny dining table.

The flat she and Fliss shared was cramped and cluttered.

Fliss sighed.

She avoided the papers, but Sylvia was not easy to deter. She stabbed at the paper with a red-nailed finger. 'It's an open letter, whatever that means,' she said. Her hair tickled Fliss' face as she leaned over the page.

'I think it means it's written anonymously.' Fliss said.

'Oh well. Oh yes!—it's just got "A woman reporter" at the bottom. Anyway, it's about the American soldiers. Listen to this, will you! "I offer the following suggestions for entertaining them". Oh my, George would love this. He's not keen on the Yanks taking over the town. "Parties…" Well, how do you like that! Parties! And coming right on the heels of all that talk from Mr Curtin about cutting back on frivolity and being frugal. Our Prime Minister won't be impressed with "parties". Ha—there's more, Fliss. She tells us what the Americans like, "swing music and redheads"—you'll be right, sis.'

'Leave off, Syl.' Fliss pushed the paper aside.

Sylvia pouted. 'You're always telling me to do my bit for the war effort. I can be entertaining, and I love swing music.' She lifted her hair and twirled around the kitchen, then turned and batted her eyelashes.

'Pfft.' Fliss located her toast and had it halfway to her mouth when Sylvia pounced on the paper.

'Oh look, they mention "strawberry blondes". I'm in with a chance. A bit of dye and I could be a strawberry blonde.'

'Did they say that? I don't believe you! They might as well sell us on street corners.' Fliss grabbed the paper. 'Oh, my goodness, you're right! Some daft woman is telling us to roll out the party rugs and deliver redheads.' Fliss chuckled. 'Ah, but you're out of luck, Syl. See—it says, "not synthetic or bottle". That's you out!'

'Who cares about Yanks and hair dye.' Sylvia headed for the coffee tin for her third coffee.

'At this rate we'll use our month's rations in a week,' said Fliss. 'Anyway, you don't need to do anything to your hair. With those gorgeous blonde locks, they wouldn't care.'

Fliss turned a page of the paper and read aloud. 'AIF Honour Roll.' She said the words absently, seeing row upon row, page upon page of young soldiers. She wondered what heroic deeds earned these handsome young men the distinction of an honour roll, until she read further and realised it was a listing of the dead.

Sylvia gripped her sister's shoulder. 'Oh God, Felicity. So many. Such a waste. I can't stand it.' She slumped onto the chrome kitchen chair. It scraped noisily. 'David has enlisted. Did Mum tell you? Our dear David. Why did he have to enlist? He's only 17. I just couldn't bear to lose a brother. Oh Felicity, when will it all end? It was supposed to be a "phoney war". Over before it began.'

'All this nonsense about dances and entertainment,' said Fliss, holding back tears, 'no time for that with my job.'

GUNS & GALAS

Ennis family home, Henry Street, Quirindi, 1955

HARRY sweeps outside his hut. Magpies have begun their orchestral notes and the early morning air is crisp and clean. Near the hut at the back of the Ennis home, Harry's army mirror hangs on a low branch of the mulberry tree. Outdoor shaving—a digger's routine, hard to shift. He gazes down the long acre paddock that stretches to the creek from the hut behind the old boarding house, enjoying the spring breeze. As he throws shaving water on a patch of bare earth under the fruit-laden tree he hears the soft hush of bicycle tyres on the concrete path beside the house. It's a light sound, but a soldier's instincts persist, even in the peaceful outskirts of country Quirindi.

It's the child, Lucy. She comes every morning to feed her grandmother's hens. Harry knows her footsteps well. Part walk, part skip. He looks forward to her visits, her quirky conversation, her eternal curiosity and the childlike awkwardness of not knowing where she fits, but not entirely caring either.

She's carrying the fat white chook she calls Esmeralda, wrapped in a doll's blanket. When she places the chook on the ground, it dances around her, head bobbing. Eyeing the other hens with cautious disdain, she refuses to enter the henhouse as Lucy steps inside, perhaps fearing her liberation will end. Lucy fills the feed basins carefully, then pats each chook, murmuring to each one with a caressing voice as if they are treasured friends. When she comes out, she snakes the hose across to the pen, slipping it through the chicken wire to the water trough. She undertakes this with watchful eyes as the water fills to just the right level.

There's a cloudless sky as the day warms. Lucy looks down at the hose and giggles. Then she spins around with the nozzle above her head, watching the water spray swirl over her in diamond spirals.

Esmeralda is not impressed with this pastime. Clucking loudly, she flies to the top of the coop where she perches, fluttering water droplets from her wings.

Lucy drops the hose and runs to turn it off, remembering she mustn't get too wet. She gazes down the long yard, shielding her eyes against the early morning sun. She sees Harry crouched on the stoop to the hut as he smears black polish over his boots, and waves, a brief cheery greeting, one that says, *I'll be there in a tick.*

LUCY flicks Harry's digger's hat onto her head and laughs when it slips down over her eyes.

'You always wear your best uniform, Uncle Harry. Is that because you still have missions and stuff?'

'Something like that.'

'Are you going to the Digger's Ball? It's on every year at the RSL, the square building on Station Street. There's funny acts, food and dancing. Last year Spiffy Davis drove 'round the showground with four men hanging off the running board of his car. Nanna said they were all properly soused. Uncle Harry, have you ever been to a ball?'

Harry barks a laugh, then coughs to hide it. 'Oddly enough, little Lucy, I've been to a good many balls.'

'Did the ladies have beautiful gowns?' Lucy spins around,

36

pretending to hold the flounces of ball gown.

'They certainly did, little Lucy.' Harry puts his book aside. 'But I'd never been near a fancy ball until I became a soldier.' Harry watches Lucy drag a timber stool from under a bench. She pats it. 'This is the story chair,' she says.

'If you say so!'

Harry leans back on his slatted chair until only two legs dig into the soft earth. 'I'd better come up with a story.

The 2/17th AIF Battalion, Sydney, 1940

HAVING left London to escape the First World War, I enlisted in the Australian Infantry to fight in the Second. Our diggers were already on the ground overseas. Heavy boots on foreign soil. Several battalions of the 7th Division.

I answered the call out and arrived at Ingleburn in the middle of June 1940, not long after the enlistment of the "First Hundred for the 2/17th AIF Battalion"—a group that was photographed and memorialised for the newspapers.

The newly formed battalion ate at the brigade HQ, there wasn't a mess for the new wave of soldiers. An earnest recruiting officer at the enlistment office at Moore Park had spoken of the gravity of the war with calm, precise words—our country needed us. Several officers had been approaching men in the street. I'd already decided.

When asked about my work background I told them I could drive anything with wheels. The officer merely nodded without looking up and wrote "vehicle driver".

At thirty, I was older than most. Arriving for training in the middle of June 1940, I was allocated to the 9th Division, 2/17th Battalion, AIF. At the makeshift barracks at Hordern Pavillion we were given ill-fitting uniforms, pills and powders, a glut of vaccinations, condoms and cures.

I was accepted as an Aussie. I hadn't bothered to tell them I'd spent the first six years of my life in London. It hardly seemed relevant. My mates were surprised to meet my mother and sister Clarissa with their British gentility and accents. I was prone to use 'poncy words' according to one drawling farmhand, courtesy of a fancy English education that I was quick to joke had failed to elevate me in life due to sheer boredom and laziness at the books. That, apparently made me more Aussie than my reckless driving and eagerness to join in any prank on offer.

When I arrived at Ingleburn, training had already begun. We were introduced to the Lewis gun, later replaced by the Owen gun—an Australian invention by Private Owen, one of three brothers in our battalion.

Hacking coughs interrupted the bitter chill of winter nights as men succumbed to Ingleburn throat. Vaccinations wreaked havoc. One poor sod, wracked with bronchitis asked what the flaming hell they were all for— 'Every bloody disease known to man, soldier,' the grim reply.

Pack, carry and march. Morning range practice at Anzac Rifle range. A Debutante Ball at the Trocadero in the evening. The men who couldn't dance soon learned; good dancers got the best sheilas.

My days were no longer concerned with shouldering boxes, signatures on delivery sheets, meeting deadlines for deliveries and negotiating traffic with only brief exchanges, fast jokes passing through tired suburbs, narrow laneways, windowless warehouses screeching metal doors and hooting horns.

Heavy lifting and handling had prepared me for many of the challenges of army life, but my legs sagged, first numb, then spongey, then stiff, and last searing heat of pain. Mind you, some men were already work-hardened machines. Country boys with pushed back hats and open smiles were often underestimated. They'd toiled since childhood from first light to the last dim streaks across the skies, fought droughts, floods, everything nature could throw at them.

There was a strange kind of power in the pounding rhythm of a thousand boots, the soft clunk of equipment as we marched in unison. Being shoulder to shoulder with his mates spurs a man on.

On our first endurance march, to Bathurst through the Blue Mountains, I shouldered the kit of a faltering young soldier for a mile or two then fell in step with a digger my own age, a bloke over six feet tall, skinny as a piece of cardboard, with the newly minted nickname of Lanky. As we were beginning to march as one man, we were learning about each other. I'd only known city life. I had made some longer runs in the truck to Katoomba through the Blue Mountains, but nothing prepared me for the grandeur and beauty on that first body-breaking march.

Welcomed at every stop on the way, diggers were billeted in homes delighted to receive them. But each mile became tougher, harder. When we arrived in Bathurst, my legs buckled.

I REGRETTED that fear had returned to my mother's eyes. The same fear I'd seen haunt her steps through London.

At least I could still send part of my pay home to her. Not that she'd starve. She'd been canny with her money, taking in sewing and piecework from factories. Our back room hummed with the sound of her industrial machines. She was fast and furious when she worked. Pity help the poor schmuck who entered her domain when she had a deadline of shirts or blouses for fancy city designers.

She hadn't survived a war to face poverty. I spent my last leave with her, and with Clarissa's family. Her young children muted the ferocity of the looming separation and shadow of war with their eager questions and open admiration of my uniform.

Mum became quieter as the days passed; her silence punctuated by sighs. Then on the last day before embarkation—a torrent of words, halting tearful advice, a fierce embrace. My last sight of her—standing like a sentinel in the window of our home in Cammeray. Her gracefully folded hands and air of stillness did not fool me. She was alone and afraid in the narrow red-brick house that had been our home since arriving in Australia over twenty years before.

'YOUR MUM must have missed you,' says Lucy, 'but it's good you had the cardboard man for a new friend.'

'Indeed it was, little Lucy,' Harry squints as he returns from the past, returns to the backyard of the boarding house, to the world of peace, far from war. 'A grand friend he was too.'

'Was? Don't you have him anymore?' she asks, tilting her head, eyes concerned.

Harry wipes a forearm across his forehead, shielding his eyes from the child's careful gaze, realising that he is slipping. He hadn't meant to bring this up, hadn't seen that Lucy listened with such focused attention.

'No, erm, ... I don't ... have him anymore, little Lucy.'

THE STUMBLING MAN

Lucy Meredith Carter, Book Of Known Facts, Quirindi, 1955

DAD AND NANNA had an argument.

I didn't hear what it was about. It was over before I
arrived, but they both looked cranky.

Esmeralda is sitting on my lap.

I can't write cursive with her here.

But my writing isn't much good anyway, so I print.

THE GARDEN'S gone a bit wild since Mum died.

Dad says he likes it overgrown. He doesn't trim the lilly pillies
or the grevilleas, even though he often prunes shrubs for Nanna
Ennis and neighbours.

Dad is fussy about the upkeep of the house. He spent all last
summer painting the outside. He even painted the doors, the
eaves and the trim Prussian Blue. It was on sale at Parson's
Hardware on account of the name of the colour being German,
even though the war has been over nearly ten years. Nanna Ennis
reckons people don't forget something like that.

Dad added a porch swing at the side of the house, his own
design. It's a secret place, shaded by the camphor laurel tree.

Nanna Ennis tut-tutted about it. 'That might be a clever thing,
George, but I wouldn't be caught dead sitting on it. It would make
me seasick, all that rocking to and fro.'

A TALL MAN is limping slowly up our street. His suit coat is thrown over his shoulder. His tie is loose and his white shirt looks new. He's very thin, leans on a cane, stopping every now and then to stare at a piece of paper, then up at the houses. He seems to be looking for something.

I wonder if he's a wounded soldier.

The fruit truck man passes on his way home so it must be near four o'clock. He toots and waves to Mrs Kingston across the road at No. 4 as she digs up daffodil bulbs, brushing them off with gardening gloves and putting them in an apron pocket. She keeps looking over here. I guess Dad asked her to keep an eye on me.

Esmeralda clucks and wriggles so I take set her down on the grass.

'Ahem.' The stumbling man is standing by our letterbox, leaning on his cane. 'Excuse me,' he says softly. 'I'm sorry to bother you but I can't make head nor tail of this thing.'

His face is tight as if he's in pain. He waves the creased paper. 'I'm looking for the Ennis place.'

'Oh, that's my grandmother's,' I say, 'at the other end of Henry Street. She's Ethel *Ennis*. She takes in boarders, working people mostly.'

He takes off his hat. His hair is the colour of burnished brass.

'Grandmother?' Blinking sweat from his eyes, he pulls out a handkerchief. There's a badge pinned to his jacket.

I recognise it. 'Oh,' I say, 'you must've been here for the Jubilee, Mister. I helped my mum, Sylvia, put those badges into the farmers' show bags, before she died.'

He jerks. 'Mother? Dead…' He falls back against the letterbox and fans his face with the paper.

Mrs Kingston starts across the road without looking for cars. She's huffing and puffing. I point to the east end of the street where Nanna lives.

Mrs Kingston looks angry. She stands in front of me. 'Can I help you?' she asks the man. A few bulbs fall out of her pocket.

THE MAN straightens. 'I was just asking young Lucy here for directions.' He shoves the paper into a pocket, tips his hat and stumbles away, heading in the opposite direction to Nanna's place, jerking along, faster than before.

How did he know my name?

Leave Things Be

Ennis family home, Henry Street, Quirindi, 1955

ETHEL thumps heavy footsteps down the back steps as she balances a full basket of washing on her hip. The side gate squeaks. She turns. 'Ah. George.' Dropping the basket into a wrought-iron trolley she tilts the tall timber struts of the rope clothesline.

George straightens the peg basket. Ethel frowns and reaches for a peg. George removes his glasses, wipes a trickle of sweat from his forehead. Silence stretches to tension.

Ethel breaks the strained choreography. 'If there's something on your mind, George, just spit it out.'

'With Sylvia ... gone I, we...'

'Leave things be.' Ethel cracks a wet tablecloth like a whip, reaches for the rope line.

George grips it. 'Ethel. For God's sake!'

Ethel flings the tablecloth down. 'Don't cross me in this, George.' The pegs screech as she shoves them onto the clothes with a tight-fisted hand. She doesn't flinch as the side gate slams.

If only George, Sylvia and Lucy had stayed on with her in the big house. Things would have been easier. There'd have been no need for boarders, for laundry services for others, for penury.

She has sacrificed enough. For family and marriage. A marriage that brought more pain than comfort.

Not another war, Ennis family home, 1939

PRIVATE William (Bill) Ennis returned from the First World War in 1918 with renewed devotion to the Imperial Hotel. Formerly cherished by his drinking mates for his bonhomie and rollicking tales he'd become a sullen drunk.

Stumbling homeward steps rarely saw him arrive at his desired destination. He was often retrieved from a sodden ditch or among tall sticky paspalum grass by the side of the road.

In the winter of '39, Bill's confusion was no longer limited to periods of inebriation. Lucid moments were rare and unpredictable. And as for the fevers and seeping sores, would they ever fade?

The local doctor took blood, visited Ethel on a slow Monday and quietly delivered the news she'd feared. They sat at the kitchen table while she filled in forms for Bill's admission to Concord Repatriation Hospital while Bill snored in the sunroom.

RADIOS hummed in homes all over Australia as Prime Minister, "Pig Iron Bob" Menzies began—'Fellow Australians, it is my melancholy duty...'

Another war. After listening to this grave news Ethel packed two leather-strapped, tan suitcases for her husband's transfer the following day.

It was late, yet Bill Ennis wandered the house, pale skin drawn across a too-thin face. A soft cotton scarf covered blood-red sores on his neck, yet he managed to tear at them. He paced, confused and angry, refusing medication. Ethel crushed his evening pills, stirred them into his tea and waited as he wound down from ranting about wars, past and impending, children who behaved like heathens, wives rejecting sick husbands.

In the morning Bill sat sullen and silent. The children kissed their father goodbye and left. Ethel turned away, fumbled in her pocket for a handkerchief and wiped weary eyes on a corner. It was the last day they'll all be together.

Bill grabbed a corner of Ethel's apron and tugged. 'What have you told them, wife.'

Ethel sighed. Trust Bill to choose that morning to be in his right mind. She leaned in. 'Shell shock. It's close enough.'

He banged the table with a jerky fist. 'A bloody lie!'

THE RAILWAY station was deserted as Ethel surrendered her husband to the care of a waiting escort nurse, who nodded sagely when Ethel's trembling hands furtively produced a crumpled folder of medical notes from inside her coat.

Ethel fought bitter tears.

God help her, she'd live with this lie for the rest of her life. *Treponema pallidum*. Syphilus.

———

PRECISELY one year after the declaration of the Second World War and Bill's admission to Concord Repat Hospital, Ethel Ennis organised her husband's funeral, a hasty affair, left out of the local papers. Family only. Ethel begged no favours, sought no help, expressed regret for the small funeral, to her friends, Bill's former workmates and drinking buddies. 'The war, you understand.'

She advertised discreetly and took in boarders. From two leather-strapped, tan suitcases, sent from the repat hospital, she unpacked Bill's meagre possessions, and burned them in the backyard incinerator. In spite of the lack of an obituary or prior notice of the funeral, flowers filled the house. With this unexpected, yet encouraging sign of goodwill, the following month Ethel attended The War Widow Society's luncheon on the arm of a friend, known since childhood.

Approached by Mrs Elisabeth Renshaw, President of the Society, Ethel was delicately reminded of her status; not technically a war widow, but welcome nonetheless.

ETHEL walked stiffly home.

When Mr Price, her neighbour, a man prone to leave bruises on his wife, chided her for walking on his lawn, she said, 'Bugger off Bruce!' went inside and wept.

CHILD-RaiSing WaSN'T MeanT For Men

Lucy Meredith Carter, Book Of Known Facts, Quirindi, 1955

I'm in a hurry today.
I'm going to see Fliss at Montview.
Esmeralda hops quickly into the bike basket.

I LIFT my feet off the pedals as the bike gets speed up down the driveway. Esmeralda's blanket is flapping in the basket. I stop behind the lilly-pilly in front of Mrs Kingston's yard to tuck it back in. Dad's there helping in the garden. I peak through the branches.

I'm about to step out and tell him I'm on my way to feed Nanna's chooks and visit Fliss when Mrs Kingston starts talking.

'She's an odd one, that girl of yours, George.'

I shrink back behind the shrub. Dad turns from pruning the roses. 'Why Marj, Lucy reminds me of all the best things in childhood,' he says, pulling a thorn from his thumb and sucking the red wound.

Mrs Kingston pulls a face. 'Oh George, don't do that. I wish you'd let me...' She ransacks her apron pockets with chubby fingers and produces a Band-Aid.

'Nature's cure, Marj, nature's cure.' Dad waves the Band-Aid aside. 'She's got spirit, my girl.'

'A little too much spirit if you ask me.' Mrs Kingston folds her arms and shoves the Band-Aid back in her pocket.

Dad gives her a hard look.

I feel uncomfortable. Esmeralda wriggles. I pat her.

Mrs Kingston pushes a tight curl off her forehead. 'I don't say you're not doing your best for the girl since her mother died, George, but child-raising wasn't meant for men.'

Dad snips a dead rose head and drops it in a pail. 'Can't see why not Marj. Anyway, the war changed things. Women are holding down jobs now. My Sylvia did.'

'Hmmph, yes I know. We were great friends, your Sylvia and I. Just the same, I often wondered if that exciting job during the war didn't ruin her for peacetime.'

I wonder what she means about Mum having an exciting job. She sometimes worked at the library. I can't see how that was exciting.

Mrs Kingston folds her hands across her round belly and puffs air from thin lips. 'I don't know about you, George, I wonder if it's a good thing for Lucy to spend so much time at that nursing home place with those … poor unfortunate people. I know she's fond of her aunt…'

Dad turns his back to her, using his pruning shears to squash the rose heads into a metal bucket. His hat shades his face so I can't see him. He doesn't seem to want to talk.

Mrs Kingston huffs and looks down the yard towards the shrub where I am, so I wander out and wave to them, acting like I haven't heard anything. Then I scrape the bike around to face the road again, slip onto the seat and check Esmeralda in the basket.

Mrs Kingston stares at the basket. 'Oh my gosh, George! Has Lucy got that blasted chook in the basket?' she says, forgetting that *gosh* and *blasted* are on her list of words to *not* say.

'She told me it was magic. Really, George!'

'Who knows?' Dad shrugs and heads to the next rose bed.

I PEDDLE as fast as I can to Montview, to Fliss. There are no secrets there. No whispers that stop when I arrive. No sharp words. No criticisms behind my back.

I LOVE going to Montview.

Sometimes Dad sits at the piano in the evening. Most of the patients are in bed asleep, or in their rooms listening to radios or playing cards. Then Fliss and I sit in the squishy brocade settee. We lean our heads together and listen. Fliss usually likes to sit in straight-backed chairs because she can get out of them by herself, but when Dad is there he helps her up. Those times we have our own concerts are treats, especially on long humid summer nights when the sun sets late and the damp heat of the day clings, heavy and still. With the ceiling fan turning slowly, the cicadas tuneless song fades, the kitchen noises are gentler as Maria, the cook, hums and sets up for the next day.

When we hear the soft-shoed footsteps of the evening sister as she moves through the home with the last medications, we sigh. Dad gently closes the piano, stows the stool.

After we help Fliss out of the settee and hand her to the Sister we walk home arm in arm. Dad said I used to go to sleep when I was younger and he would piggyback me home. I don't know how he carried me that far.

Sometimes I read to Fliss. Even though she lost her words we understand each other just fine.

DEAD THINGS

Lucy Meredith Carter, Book Of Known Facts, Quirindi, 1955

Nanna takes me with her to help with the weekly grocery shopping at McDonald's Corner Store.

NANNA IS wearing her Going Down The Street clothes. Her hair is pinned in a tight bun. She's wearing her second-best winter coat over a flowery dress. A thin blue belt has crept up under her bosoms because she's hasn't got a waist anymore.

She meets her lady friends, gives me a list, tells me not to dawdle as she and her friends huddle together, their hats almost touching, just inside the door, their purses tucked firmly under their arms as if purse snatchers might be on the loose.

Pretty soon they start on about how different life has been since the war: how cheap tinned fruit is; and how marvellous it is to buy as much meat and butter as they like.

I wander the aisles with Nanna's basket, looking at the list she made. I can't make out whether she wants brown or white onions so I have to interrupt her. As I wait for her to notice me, she says, 'George would have me tell all, but ...' Nanna shakes her head. One of her friends points to me.

'Don't sneak up on a person, Lucy.' Nanna puts her hand over her heart and takes a step back.

Mr McDonald clears his throat loudly and calls out, 'Next

please!' He doesn't like people clogging up the doorway. Nanna says it's because he doesn't like chatter about the war. Near the back door of the store, next to rat-traps and candles, there are two dusty pairs of working boots that once belonged to their sons who died in the war.

NANNA doesn't approve of them. She calls them 'dead things'. I don't remind her that she has an upstairs room of dead things. I poke around in there sometimes, when Nanna's in the garden or settling in a boarder. There are tea chests with black stencilled signs like PRODUCE OF INDIA, and others with BUSHELLS, Tea of Flavour.

Downstairs, in a glass cabinet, Nanna has heaps of newspapers about the war. In the newspaper printed the day I was born, people in heavy winter coats are dancing the Hokey Pokey in the streets, with long white streamers scattered on the ground like snow. None of the papers have pictures of the fighting, just stuff about the edges of it, like why the men should join up and fight for their country and loved ones, and why women should knit socks.

It's a tricky subject, the war.

War is like those boxes in the upstairs room. Memories in dark, dusty corners. There, but not there.

A Pliable Man

The Ennis family home, 1955

GEORGE Carter oils the hinges of the side gate to his mother-in-law's house. Ethel watches this activity with folded arms. 'Making it easy to sneak up on me, George?'

His back to her, George swings the gate back and forth to test it. 'A tantalising idea, Ethel.'

'You used to be so pliable, George.'

'Why Ethel, you make me sound about as interesting as plasticine. But if I was fixing the squeak to sneak up on you, I'd have done it while you were out.'

'So, you've never been sneaky, George?'

'I didn't say that, Ethel.'

——————

Across the border, Queensland, 1951

ARRIVING home from work, George found Sylvia's suitcases at the door, lined up in awkward precision.

The sight galled him. Even though the war had ended years before, Sylvia's visits to the farm continued. She'd been spending longer each time. Any conversation about the long weeks she spent there was quickly sidelined, which was easy to achieve given that her mother might be in the next room.

George heard pots and pans jangle in the kitchen, saw a quick flash as Sylvia ran into the bedroom, then out, carrying a large hatbox.

'Ah, George. There you are.'

'You're leaving Sylvia? Again.'

'No flies on you, George.'

His jaw clenched as anger rose. 'We were going to talk about moving out, getting our own place. I'm fed up. We've lived here ever since we got married.'

'But living with Mum is so much easier. Shush, you'll offend her. Anyway, I'll write.'

'I beg your pardon? *You'll write!*' George jammed hands into his pockets, then stepped back, craving distance and reassurance in equal measure.

'I have an out-of-town job next week,' he said, 'at the army training camp.'

'The army base?' Sylvia stiffened and straightened the suitcases slowly. 'Oh. Which one?'

'Tamworth.'

'Oh! Right. That one.' Then she spun around, kissed his cheek, laughed and rubbed the lipstick off. It was the first act of affection in months, but it chilled him to the marrow.

Driving on the highway, Sylvia was on his mind. He couldn't shake her swift mood change before she'd left. Why had she reacted? Which army base had she thought he was talking about? Why hadn't she ever told him where the farm was? This only showed what a consummate fool he'd been.

IN TAMWORTH, at the Manilla Road Training Camp, George drummed the steering wheel of his FJ Holden Ute with anxious fingers. Completed plans for the barracks expansion were spread on the vinyl seat beside him.

Stopping at a service station on the highway he filled the Ute with petrol, bought a map of Queensland and clipped it to an address he'd found in Sylvia's scrawled handwriting in a kitchen drawer and headed north.

ACROSS the border the heat was suffocating. At the end of a long gravel drive sat a rundown bungalow with paint peeling off aged timber boards in sheets, not the sprawling Queenslander George had conjured in his febrile imagination.

A buzzing fly bashed against the screen door.

An ancient Kelpie lounging on the porch, opened one eye, stretched and fell back into languid sleep.

George rapped on the door frame.

The door creaked. 'Oh my God! George? This is unexpected,' Sylvia said. The door groaned a protest as she opened it slowly. 'You've come a long way, George.'

She leaned on a verandah post. Tired strands of hair hung over her damp forehead. She wore a stained apron. 'You could have waited until I came home.'

George flinched, *home*. 'I wasn't sure if you were coming … back.' He shuffled on the porch, holding his hat up as protection from the fierce sun. Sylvia heaved a sigh. 'Come inside.' She moved aside as George ducked his head through the doorway. 'Eric's not here.'

The truth was out, a simple sentence, no regret or explanation. One word for the truth. "Eric".

THEY SAT at a red-marbled laminate table.

The odour of days' old lard permeated the room.

Sylvia shrugged, pulled out a cigarette and lit it.

George sneezed. 'You don't smoke, Sylvia.'

'I do now, George.' She took a long satisfying drag. 'I don't want to fight.'

'I've bought a house,' George said, suddenly sure of at least one thing. Matt Pascoe had been trying to get a buyer for his mother's house for months, the old settler's cottage at the edge of town. 'You'll be able to live this new version of our life there.'

'You've what?' Sylvia's head jerked up, the old fire in her eyes. George's jaw was grim. 'Now, dear. Do try and remember your policy of non-combatancy.'

'You've always said you wish I had more go, more initiative. So … I'm buying the old Pascoe place.'

'George! You shock me. But Mum is depending on us.' Sylvia held his gaze for the first time since he arrived.

George laughed, a rough grinding sound. 'Think of it as compensation. Compensation for me sharing a bed with a wife who sleeps with her back to me.'

Sylvia brought a jug of iced tea from a wheezing, chipped refrigerator and thunked it on the table.

A large ceiling fan disturbed humid air while the minutes got up and slowly left the room.

'I care too much to fight with you, George.'

'You don't love me enough to fight with me, Sylvia.'

Sylvia paled. She paused. Cigarette ash fell as she leant forward. 'Anything else, George?'

'Yes.' George stood, scraping the chair across the dull Lino floor. He spoke softly, precisely. 'Lucy. If you leave me, you won't take her away from me. Take anything else. Hell, take everything else.'

'I never would, George, I…' Sylvia stared at the table, clinking a mottled fork against a cup. 'I'll be back at the end of summer.'

George slipped quietly out the door, ramming his hat on his head, tilting it down over his eyes.

Fear clawed at his gut as he slammed the car door. He wound

the window down and dragged in gasps of thick, moist air. What had he done? He had known her secret, known it some place deeper than heart, or mind. Now the truth had life, shape. It was a sharp thing between them, not a shifting, smouldering thing they avoided.

Trembling fingers jammed the key in the ignition. He crept down the long, dirt road, idling the engine, delaying the moment. Then, he gunned the engine, thrashing the gears, leaving an exhilarating thick cloud of dust that blocked out the farmhouse, the landscape and Sylvia.

WHEN Sylvia returned, Lucy and George were already installed in the cottage. Sylvia picked her way through the chaos and closed the guest door behind her.

I Leave My Hand Out

Lucy Meredith Carter, Book Of Known Facts, Quirindi, 1955

I don't like the dark.
I don' t like it when the world disappears.
Dad lets me have a light on.
Sometimes Mum held my hand until I went to sleep.
I miss her.

THE LAMPLIGHT is dim. It's hard to see what I'm writing. I put the pen and book on the side table and wish I could turn all the thoughts in my head off. Dad says I think too much.

Whoot whoot. The night owl is saying goodnight as I creep further down the bed. I stay still and listen for the thud of my heartbeat, *lub dub, lub dub.* There are other sounds too; the groaning and creaking of the house as it settles into the cool of the evening, the cooing of the other night birds.

All those noises used to frighten me, until Dad explained that our house is made of timber and the boards expand and contract with heat and cold, and some birds like to sing at night.

Understanding why things happen is important. I was afraid of the tapping and scraping of the eucalypt branches on the window so Dad cut them back. He said 'that ruddy noise would bother anyone'.

There was a time when I thought all the colours disappeared at night, leaving dull greyness until the sun brought the world to life again in the morning. Now I know that doesn't happen, but I still like the glow from the lamp in the corner of my room. It's covered with Fliss's shawl, one she had when she was young. It's the most colourful thing I've ever seen. As it flutters in the night breezes, it sends shifting colour around the room.

Dad has just been in to kiss me goodnight and turn the lamplight down low. When Mum was alive, she never allowed this, saying it was 'giving in to the foolishness of childhood fears'. As I lay still and quiet, I hear the rustle of pages as Dad reads in the lounge room. I turn over and the bed springs creak.

'Dad,' I call to him, 'can I have just five minutes to write in my book?' I ask. 'I don't want to forget anything. Please?'

His voice is a low rumble. 'Just five minutes then. I'm keeping an eye on the clock.'

'Thanks, Dad. I'll be quick. You're terrific.'

'Yeah, yeah. Five minutes.'

I write in my book nearly every day. Nanna Ennis says she'll buy me a proper diary when I'm twelve and going to high school. I don't want that; I like this book. It's made of tapestry and leather. I love the feel of the fabric and the smooth hide. It's special because it was Mum's and had pressed wildflowers in it. I tried to dry some flowers myself. It didn't work for me, it just left stains. Mum must have had a special way of doing it, I guess.

The book has a stamp Mum used to put her name in all her books—"This book is the property of Sylvia Jane Carter". I wish I had a stamp with my name to put in all my books.

EVERY night before I go to sleep, Dad lets me check my favourite things one last time, so I quickly touch them: Mum's button collection, Dad's draftsmen's pencils and last of all, my Book Of Known Facts. The eiderdown quilt Nanna made is soft and warm.

When I'm all snuggled in, I slip my hand above the covers.

I'm remembering Mum. I remember her sitting here, humming and holding my hand until I fell asleep.

So, I leave my hand out, even if it's cold.

THERE'S a soft kiss on my forehead.

It's Mum in a soft silver dress.

We dance and twirl across the sky on moonbeams.

We swim in the ocean, under the water and above.

'Mum. Why are there more colours down here than on land?'

'Because there are many other worlds.' Mum says.

She spins. Her hair swirls above her.

'Mum. Why are all the colours brighter?' I ask.

'Who knows?' she says.

'Mum. You're starting to sound like Dad, that's what he says.'

She laughs a tinkling sound.

Then she drifts away through the seaweed.

I reach for her.

It's cold and I scream, 'Where have you gone?'

'IT'S ALL RIGHT, Buttons.' Dad pulls me out of the bed onto his lap. 'It was just a dream.'

I curl up into Dad's arms with my head under his chin. 'I hate dreams,' I sob. 'They're supposed to be beautiful, not sad.'

'Too much like real life, hey Buttons?'

The quilt is on the floor and the sheets are all tangled. 'Did I call out again, Dad? I'm sorry.'

'It's okay. Let's have breakfast. Aren't you visiting Fliss today?'

'Oh yes!' I jump to the floor.

'Good. Don't forget to feed Nanna's chooks before you go.'

'Oh Dad! I never forget the chooks. You know that. I feed them every day.'

'Well, don't dawdle.'

'Okay.'

Dad ruffles my hair. 'Come on, Lucy. You'd better throw some water on yourself and … why are you laughing?'

'You're funny. Mum would have told me to scrub myself clean, wash behind my ears, a whole list of things.'

Dad smiles and scratches his head as if he doesn't know what to say to that.

My voice goes soft. 'You know, Dad, sometimes I think I dreamed Mum—that she was never really here. How old was I when she died?'

Dad looks out the window, his eyes look tired. 'Six.'

'I was just a kid really wasn't I?'

'What do you think you are now, Buttons?' Dad laughs and pushes me gently towards the bathroom.

I turn when I get to the bathroom door. 'Dad. Where did Mum go, all those times she went away?'

Dad scratches his head and it ruffles his hair, it's thinning on top and tufty bits stick up.

'One day, Buttons,' he says.

His eyes are very sad and I'm *almost* sorry I asked.

Oceans & the Queen Mary

Ennis family home, Henry Street, Quirindi, 1955

LUCY sits on the chrome seat in Harry's hut, breathing mist onto the window. 'I can see right down to the creek from here.'

'I dream about Mum,' she whispers, 'I dream we're swimming in the ocean. I've never seen the ocean—Mum promised to take me there one day. Have you seen the ocean, Uncle Harry?'

'Oh my yes! I've seen more of the ocean than I ever wished.'

'Tell me about the ocean, Uncle Harry. I've only seen pictures.'

Farewell, Sydney Harbour, October 1940

I SAW LOTS of oceans when we came to Australia from England. I don't remember much. I was only six and spent my time wandering the ship, following the sailors around, getting into mischief. Then, when I was a soldier heading off to war it was an entirely different experience, I can tell you that.

All of Sydney seemed intent on farewelling the troops. It was a spring day, cloudless and optimistic. People lined the dock, waving banners and throwing streamers. The harbour was filled with small craft with the same patriotic mood. It was October, 1940, and after months of training, the 2/17th Infantry Battalion was finally heading overseas. On the Queen Mary, no less.

The luxury of the ocean liner momentarily overwhelmed most of us. The regal ship had not lost the trappings of its former use as a first-class passenger liner, but the enormity of the ocean was a powerful reminder that our former lives were far behind.

'Good crowd,' said a voice beside me. It was Frank. Over six feet and skinny as a piece of cardboard, he always stood out, earning the nickname of Lanky. We'd been together from the start, signed up the same day, theatrically moaning about our jabs, then endured all the prodding, "shearing" and endless paperwork together.

A solicitor from the city, he'd been challenged by the training more than most. Like me, he was older than many of the blokes. I guess that was one of the reasons we'd become fast friends at Ingleburn. That, and the fact that his measured approach to life was a foil to my impulsive nature.

Thousands of Sydney-siders were there to farewell the troops.

'Struth,' said Lanky. 'Thousands of 'em!'

I frowned. 'I thought our departure was a secret!'

'Oh, it is, mate. It is. This is a secret you're looking at, old son,' he said, pointing at the crowds. 'Welcome to the Australian Army, mate.' He flicked open a cigarette case and lit up. 'I expect Hitler's preparing a high tea served with mortar rounds as we speak.'

'Shit. I hope they're better at keeping war strategies under wraps,' I said, wondering how Lanky always seemed to be one step ahead of the rest of us. 'Thought of going into army intelligence, Lanky?'

'Lord, no! I've neither the inclination nor the psychic ability to carry off that lousy job. However, that doesn't stop me questioning every bloody decision. Not an affliction you share, Harry?'

I shook my head. 'I'm just a simple man, Lanky. Head down. On with the job.'

'Good man, the army needs men like you.' Lanky slapped my back.

The 2/17th was heading overseas. After boots thundering in unison, deft and swift handling of weapons, fastidious care of equipment, disease prevention and of course, obedience.

The huge liner was dwarfed in the Southern Ocean. Reminding us powerfully that our previous lives were far behind. The "Queen" carried over six thousand soldiers from battalions across the country.

Long corridors criss-crossed.

Fights broke out in hallways crammed with lost anxious soldiers. I'd been a lorry driver and delivery man so I could read a map upside-down, sideways or as it fluttered around the cab of my truck so I found my way easily with the schematics. Lanky ducked and followed.

'Couldn't find my way out of a paper bag, mate,' he declared as he ducked and followed me from deck to deck.

There were over six thousand men aboard. All from different battalions. This made the ship a prime target so we sailed south towards the Antarctic. The HMS Venetia had been destroyed by a mine in the Thames Estuary the day before embarking, a sobering reminder of the war.

The Germans were dominating the seas. The Queen Mary with its precious cargo of soldiers would take no risks.

The ship sailed silently at night, all lights out. Lanky and I, and some of the others sat on deck in the still of the night, enjoying the familiarity of the southern skies, watching the phosphorescence in the ocean. The ocean rolled and dipped that first day, its depths an unfathomable indigo. If, as the scientists claim, the seas are a mere reflection of the sky, then the sky that night was a tempestuous thing.

Then, a placid, flat sea prevailed. Flying fish slapped the steel sides of the ship, until the ocean changed. The decks swayed—a slow sick rhythm. Some of the men were brutally seasick. I felt for them, although I was glad I didn't join them at the bucket, the porcelain bowls or over the side of the ship.

They diggers seemed so young to me. Green men off to war. Raw lads with grand dreams and schemes. There was excitement in their voices—some talked of finding adventure, some would make fortunes, get trades and careers. Many would fall. And those of us who survived...

They teased me about my resigned attitude.

'You're an old man to them,' Lanky said. 'Practically a geriatric.'

Lanky and I had been together from the start, signed up the same day, took our jabs, and endured all the prodding, "shearing" and paperwork together. He was younger than me, but he seemed older and wiser than the teenage soldiers.

'I went through a world war before some of these lads were born,' I said. 'Lived through the London bombings.'

'You should be ready for what's ahead, then.'

'You're never ready, Lanky. That's one thing I've learned in life.'

He leaned over the railing and gazed at the ocean. 'You'd have come to Australia by ship,' he said. 'Was it like this?'

'A little less heaving over the side, maybe,' I said. 'It was hardest on my mother. A war widow with two small kids.'

'Want a fag?' he asked, extending the packet.

'What are they?'

'Capstan, the Prime Minister's favourite.'

I laughed and accepted one. 'From what I hear our PM has quite a few favourites. Loves his smokes.'

'They'll be scarce as hen's teeth where we're going,' Lanky said, enjoying the draft as he inhaled. 'Some of the blokes are already sussing out black market opportunities.'

A young digger rushed to the railing, hurling wretchedly. 'Shit mate! Stay upwind, will you!' I said, flinching. I patted the boy gingerly on the back.

'What's y'secret?' he asked. 'You blokes haven't hurled once. Must've misplaced my sea legs. Arrgh!'

'Keep on deck and stare at the ocean,' I said, but my words were useless; the poor bloke was back over the railing, too busy to care.

Wiping his face with a much-used handkerchief, he leant on the railing, exhausted. 'I can't even remember signing up,'

He dragged stubby fingers through short, spiked hair. 'I do know I was getting acquainted with a few very attractive schooners of Resch's Pilsener.' He chuckled. 'Great yarn to tell the grandkids hey? "Why did you join up, Grandpa?" he mimicked a child's voice. "Resch's Pilsener, son",' he said, lowering his voice.

'You're not the only one, mate.' Lanky helped him to his feet, and he staggered across the deck. 'You're not goin' back below deck are you, son?' asked Lanky.

'Yeah, sure. There's a pack of cards, and a good hand with my name on it.'

ON-BOARD, the army kept up training, even delivering lectures on life as POWs if we should fall into enemy hands.

A few boxing matches were held, bets laid. These were intense as we each cheered our favourites.

'You'd be good for a few rounds wouldn't you, Harry?' suggested one of the young blokes who'd been with me in one of the lifeboat drills.

Lanky laughed. 'That'll teach you for bragging about the enormous weights you carried on deliveries.'

'Yeah. C'mon, you're a nuggetty sort of bloke. You'd do.'

'Not me mate. I might've carried more sides of lamb and

Christmas hams than I can count but I'd be a poor show at that malarkey. But give me a go at the sandbag race and I'll show you a thing or two.'

I threw a bag over each shoulder.

Then as the men cheered, or hissed, I crossed the line ahead of the pack. If only they'd known what I'd carried as a driver.

'Bravo,' said my lifeboat class companion. 'You're a nuggety bastard. I won a few quid on ya today.'

That's how I got the nickname, Nugget. Lanky thought it was hilarious. 'Suits you. It's better than your lame jokes.'

'Go on with you!' I said. 'Have I told you the one where Churchill, Hitler and Mussolini go into a bar?'

Lanky told me to shut up.

AN OFFICER walked towards us, with sure brisk footsteps. He had his sea legs. We saluted.

'Indian Ocean now, fellas,' he said, eyes warning to ask no more.

'Where do you think we're headed?' I asked Lanky when the officer had gone.

'Dunno, but if I was a betting man, I'd say the Suez,' Lanky said.

———

LUCY squeaks with delight. 'I like your nickname, Uncle Harry. You might have been a gold nugget.'

Harry bowed forward on the slatted chair.

'You're too kind, mademoiselle.'

EMPTY NEST

Ennis family home, Henry Street, Quirindi, 1955

SUNLIGHT gleams on sudsy puddles on the back porch, where Ethel has recently swished a tangled mop over pale decaying timber. George has politely offered to seal the boards, but she would have none of it.

Ethel wipes her brow with a cleaning rag.

How could there be more work than when all three children were home?

She flops onto the couch opposite the glass display case, where rows of family photographs stand.

Was it really that long ago?

Leaving, Ennis family home, 1940

IN THE MIDDLE of a bitterly cold winter, in 1940, David Ennis, seventeen, fudged his age, forged his mother's signature, and enlisted in the AIF leaving his mother a scrawled note—'Doing my bit. Love, your son.'

Sylvia packed her father's two leather-strapped tan suitcases and caught the early train to Sydney.

She left a messy room, but no note.

After moving into Fliss' tiny flat Sylvia landed a job with a law firm, becoming a brisk, efficient employee, making her mother proud.

With a new hairstyle—heels and makeup, she passed for twenty-one out on the town, where she met shy diggers, larrikin airmen, lusty sailors and charming Yanks with money to burn, a fondness for swing music and Miss Sylvia Jane Ennis.

These latter activities were omitted from glowing stories to Ethel, whose anxiety for Sylvia was taken over by Fliss.

If there were any signs of Sylvia's night life or hijinks Ethel pushed those hints aside, preferring the new version of her offspring; the elegant woman, the dutiful daughter that came home on weekends with tales of industry and diligence.

It was a reality so desirable, so palatable that Ethel ignored wine stains on lace handkerchiefs, photographs, briefly seen of sailors, soldiers and airmen.

Ethel discounted the most blatant changes in her errant daughter, even when Sylvia wallowed in misery over a Yankee pilot who had called, adored, brought flowers, plied with silk stockings.

Until deployed to Darwin, he found another love to adore, bring flowers, and ply with silk-stockinged charm.

After all, Sylvia was more circumspect, more pensive and spent all her time when she was home with sensible George Carter, attending church and going on picnics.

Past Terrors

George Street, Quirindi, 1955

GEOFFREY McDonald, owner and proprietor of the corner store on George Street, sweeps the pavement, enjoying the early morning quiet. He looks up, eyes jagging on the sign above the store. "McDonald & Sons, 4Square Store". He blinks, filches a crumpled handkerchief from a back pocket and blows his nose noisily. Geoffrey McDonald has no more sons. They were both killed in the First World War, on the same day, rushing forward to battle on the beach, still wet from the Aegean Sea at Gallipoli.

Geoffrey McDonald hears a light sound, the scraping of a rubbish bin lid. It's Old Pat, the long-bearded vagrant, scrounging in the shop bin. The old man finds the half loaf of bread that Geoff left there in a tightly-wrapped brown paper bag, doffs his diggers' hat and whispers, 'Sir'.

Old Pat scans the sky for German fighter planes from the First World War—an Albatross, a Panzer Einsitzer, a deadly Fokker, I, II, or III. Old Pat knows them all. Then, seeing no threat, the old man flees, coat flapping, bare feet thumping, back to his canvas humpy by river's bend to the war he brought back home with him, where no wife or child can hear his shrieks or moans, where no wife will ever feel the grip of his hands on her throat, where he can howl his wartime terrors to the dark night sky.

Broken

Lucy Meredith Carter, Book Of Known Facts, Quirindi, 1955

There are things I don't want to remember.
Like my Mum dying and always going away.
No one will talk about it.
They don't think kids need to know stuff.

MUM usually went away in early spring and came back in summer just before Christmas. Nanna told me I clung to her leg and cried when I was little. Whenever I asked where she went, I was told she had to go to the country. I guess I thought everyone's mother went away.

Until I started school.

Charlotte Renshaw came up to me on my first day of school, with a crowd of small girls behind her. She was in Grade Two. 'Your mum doesn't live with you,' she said, twirling her hair around plump fingers and watching me closely.

'Does too!' I yelled. My face was hot.

'Not all the time,' she said, swaying her body as she moved closer.

'She's got … an important job.' I wanted to step back but I didn't.

'Don't be stupid. Only fathers go away to work, not mothers. Your family is broken.'

'Is not!' I screamed. That's when I realised that even though no one in the family talked about Mum going away, everyone else was talking about it.

Sitting alone at lunchtime, I wondered how far it was to home. I would have to walk along the road where big bony Jersey cows straggled across the road, lowing and bumping.

'Don't worry about Charlotte. She's mean to everyone.' It was Jenny Baker. She was in my class. Thin blonde hair fell over her face as she leant towards me. I decided I liked her.

AFTER SCHOOL that day I ran home in the rain, crying, wanting Mum's hugs. It was a wintry Monday. I stumbled over the back step. I'd forgotten my yellow-caped raincoat again, and my hair was sopping wet. I grabbed the old towel Dad used to wipe his boots and rubbed it roughly through my hair so Mum wouldn't know that I'd been caught in the rain without my raincoat.

I found Mum's suitcases in the hallway by the front door. There were tags on them with Mum's beautifully curved writing. I was halfway through Grade One then. I couldn't read much but I saw the letters "QLD". I didn't know what they meant until later. But I knew those suitcases only came out when Mum was going away.

It was July. Mum only ever left after Christmas, after stockings after roast dinners, or after my birthday.

The air was thick with the smell of hairspray. I sneezed.

Mum's wool suit was a blur as she rushed down the hall calling out to Mrs Kingston over her shoulder, 'I won't need that coat Marj. It'll be too hot'. She saw me. 'You're home early pet,' she said, leaning in to kiss me.

I turned my head away quickly.

'You're leaving!' I yelled. 'It's only July. Why do you keep going away? What is wrong with you?'

'Lucy! We've talked about this.' Mum smoothed her hair.

'No we haven't! We haven't talked about it. We never talk about it. We never talk about anything. You know why? Because we're broken, that's why. We're a big old cracked broken family! We're broken people!'

Mum's face went very red. She raised her hand as if she was going to slap my face, then dropped it. She yanked hard to pull on her gloves and spoke to me through her teeth. 'You will not speak to me that way again, Lucy Carter. Mrs Kingston is taking me to the station now. Be good for your father.' Her face was twisted.

Mum stared past me and pinned her hat with a silver pin.

I yanked her sleeve hard. 'Why!'

The hatpin fell. Mum bent to pick it up.

I grabbed it and stabbed it in the wall, tearing the wallpaper. I yelled all the horrible things Charlotte had said. I kicked the suitcases that only appeared when she was leaving.

Mum's hands shook. 'Tittle-tattle kids!' she said. 'Telling silly tales they've heard at home.'

She took a step towards me I shrank against the wall and yelled. 'Don't touch me, Sylvia!'

Her face went pale then. She flinched and moved away. I heard Dad scraping mud off his boots on the back step. I turned and saw him standing in the doorway in his socks, his face stiff and white. Running to my room I slammed the door.

After a few light taps on my door, I heard Mum's footsteps then the click of the front door.

I cried then, great bunching sobs that cramped my stomach. I stuffed a pillow in my mouth and cried so hard my throat hurt. These were sounds I could never let my mother hear.

Dad made me a banana sandwich. I asked how much he loved me. 'More than the stars in the sky, or water in the oceans.'

The day before, the whole class had been to Beth May's sixth

73

birthday party at her three-storey house in George Street. It had taken me ages to fit in, to be invited to the best party. Beth was the only one who invited all the class. Of course we all went. None of us wanted to be left out, or picked on. At the party she was like a princess, all froth, lace, ringlets and royal airs. So I had head full of princesses, parties and games when I tripped through the back door. It would be my sixth birthday in a few weeks and absolutely everyone at school had a party for their birthday. I was sure Mum would love to give me a party.

The year before, 1950, had been the Diamond Jubilee for Quirindi and Mum had helped sew costumes for the pageant girls. The celebrations went for a whole week in November and Mum had been happy right in the middle of everything. She'd even put off going away for a couple of weeks. But not for me, not for my birthday.

IN THE END, a few weeks later, Nanna tried to make up for things, like she always did. She put on a small birthday party. She made a Dolly Varden cake with a pink lace dress. It was too nice to put candles on so she made a number 7 in silver icing buttons on the cake. My friend from school, Jenny, and her Gran came. Nanna knew them from the CWA, but then Nanna seems to know everyone.

It was a stormy Sunday and hail pounded on the tin roof. Nanna let Jenny and me run outside catching hailstones in the big green mixing bowl she used for making bread. Jenny and I tasted the icy hailstones. We pulled faces and said they tasted horrible, like earth and grass.

'Well, what did you expect, you silly kids?' Nanna laughed and let us spread pink icing on the cupcakes with hot knives. She even let us run our sticky fingers around the bowl to get the last smears of icing, something she never allowed any other time.

Jenny's Gran and Nanna sipped tea at the kitchen table while Jenny and I lay on the rug in front of the hissing fire, playing Chinese Checkers. Because there was just the two of us we had three colours each and got really muddled, but we didn't care.

Jenny told me she lived a long way out of town on a property with just her Gran and Gramps. She was glad to have a friend at school because there weren't many kids and farm life meant visits didn't happen often. She said Charlotte teased her too because she lived with her grandparents. Jenny was right about Charlotte being mean to everyone, although she had favourites—Jenny and me, Nikita, the Czech girl whose mother wore a scarf over her hair, and Rosalie, who didn't have a father and lived with her mother and brother in a rundown house on the edge of town.

Jenny and I moaned about our hair, we both hated our hair. Hers was fine and wispy and wouldn't stay tied up in a ponytail or plaits. I couldn't believe it when she said she'd give anything to have hair like mine.

'But it's horrible,' I said. 'No one wants red frizzy hair that's hard to brush.' We laughed, and I forgot about Mum leaving, and jobs far from home that no one talked about. Mum had sent a parcel with books, pencils and doll's clothes so I tried not to be angry with her for not being there.

Jenny's Gran braided my hair and promised to have me sleep over at the farm sometime.

Dad wandered in and moaned when we told him we'd already licked all the spoons. He was supposed to stay away because it was a Princess Party, but he said no one in their right mind could expect a man to resist cake. As Dad piggy-backed me on the way home I had to fight to stay awake. The sun was falling below the trees. The moon was a see-through ball, the way it is when it arrives early in the evening. The magpies were warbling their afternoon song as Dad clicked the door behind him.

MUM'S SUITCASES were inside the door, just tossed carelessly there, one was on its side resting on the other. Dad stood very still. A cold hard feeling hit me. Mum walked into the hallway. Her eyes were red and puffy, like she'd been crying. She and Dad went into the loungeroom. I didn't know what to do so I slumped to the floor in the hallway, put my head down and hugged my knees. I heard their murmured voices.

Through the crack in the door I could see Dad holding Mum's hand. She was shaking her head and whispering in a raspy voice. They looked up at the same time. They didn't see me at all, or anything else. Something was wrong.

Mum was back too soon.

It was odd. They were sitting close to each other, but they never sat in the same lounge, never touched.

I was afraid. Mum's hair was messy.

Dad called me in and started talking.

A disease was growing inside Mum, a disease called cancer. She was sick.

They took turns telling it.

I shook my head. Mum looked great. She was pretty, glowing from the sun. Her cheeks were pink.

WE VISITED Fliss to tell her. I stayed with Fliss as they went off to tell Nanna Ennis. Fliss lived in a tiny nursing home then, an old cramped house run by the Ingram sisters. I wanted to be with Fliss. She cried easily any time, because of the stroke, but not that day.

She patted my hand and motioned for me to sit on the floor while she brushed my hair with her good hand. Everything started to feel normal. People got sick all the time. And then they got better. Mum would be okay.

THαT HOUSE OF HELL

Montview Lodge, George Street, Quirindi, 1955

FLISS' right leg jerks. She taps the muscle with a closed fist. The pain of cramp sears again ... perhaps when Katya returns... Fliss has pinned her hopes on Katya. She's been away studying Physical Therapy. Perhaps Katya will understand that when Fliss jabs a finger at the door she wants something other than to have the door closed, or open, or to be ushered to the outdoor terrace leaning on a walking stick and a supporting arm.

She wants something farther, bigger. To stumble through the pain until her muscles remember and obey. She does not hope for miracles for her slow jerking leg. But to move alone. To have time to linger among the trees beside the garden. To touch the waxy leaves moist with dew, the rough sinewy trunk, to pick a blossom or a crimson lilly pilly berry. To whisper with the breeze.

In a straight-backed chair near the window Fliss hooks her right foot with the crook of the walking stick and lifts it, forcing it free from its stiff prison. She moves it in circles with white-knuckled grip, persevering with patience learned at the Ingrams. The Ingrams, that house of hell run by the Ingram sisters, Ernestine and Evelyn.

The cramp grips with iron force. Fliss moans. It's a relief to release sound, for she was once not free to do so.

'FELICITY will be one of the family here, Mrs Ennis.' The voice was smooth and confiding, but Fliss suspected the speaker, Ernestine Ingram, was not.

Miss Ernestine Ingram was exceptionally tall, with straight-backed posture that was neither forced nor elegant. She exuded confidence and efficiency. Perhaps she knew this place was Fliss' only option. Fliss wasn't ill enough for hospital, but months of pneumonia had weakened her, making a return home to Henry Street out of the question. Ernestine wrote "indefinite" in the section titled "Stay". Fliss shuddered. She raised panicked eyes to her mother, but Ethel sagged with weariness then sighed with something akin to relief.

As Ernestine stacked the completed paperwork with a satisfied snap, her eyes merely grazed Ethel, and didn't rest on Fliss at all. Ernestine's hands were fast, handing a sheaf of papers to Ethel. 'These are your records, Mrs Ennis. Now, don't worry. Felicity will be happy here. She'll have the best of care.' She patted Ethel's hand, her words the perfect pitch of reassurance and calm.

'Oh, thank you Miss … Miss Ingram.' Ethel smiled weakly.

'Call me Ernestine, Mrs Ennis.' The woman smoothly filed the remaining papers and locked the cabinet.

There was a coldness about her, a formality. Fliss had learned to read the nurses in the hospital, know which ones were kind, which were indifferent, or plain cruel. Fliss wasn't sure about Miss Ernestine Ingram.

The formalities over, Ernestine turned to Fliss, tugged and smoothed Fliss' skirt hem then stood back. Regarding her with narrowed eyes, Fliss resisted the temptation to skew the hem back to where it had been. Ernestine's sister, Evelyn Ingram, plump as an over-stuffed pillow, was all bustle and clatter as she entered on her sister's summons. She flashed a perfunctory smile at Ethel, then tucked a knee rug tightly around Fliss in the wheelchair, before lifting Fliss' suitcase with a satisfied humph.

Ernestine gripped the handles of the wheelchair. 'We'll take her from here, Mrs Ennis. She'll need to rest after the ambulance journey. We have a lovely corner room prepared, with a view of the creek.' There was a vague warning in her eyes.

Ethel took a step forward. 'Oh...I'd love to see Felicity's room...'

Ernestine blocked the doorway. 'And you shall, Mrs Ennis, you shall, once Felicity is settled in. Anyway, we encourage patients to spend their time downstairs. So much better for their health, don't you think? And we encourage visitors to make use of the lovely downstairs sitting rooms.'

'But I thought...' Ethel straightened her shoulders, a stance that had always intimidated Fliss but had no effect on Ernestine Ingram.

'Best leave the nursing to us, Mrs Ennis. It's rather late. The nurses are settling the patients now,' she frowned, 'busy with bedpans and the like...'

A woman in a pale blue uniform hurried towards the stairs with a flimsy fabric cover over a metal bowl.

'Oh. Alright, I'm not ... I wouldn't make a nurse's bootlace.' Ethel blanched and leaned back. 'I don't know how you girls do it.'

Ethel left with a curt nod.

Ernestine swung the wheelchair around. Fliss caught sight of her walking stick and pointed with a yelp. With a firm grip Ernestine returned her arm to her lap.

'Keep your arms in, dear. We don't want you getting skin tears. There's not a lot of room in the lift.'

Fliss' 'tsk tsk' was ignored.

A MIDDAY storm announced Fliss' arrival to the room prepared for her. Even as clouds bulked and the sky turned to inky charcoal as midday mimicked twilight, Fliss could see the dark shine of mahogany furniture, promising warmth she feared the Ingram sisters could not deliver.

Beside an unmade bed, Evelyn propped Fliss in a cold, chrome chair where Fliss saw dull timber floors worn by years of indifferent polishing, a tattered circular rug, rectangular shadows where paintings once hung.

A Slavic woman entered, wearing a capacious apron that spilled cleaning rags. 'No English,' she said as she set about cleaning. A pale headscarf partly covered thick greying hair that had once been golden blonde. She didn't look up from her work, humming as she swept strong arms in circular movements.

Fliss knew the tune and hummed along.

The woman turned slowly, cleaning rag hanging limply. 'Hmm, vell, vell…' She wagged a stubby finger.

Fliss turned her hands upwards in helpless gesture.

'Ah, no verds.'

Fliss shook her head, *no words*.

'Zilent we are then, both, yar.' The woman rolled up the rug, shrugged in apology, then left.

Fear gripped Fliss. What other comforts would be denied?

VISITORS were not permitted upstairs. Only Sylvia braved the wrath of the Ingrams, smart heels clicking, bounding up the stairs two at a time, waving a negligent hand. Sylvia, with her brash confidence, sharp eyes, fierce mutterings of fetid urine smells and hell-holes.

Fliss came to know the difference between the brisk footsteps of Ernestine, the rolling gait of Evelyn and the heavy shuffle of Dr Emmerson. As for the footsteps or appearance of other staff—

there were none she could discern. They wore the same uniform, a pale blue military-style dress.

Fliss longed for the agony of the rehab ward, with its relentless stretching and straining. She craved the punishing exercise program she once loathed. She remembered the exhaustion and the satisfaction, and wished she could push her body until it relented and gave her rest. The meagre stretches she could manage in bed failed to bring relief. Anger roiled. She had walked in the rehab ward, stumbled with a walking stick, crossed the room alone. But not here with the Ingram sisters. Any walking sticks she purloined, left by departing residents, soon disappeared.

THUNDER began a drumbeat. The Ingrams would be tucked up in bed in their downstairs flat with only an ancient call system to disturb their slumber. A flash of lightning poured light into the room. The porcelain clock showed the time. Nearly midnight.

After years of studying the Ingrams' routine Fliss knew the sisters turned the call system off between midnight and 4am.

Evelyn had forgotten to close the window. Evening breezes, delicious as cool clear water, crept in. Fragrance from a native frangipani came whispering. Gauze curtains were flung aside with a screech of rings on railing as lightning slashed the purple sky above the Quirindi hills.

At the centre of nature's sovereignty, Fliss revelled in the storm's power and longed for her own. She yearned for the sweet smell of rain, for silky night breezes to touch her skin. In that one wild moment, freedom seemed possible. If she was found outside on a stormy night, surely then Ethel would realise her plight, surely the Ingrams would be exposed.

Fliss slipped her left leg over the side and yanked at her right leg.

Using the bedhead as ballast, she stood and moved along the bed to the wardrobe.

Probing her fingers into the crevice behind it, she found what she was seeking. With escape on her mind she had filched Nellie Stockton's crutch from her room several nights before. Nellie had no further need of crutches, having suffered a devastating third stroke and been bedridden for weeks.

Fliss had overheard Ernestine's low conversation with Dr Emmerson, a sour portly man with dull eyes who wheezed his arrival up the old timber staircase as he followed Ernestine's clicking steps.

Gaining the crutch had been a triumph.

Its midnight procurement had been exhausting.

Fliss remembered how many hours it had taken her to cross the hall with an awkward half-slither, half-rolling crawl as her joints gave sharp protest. Her elation had been sweet when she grasped the crutch beside Nellie's bed. The urge to sneeze at the fetid, urine tainted air had nearly brought her undone.

Fliss' trembling fingers found Nellie's crutch beside her own wardrobe and tickled it closer. It fell into her hands. With juddering movements she jerked across the room along the wall, flexing, moving, heedless of the cramping ache of her body, forcing her dead leg along, step, slide, drag, step, slide, drag. Fliss knew she would be in agony the next morning but she didn't care. Only one thought pierced the fog of her mind.

She had to keep moving, stay awake, stay alert. She thought of old Nellie, lying in the next room. Nellie who chanted 'brain in a coffin' in her waking hours. Fliss would not become a frozen caricature.

With ungainly steps she inched her way to the lift, then leaned panting against the wrought iron cage as she summoned the lift. Once inside, she pressed the down button. The lift lurched into motion with a squeaking of pulleys. How Fliss would secure the rest of her escape was unclear but she was desperate.

When the lift doors clattered open noisily downstairs, the Ingram sisters stood in the hallway opposite the lift, waiting as Fliss leaned out of the door, her stained nightie twisted around her. While Ernestine flayed with her vicious tongue, Evelyn wrenched the crutch from Fliss' grasp and rained slapping blows, dragging Fliss into the lift by her bad arm, causing her to howl in pain.

Fliss fought, kicking and gouging, arms flailing ineffectually, surrender inevitable. She must have looked like a madwoman, wild-eyed, unkempt, filling the air with banshee screaming.

Back upstairs, she was tossed swiftly into bed Evelyn with her pinched-sour eyes delivered a sharp jab in Fliss' thigh.

Fliss' heart thundered in her neck as she fought the slow advance of the sedative, vaguely aware of a sheering new agony in her shoulder. As the fog of the drug descended, Fliss cursed her impetuous actions.

In those fierce moments of heart-racing conflict she feared another stroke. She had risked too much for too little, courting new wrath from the Ingrams. Would they write hasty notes for the doctor, speak of madness? Assess her as aggressive?

The sedative hammered its way into her brain. This was no soft retreat into somnolence or peace.

As consciousness flickered Fliss vowed to accept any punishment, offer any penance.

She thought the sisters would ignore her for days, like they had many others, leaving her to lie in a darkened room, sleeping off her rebellion, but in the morning, while still drug-hazed and disoriented she was wrenched into a wheelchair by Evelyn who secured Fliss with torn strips from an old bedsheet. With only a thin nightie to cover her, Fliss was taken down in the rattling lift.

She stared at the floor. Why downstairs?—to remind her of the freedoms she would be denied until her capitulation was complete? Fliss panicked as she heard Ernestine murmur smoothly to Evelyn about moving her to share a room with mad Alice Fenchurch, a poor soul who counted all day, loudly reciting numbers with the bombast of a preacher.

Fliss heard the flurried wheezing of Dr Emmerson.

Ernestine pulled the nightie off Fliss' bruised shoulder, revealing her nakedness to the crowded dining room.

Fliss fought tears—to withhold them, her last dignity.

The doctor strapped her shoulder with gentle enough care, ignoring the bedsheet restraints ensuring her confinement. He shrugged and looked at Ernestine.

'Dislocated shoulder. Good Diagnosis, Sister.'

He gave a brief nod of approval at his handiwork, never seeing past Fliss' bruises and pained flinching. In the four years of her stay with the Ingrams he'd never looked Fliss in the eye. What did he know of her? Patient records, if they could be called that, were school notebooks, locked in the tiny office, seldom brought out, even for doctors' visits, never for relatives' perusal. All he knew of Fliss was contained in those brief scribblings, distorted by the Ingram sisters. Would he prescribe the cursed sedative Largactil regularly? A medication reserved for the intractable and violent? Fliss suspected Largactil had been the drug chosen for last night's sedation. Her vision was blurred. Her head ached with a pounding rhythm.

RETURNED to the upstairs room, Evelyn secured Fliss once more to the bed.

There, she was torn through shuddering dreams that belonged to neither night nor day.

Was she asleep? Awake?

Around what seemed like midday, a storm broke again. Dazed and restless Fliss fought her way clear of the bedsheet.

Escape had been a dream the night before. The following day it was a necessity.

Fliss could never know how often they would drug her.

Sliding to the floor, she inched her way to the lift.

A searing cramp gripped her leg, throwing her down. Fliss felt a sting as her forearm tore, blood, then a dull thud as her head hit the floor. She lay moaning softly, her hand over her mouth, lest the Ingram sisters heard.

Footsteps, echoed up the stairs, louder, coming closer. Preparing for Ingram fury Fliss shielded her head.

Ernestine stood over her.

'Get dressed. Your brother-in-law is here. Your sister's dying.'

FLISS heard the thundering of footsteps up the creaking timber staircase as George ran up the flight of stairs and rushed into the room.

Fliss raised tear-drenched eyes.

There were dull bruises and cuts on her face.

A shoulder, confined in a sling. The sisters threw a sheet over Fliss at the sight of George, standing, arms folded.

'What the hell...?' said Ernestine. 'I told you to wait! Mr Carter.'

'I will wait.' George moved closer. 'In this room. As you dress my sister-in-law and organise discharge papers, while I pack her belongings. To take with us when we leave here. Today. Now.'

George threw open the wardrobe doors, took out Fliss' battered suitcase and threw her clothes willy-nilly into it. Fliss thought of George's well-ordered workroom and shed, and knew how angry he was.

THE HOSPITAL

Lucy Meredith Carter, Book Of Known Facts, Quirindi, 1955

Fliss was a nursing Sister before the stroke.
I wish she didn't have the stroke.
I wish she had some words left.
Nanna says wishes are for fools.

AFTER DAD rescued Fliss, she often sat with Mum in the hospital room. Lots of the nurses knew Fliss from when she worked there as a Sister. They often called by to see her.

I think Fliss had more visitors than Mum, but Mum didn't mind. In that hospital room it didn't matter at all that Fliss had no words. The nurses treated her as if there had never been a stroke, or a tragedy. I'd never seen her so happy, sitting with old friends, sipping tea.

I think it helped her sadness about Mum being ill, but back then we all thought Mum would win against the cancer and be herself again as soon as she got home.

When Fliss wasn't brushing Mum's hair, pouring water for her with her good hand, she shuffled around the room with a walking frame the Matron had found for her to use.

Fliss arranged Mum's magazines or fruit brought by friends. She sat quietly, as if she belonged there.

For the first time I could imagine Fliss as a nurse gliding down the corridors, caring for others instead of being helpless.

But Mum shrank into herself, slipping down the bed, just listening watching, faded and lost. It was harder to avoid things when the treatments started.

Matron came every day to visit Mum and she often sat for a while with Fliss while Mum slept. She took Nanna and Dad aside to talk about things, then Dad would come and explain to me, in bits he thought I'd understand, about pain and scars, surgery and exercises, about radiation like X-rays to kill the cancer. I would nod. I didn't really understand much at all but I was glad he tried.

ON THE DAY Mum was allowed to come home Dad told me that Matron had found a new place for Fliss to live. Some people she knew owned a big country house that had once been the main house on a large farm. They'd turned the house into a hostel, for patients recovering from illness or needing a home because they couldn't care for themselves. The place was called Montview.

Fliss cried buckets that day. It seemed a funny time to cry. Mum was coming home. She was doing well after the surgery. But things were like that with Fliss, she'd be happy over odd things and cry for funny reasons. That's what strokes did, Nanna Ennis said. But Fliss shook her head as if none of us understood anything.

VIGIL

The Settler's Cottage, Henry Street, 1951

SYLVIA stared into the wardrobe as if it held the secrets of the universe, if only she could decipher the message. She turned, her eyes following George as he entered the room.

She savoured a cigarette and regarded George with fuggy eyes. Even through opiate dulled eyes she saw him recoil from the cigarette smoke. 'Have you no vices, George?' she said, tapping ash into a coffee mug that rested on her frail midriff. Her voice was thin, a tenuous strand between them. She exhaled a thick clump of smoke through pale blue lips.

George ignored the question and leant on the doorjamb. He'd always hated her smoking, especially inside the house but he had relented, first on frost-chilled days, then, as she grew weaker he resigned himself to the inevitable—she could smoke in the room that had become her hospice, but only under his watchful gaze. His vigilance no longer insulted her, she was too tired to fight, another reminder of how ill she was.

She closed her eyes and George flinched as her hand wavered and the cigarette dangled precariously. She was far more affected by the morphine than she realised. She had spent the previous two days drifting in and out of consciousness. He crossed the room wordlessly and plucked the cigarette from her hand. She sighed, a thin whistling sound. A tear ran down her cheek. George held the cigarette to her lips. She grasped his forearm in gratitude. In the six years of their marriage he'd never been able to deny her anything.

She placed a slender hand on armchair by her bed. 'Sit down, George. Not yet. Please. The medicine.'

The doctor had visited, earlier in the day, shaken his head sadly and increased her dose of liquid morphine. He'd also managed to talk George into administering it, an act George had resisted, fearing gossip from those who would judge him for being the one to dose her. The rejected husband. Sylvia didn't understand that. What others thought was never her concern.

'How did we get here, George?' she asked.

'We were born, I suppose.'

'So droll.' She chuckled lightly. 'You know what I mean. You always have.'

'Have I?'

'Yes, George. I could never say, "My husband doesn't understand me". Not that.'

'What then?'

'Perhaps…' she rasped, 'Perhaps you understand me too well.'

George reached for her, leant her forward and rubbed her back until the convulsive spasms passed. Falling back on the pillows, her breath came in gasps. Pneumonia had gripped her weakened lungs.

'Rest, Sylvia. Don't try to speak.' George wiped a forearm across his eyes to hide the tears that gathered.

FLISS reached to wipe her sister's forehead with a damp flannel, pleased Sylvia was too ill and too drugged to notice George's grief.

Sylvia's head turned towards the sound of the Jubilee Celebrations, the cheering, horns honking and brass bands playing. Life was going on without her.

The daybed was covered with rugs and cushions, handmade by friends. Friends who shrank from her in life, gathering to bring gifts in death, handing them across the threshold of the open door, eyes sliding away from the inside of the house, afraid to see her. Afraid to comfort.

'Yoo hoo!' Ethel peered around the door. 'How's the ... patient?' she asked, voice falling, discordant. When she saw Sylvia and heard her laboured breathing, she paled and whimpered.

Sylvia winced.

Ethel's face contorted as she fought tears. 'I'll just get the medicine, shall I?' she asked, unable to call it anything else, unable to use words that relate to the end of a life.

George slid a glance at Sylvia's pained expression and nodded.

When Ethel returned with the glass medicine cup, she and George leant Sylvia forward. Her body was limp and pliable, her nightgown damp with sweat.

'We should change her,' Ethel said, 'should we George?'

George shook his head. He guided Ethel's hands to Sylvia's feet.

Ethel covered her mouth with a hand. 'So cold,' she said, 'I see.'

Sylvia sipped the fluid, rejecting the water Ethel offered after.

Exhaustion etched in her face Sylvia turned to George. 'Lucy?' The word was a question; it held a hint of panic and longing.

'At school,' he said, adding a pillow behind her.

Sylvia's breathing slowed, taking on a peaceful rhythm in spite of the whistling rattle in her chest. Her eyes were glassy as she drifted. Then fixing her eyes on Ethel, she said, 'Dad came. Sat on the bed and chatted. He looked well.' Her voice was absent, disconnected, but oddly clear.

Ethel flinched. Bill had been dead a dozen years or more.

Fliss stroked Sylvia's face and nodded. She'd been a nurse, around the dying. What did mortals know of this final chapter?

'LUCY?' said Sylvia.

George stood and paced the room restlessly then turned to Ethel. 'Will you be okay here for a while Ethel?' He grabbed his coat and hat, pausing for a response.

'But George …'

'I have to get Lucy.' He thrust an arm into a coat sleeve.

'But George. You've only got the school bus. You can't take that…'

He crossed the room and took Fliss' hand.

Fliss smiled and nodded.

Ethel met him at the door. 'George, is this the right thing?'

'There are no right things any more, Ethel,' he said.

THE SCHOOLROOM door was open to catch the summer breeze. George waited, hat in hand. It was a short drive home. Lucy's face was pale as she gripped her father's hand and looked up at him.

'Do you want to say goodbye, Buttons?'

She nodded, but kept her grip on George until she saw Fliss. She rushed at Fliss and climbed into her lap. With one arm around Fliss' neck, she bent to kiss her mother.

Sylvia moaned softly. 'Ah, Lucy.' She raised one arm and pointed at the window overlooking the back yard. Ethel pulled back the gauze curtains and George opened the window. Sylvia drank in the breeze with thirsty abandon. Magpies flitted to and from the grevilleas enjoying their afternoon frolic in the birdbath, as they sang their varied harmonies and chased the noisy minors away.

Lucy settled into Fliss' embrace. George put a cushion under Lucy's head and covered her with a crocheted rug as her eyes drooped, then closed in sleep.

Ethel perched on a footstool, her hands arranged tensely in her lap, her eyes pained.

91

Fliss was grateful to George for insisting on her presence. For this goodbye, to be with Sylvia for this last act of life. She treasured the small, tender considerations she could give. She was glad that George had brought Lucy home. For this goodbye, and for all the goodbyes the child had missed and mourned for, when her mother went away. If not today, then some day, Lucy would be glad too.

A NEW, sombre mood filled the room.

The last silent vigil of death had begun.

The hall clock metronomed the minutes as they stretched.

Sylvia's eyes fluttered. She reached a frail hand towards George. 'Will you...' Dry lips struggled to form words. 'Tell...'

A tremor of air escaped, and she was gone.

SCENT OF A MOTHER

Lucy Meredith Carter, Book Of Known Facts, Quirindi, 1955

> Fliss wanted to give me her hairbrush.
> She found out that Nanna threw Mum's out.
> Nanna is bossy. And sneaky.
> I bet she would read my book if she found it.

AS LONG AS I can remember Nanna Ennis has been the boss of our house. Even when Mum was alive there were arguments. And when Mum died Nanna nagged Dad to tidy out Mum's things, but Dad is more stubborn, even than Nanna and he told her that he would do things when he was good and ready.

After Mum died I liked to go to her room. It was the only place that still had her scent. I loved to touch her clothes, slip on her shoes and remember her. I liked to hold her silver hairbrush, touch the strands of hair.

Even when Mum lost her hair from the cancer she kept that brush, her hair tangled with mine.

Then, one day none of Mum's things were there. No clothes, no pretty soaps, no 4711 perfume. No hairbrush. Nothing. Not even the dust was left behind. I smelt disinfectant. Nanna!

I took off up Henry Street to her place, punching the air as I ran, crying angry tears all the way. Past Mrs Kingston, sweeping her paths. Across the main street. Past the postie on his bike. Past

Mr Evans lifting the flap on his vegetable truck.

Nanna was putting out the fire under the copper in the laundry. Her sleeves were rolled up and her face was sweaty.

'What have you done with Mum's things?'

I threw wet washing on the floor. Mum's smell would be washed off everything.

'*Lucy Meredith Carter.* Stop that! Some poor soul could use them. You can't keep dead things.'

With muddy shoes I stomped on the washed clothes.

'You're a dead thing, Nanna! You're the deadest thing of all!' I yelled as Dad came panting through the door with long bits of his hair on the wrong side.

'What possessed you to do that, Ethel?' He leaned on the wall and pushed his hair back to the right side. 'The child only wanted something of her mother's.'

I WALKED straight out of Nanna's house.

Past the cabinet where she keeps Grandpa's old pipe, past a wooden spinning top of Uncle David's, past the black cast-iron doorstop that Nanna's mother gave her.

Wanting to take them all away from her.

Dad found a suitcase of Mum's, from when she went away. There wasn't much—a scarf, some hairpins, but Mum's scent had gone.

That's when we found the notebook with silk-embroidered peacocks and pressed flowers. I held that book, turning every page, sobbing on the bench swing Dad built, where Mum would brush my hair for ages. I sat there, wanting to remember those hours with Mum and forget all the times she went away.

The memory of Mum leaving sometimes seems stronger than the memory of *her*.

BOOTS, a BOAT anD a GOAT

Ennis family home, Henry Street, Quirindi, 1955

LUCY skips through Harry's door. 'Uncle Harry, I was born the day the war ended.'

'I know,' he says.

She frowns. 'How'd you know?'

'Doesn't everyone know?'

'That's Nanna and Dad arguing.' Lucy jerks her head at the house. 'Nanna wants to get a goat. Dad says goats are nothing but endless trouble.'

'Oh dear, I'm afraid I have to vote with your Dad.'

'Have you had a goat, Uncle Harry?' Lucy sits.

'Phew. Almost."

The Rohna, India, 1941

MY EYES strained through the early morning haze. Dark, dull shapes formed—the mountainous coastline of India. As we sailed closer the cityscape of Bombay appeared.

Seven miles from land. 0830 hours. The propellers spun the sea into mud. Heat spilled onto the decks of the halted Queen Mary and permeated below. The harbour was a chaotic clutter of vessels, noisy and exotic.

The 2/17th parted company with the other battalions, boarding the British India line vessel, Rohna, which ferried us to the docks. WE CAUGHT the midnight train, designed for troop transport, to Deolali, a small town in the Nashik district of Maharashtra. It's a six hour journey through the night. We hadn't washed and the air was thick with the smell of grime, sweat and tobacco. At last we surrendered to sleep after the excitement of our arrival in the exotic East. The train was cramped. Some men slept on the luggage carrier near the roof of the train as it jagged across the country.

At a rest camp near Deolali spacious huts were organised. We were welcomed and surprised to find that each tent had been assigned an Indian servant, eager to assist and acquire anything we might desire. The camp was set in a basin. The mountain air, a welcome relief. We were soon introduced to the British troops.

After we'd cleaned up and rested, we wandered. We passed by bazaars and temples, saw snake charmers with reed pipes, magicians and fortune tellers, willing to take our money. The clothing was as colourful and rich as the aroma of spice, colours never worn a world away.

'Not everyone wants us here,' muttered Lanky, as we wove our way down the streets.

'What do you mean?' I asked.

He pointed at several narrow-eyed men with their dark faces hidden by white turbans, curved blades hanging from the sashes at their waists. 'No everyone's on our side in this part of the country, Nugget.'

I rested a hand on my Webley revolver.

Lanky frowned. 'Don't be too quick with that thing.'

I merely nodded. Lanky had sharper wits than me. I remembered the lectures when we arrived that dangerous undercurrents existed and not everyone welcomed the presence of soldiers.

Our initial leave in Bombay had been limited. While repairs and restocking were underway there was time to explore a city where the customs were as strange and violent as the undercurrents we'd previously encountered. Homeless thousands with no other life or memory crowded the streets of Bombay. Narrow-eyed men stared, dark faces hidden by loosely worn, tasselled turbans, curved blades hanging from sashes at their waists. We wandered past bazaars and temples, snake charmers with reed pipes, magicians, fortune tellers, sellers of fabric and wares—all willing to take our money.

We passed the Tower of Silence at Malabar Hill, where the bodies of the dead were laid bare to the elements, gifted as a final act of charity, to nourish the birds. Vultures devoured a body in minutes. We saw the Burning Ghats, were bodies were cremated on the steps leading to the river, the ashes washed away. Homeless thousands with no other life or memory crowded the dry streets.

On Grant Road, both sides of the street were lined with black-eyed, brown skinned prostitutes in cages, under the watchful eyes of their minders, their singsong voices rising, offering themselves for a shilling or two, their dark eyes pleading. For most of us, this was an image that competed with the treatment of the dead to shock our Western sensibilities.

AFTER this brief rest and taste of the orient, we again boarded the *Rohna* with its cramped quarters, swaying on hammocks strung up randomly on deck. Back onboard, we became attached to a goat belonging to the Indian crew until it developed some alarming habits.

'Strewth, Sarge, the bloody goat has eaten me chin strap!' shouted one of the men. The rest of us laughed until we found we'd all suffered the same fate.

'Goat stew is what I fancy right now,' muttered one of the cooks.

But the Sarge took great pains to explain the religious significance of the animal to the crew and the consequences if anything befell the goat.

That night we were wakened by more yelling and cursing.

'Fecking goat's pissed on us. M'uniform will take ages to dry, and god only knows how I'll wash it,' moaned Slippery Murphy.

He wasn't the only one the goat caught this way.

'Fecking animal must have a bladder the size of China,' muttered Slippery.

———

LUCY SQUEALED.

'OH, YUK!' she said. 'That's one mean goat.'

The child doesn't notice Harry's face pale as he remembers the days after disembarking and beyond.

It's time he reconsidered the stories he tells the child. How could he relate the events at the Tower of Silence at Malabar Hill?

THOSE SMALL FICTIONS

Montview Lodge, George Street, Quirindi, 1955

FLISS taps the table with her walking stick, hoping to catch the attention of a nurse. Elvira Bertram, the new woman, admitted a week ago, is on the move, zig-zagging through the lounge. Fliss recoils. She's lost count of the times that her tender shins have been bashed as Elvira passes.

Elvira Bertram has an alarming state of dementia that rises and retreats like a tide. She's also a zealous bowerbird. The nurses are forever trying to get hold of her purse to search for small things she's purloined from other patients or staff.

Flopping down on the settee beside Fliss, Elvira turns her purse upside down and shakes it, spreading the contents on a small table. There's: a man's comb, one shiny earring, a tiny pair of ornate scissors, buttons and tacks, a military style cufflink, half a dozen mismatched teaspoons, an assortment of paper clips, a stained medicine glass and a coin purse in oriental fabric.

Fliss leans forward, fascinated. Elvira hides all this so carefully, yet here it is spread before Fliss.

Suddenly, Elvira jumps to her feet and scurries off.

'Tsk tsk!' Fliss waves the oriental purse, but the woman is gone. Something falls out, clinking on the table. A pearl ring!

Ah, the memories of a pearl ring!

Secrets, Ennis family home, 1944

A PEARL RING on a silver chain around Fliss' neck swung in time with the rhythm of the Quirindi-bound train. The growling beast echoed Ethel's grim words—'Bring me no soldier for a son-in-law. Bring me no soldier.' The grinding of the train seemed to whisper.

Black trees rushed past grimy windows, places to go, places to go, there'll be woe, there'll be woe.

THE COUNTRY-link train jerked and jagged. Darkness descended, thick and complete. The train entered the first of the Hawkesbury tunnels on the long journey from Sydney to Quirindi. Fliss felt the smooth perfection of the engagement ring nestled on her gloved hand and rested her head against the seatback, savouring the memory of his lips on hers as he'd slipped the ring on her finger. Fliss put aside the gnawing worry of how Ethel would react to the news. Fliss hadn't even told her mother that she had been dating, much less planning to marry a soldier. Ethel had been angry when their brother David had enlisted and was barely coping with the anxiety of him serving overseas in New Guinea.

There were soldiers on the train in the next compartment, heading back to barracks at Tamworth, jostling and laughing, smoking, playing cards and flirting. Several slept, their slouched hats tipped forward, arms crossed as their bodies swayed to the rhythm of the train. In Fliss' compartment an old woman knitted, socks for the troops. Even in the gloom of the carriage through the tunnel the clicking tempo of her knitting needles had continued unchanged.

When they came out of the tunnels, the woman put her knitting aside and tried to tempt Fliss with a pickle and ham sandwich, a rare treat. Normally Fliss would have been glad of it, but she was nervous.

She hoped Sylvia would be on her side about the engagement even though she hadn't seen much of her sister. Sylvia had been coming home to Quirindi more often, relying more and more on George Carter, whose patient wooing seemed at last to have borne fruit. Her appreciation of George had moved from pity to comfort after her heart had been broken by an American soldier with a thirst for dancing, drinking, and Sylvia. A tall charismatic guy with a New York accent, he'd charmed Sylvia, until he'd been deployed to Darwin where he apparently found fresh talent.

Sylvia had been devastated, weeping every night and refusing to go out. Fliss' remonstrations that she was only seventeen and had all the time in the world had only brought on greater outbursts. Then she'd been stiff and calm, too calm. Fliss worried but Ethel was delighted.

It was a long walk from the station. Few streetlights shone in the twilight. Fliss was comforted by the old neighbourhood with its mix of old and mismatched houses. Cars were parked in driveways and on the street haphazardly. Some of the houses were already in darkness. There was low music from one of the windows as Fliss passed.

A full moon lit the front yard. The gate squeaked in protest as Fliss opened it. Soft light was coming from the dining room, but the kitchen was in darkness. Fliss walked faster. Something wasn't right. The kitchen light was always on late into the night.

'Mum!' Fliss called out, flinging the front door open.

Ethel was crumpled on the kitchen floor, groaning, the most dreadful sound Fliss had ever heard. She sat beside her mother and pulled her into her arms. Ethel surrendered, mewling like a child. Fliss stroked Ethel's damp hair, pressing her for details, but she had no words, only fresh howls. Her hand was fisted around a piece of paper. When Fliss couldn't prise her mother's grip Fliss rocked Ethel in her arms, offering comfort with a growing sense of dread. Ethel tore at her apron as she used it to wipe tears and mucus from her face. Her legs were skewed at strange angles as she lay against Fliss. Fliss scanned her mother for signs of injury. There was no blood. What then? She battered her chest with the fisted hand. The paper was yellow. A telegram. Fear gripped Fliss Ethel waved the fist in Fliss' face as the animal sounds continued. Fliss recognised the elemental sound of mourning, of rent grief past understanding, of visceral pain too large to measure or control.

Ethel emitted one word, 'David', and then Fliss knew, knew the whole, even though it was much later that she read those awful words "Killed In Action". Ethel slid down to lay on the floor. Holding her mother's face between her hands Fliss soothed her like a babe. Ethel looked up at Fliss with wild eyes. Fliss called her mother's name again and again, to bring her back, but it was useless. She was an empty broken thing.

George came and helped Fliss carry her to bed. The doctor came and gave Ethel a heavy sedative. Fliss watched her mother's eyes change from fear to glassy confusion then close.

Fliss slept fitfully in the creaky camp bed beside her mother. Ethel stayed like that for days, accepting sips of broth and thin slices of toast.

Ethel's sister, Bea arrived, washed and dressed Ethel, coaxing a response the others could not.

There would be no funeral arrangements, no place to lay flowers, nowhere to mark his passing. Those ceremonies would be attended far away, with his fellow soldiers on foreign soil. The sisters walked the cemetery rows, stopping here and there, remembering other lost loved ones and creating those small fictions, those alternate memories that comfort and sustain the bereaving.

GEORGE picked Sylvia up from the station. Bea organised a wake, filling the house with food and company. A day later Sylvia told Ethel she had accepted George's proposal and wanted her mother to walk her down the aisle. As the three of them admired Sylvia's ring, Fliss slipped her engagement ring into her purse.

'I'm moving back home, Mum.' Sylvia slid Mum a quick glance over breakfast. George looked surprised and cleared his throat. Sylvia hushed him with a sharp look.

Sylvia and Fliss were solemn at the station with their winter coats buttoned tight against the cold, their breath steaming.

'You're not just doing this for Mum, Syl?'

Sylvia shrugged. 'I've never seen her like this. This war, it's horrible. It's true, it is a world war. The grief and pain spreads like a tornado, wreaking havoc in everyone's lives. No one's free.' Tears streamed down her face. 'It's like I can't grieve for David yet. Mum's pain is so huge, so heavy. Oh Felicity. What will become of us all?' They held each other and wept.

'I'm glad you'll be with Mum, Sylvia.'

With a quick tugging motion Sylvia pulled her gloves up. 'It's time I grew up Felicity. How silly I've been, thinking of all the new opportunities. Parties, friends, falling desperately in love. Well, that's all over now. It's time to settle down. Get married. George and I will live with her. That's what she's always wanted.'

'Doesn't sound very romantic. You're sure about this?' Fliss twisted the ring under her glove.

'I'm quite sure. Romance is for movie stars and teenagers.' Sylvia reached for Fliss' hands and held both in hers. Her forehead wrinkled as she found the stone of the ring. 'What is this Felicity Ennis?' In one quick movement she removed Fliss' left glove. 'A ring. Fliss! Your soldier?'

Fliss nodded.

'But this is great news. Why didn't you say? Mum would be…

Oh, I see. "Don't either of you girls ever come home with a soldier", I know that's what Mum said … but…'

Sylvia's eyes clouded as Fliss shook her head slowly and replaced the glove. 'Not yet,Syl. He's off overseas again soon. It can wait until … he comes back.'

'Of course. If you think it's best. When he comes back.'

COMPANY POLICY

North Sydney, 1944

SYLVIA had delayed informing her workplace about her engagement, only relenting when work gossip outed the news to the boss—a bulky man with florid face and meagre manners.

When Fliss called to collect Sylvia for lunch the office girls were crowded around her.

Shooing them away Sylvia closed her drawer, pushed in her chair and clutched her purse.

Gravelly noises from a phlegmy throat announced the presence of the boss.

He required Sylvia in his office. Immediately.

The door shut with a thunk.

'*Oh oh.*' A tall redhead shook her head.

Whispering, Fliss asked what she meant.

'Oh sweetie, it's company policy to let married women go. Where do you work? On Mars?'

When Sylvia emerged, she swept the papers on her desk to the floor, yanked her desk drawer out, tipped it upside down.

She grabbed Fliss by the arm and headed out the door.

'Two weeks' notice,' she said, setting up a punishing pace down the street. 'Can you believe it. Two weeks to clear my desk, for Janine from Accounting, single and thirty.'

GEORGE'S SOOTHING words infuriated Sylvia.

'It's okay, love. I'll take care of you.' With no other choice Sylvia moved back home and threw herself into bridal preparations like a woman possessed. Ethel lost no time signing the paperwork needed for a seventeen-year-old bride. She'd averted the threat of a soldier husband for at least one of her daughters. After a modest wedding the couple moved in with Ethel.

That decision, made when Ethel was torn by grief was far less attractive in its stark new reality. The mother bowed and torn by sorrow was a transient apparition that faded, only returning when crocodile tears were deemed necessary for the management of the household.

These manoeuvres, if noted by George, were not remarked on, nor did they elicit interventions with any measure of success.

As for Sylvia, no silk stockings were forthcoming from George. Exams were imminent. Music upset his study systems. Dance venues were deemed enjoyable but best kept to a minimum.

The mere thought of the expense of hair dye and beauty treatments caused him such fiscal anxiety that Sylvia resigned herself to a life free from the burden of romance and pleasure.

George Carter was saving for a house.

Ethel brought home glowing reports of the providential opportunity of two-days-a-week employment at the Wallabadah Municipal Library. Sylvia lasted a month.

DROWNING in misery, Sylvia facing the growing realisation that she'd been in love with the idea of George.

From a high shelf in the attic she dragged out her father's two leather-strapped tan suitcases and joined The Australian Women's Land Army.

AT ROPE'S END

Lucy Meredith Carter, Book Of Known Facts, Quirindi, 1955

I have a new dress for church today, for Sunday School.

I wanted to put it on early but I didn't want to get grubby.

Church is somewhere I can't take Esmeralda, or school, except for Bring A Pet Day.

ESMERALDA pecks at the page as I write, then looks up at me.

'I was just writing about you, Esmeralda.' I pat her head. 'But you know that, don't you. A magic chook knows a lot of things.'

Esmeralda is pleased and takes high dainty steps along my arm so she can nestle under my chin.

The morning sun is moving across the book. I put it down on the slats of the porch swing. 'Enough for today. I have to go to Sunday School.'

Dad has always been good at braiding my hair. I guess that's the craftsman in him. I love the silky feel of it. I like it neat and smooth for Sunday School. There's no recess or running around so it usually stays looking tidy. Not the frizzy mess it is on schooldays.

My new dress has soft fabric, puffed sleeves and a satin sash that matches the ribbon tied at the end of my braid.

I sit with Jenny, waiting for the song sheets to be handed,

smoothing the skirt as an excuse to touch and enjoy it.

Charlotte Renshaw waits at the door until everyone is looking at her. I sink down in the red metal seat, but she sees me, walks down the aisle, sits right behind me, waving her friends to sit beside her. I flip my braid to the front out of her reach. I've been caught out before when she pulled my hair in class and cut the end. Then lied to the teacher.

Charlotte laughs, a low grinding sound, *har.*

She leans forward. I feel her hot breath on my neck and I flinch. She brings her mouth close to my ear and whispers. Charlotte's friends sputter and giggle, the sound muffled by hands over mouths, not knowing what she's said but enjoying the sharp barb of triumph.

Mrs Fryberg, the pianist, stacks and sorts white song sheets. Miss Bladen, the teacher is organising felt pictures of Jesus and the Pharisees.

I swing around to face Charlotte. Dull, brown curls bounce around her face. Her mother takes hours winding those curls with rags on Saturday nights.

She folds her arms, looks hard at me eyes waiting for my pain.

When I flinch, she smiles slowly, her top lip thins to show pink gums. A hating smile.

I hear the clock ticking, rustling of papers.

I PUNCH, swift and angry, before thoughts have lined up properly in my head. Charlotte wails like a wounded pig. There's a gasp as everyone gawks at me, at her.

I turn back to the front, quietly fold my hands in my lap and stare at the front.

The song sheets in Mrs Fryberg's hand flutter to the floor, soft as snowflakes. Miss Bladen stops pointing at the felt storyboard of Jesus and the Pharisees.

Then she runs to us, whipping out a lace handkerchief from the deep crease between her breasts like a magician's trick. Holding it up, she drags Charlotte into the aisle, presses the handkerchief to her face and coos like a dove.

With an arm wrapped around Charlotte's shoulder she moves down the aisle, stopping to give me a sharp tilt of the head that says, *come with me.*

UNDER the Jacaranda tree, thick with lilac flowers, Charlotte's howls disturb the butcher birds. There's a dark red splotch, shaped like Tasmania on Charlotte's dress.

In spite of Miss Bladen's efforts, blood gushes from Charlotte's nose into the teacher's cupped hands. Her ruffled sleeves tremble as she pushes Charlotte's head under running water from a drinking fountain beside the chapel. The rag-curls hang limp and wet.

Charlotte's shrieking turns to muffled sobs. The lace handkerchief is now a rusty brown. Miss Bladen's face as she looks at me is slack with disappointment.

'Lucy Meredith Carter this isn't like you.' She swings an arm towards Charlotte, whimpering on the bench. 'Look what you've done. Are you satisfied now?'

I don't answer her, but years of Charlotte's schoolyard jabs, pinches, and taunting flash through my head. Bullying that started on my first day at school, before I even knew her name.

Miss Bladen sucks air through her teeth. 'Lucy! What on earth got into you?' she asks, but there are things can't be said, shouldn't be said, things that won't be heard.

When I visit Nanna I don't tell her about the angry words Charlotte whispered that morning. I wonder why I'm so wicked that I feel no regret, not even later. I just remember the blood crusting on Charlotte's face outside the Sunday School room.

I tell Uncle Harry. I tell the horrible words she said nearly every morning when I came through the school gates. And the worst, today's—

'Your mother never wanted you.'

WILD RaG OF a CHILD

Quirindi Police Station, Henry Street, Quirindi, 1955

CONSTABLE Peter "Blue" Winters takes a terse, clipped complaint from a woman who introduces herself with, 'Do You Know Who I Am?'

Mrs Elisabeth Renshaw, President of the local War Widows Society 'knows people'.

She has brought her pudgy, sour-faced daughter, Charlotte, who sobs whenever her mother looks her way, without the least sign of a tear. Sweet little Charlotte, has been assaulted.

Punched cruelly on the nose, at Sunday School, no less, by that Lucy Carter, with a temper like the very devil.

A fiery, red-headed brat.

Peters who acquired the nickname "Blue" for a similar red shock of hair is instantly offended and inclined to take the side of the alleged perpetrator, especially as "sweet little Charlotte" is now vigorously banging a foot against the desk, despite a polite request to desist.

When questioned on the matter of provocation, Mrs Renshaw demurs to respond, thumping the desk with a dripping, black umbrella while raging about the inability of some to discern the victim from the tormenter.

'What else can one expect from a wild rag of a child left in the care of her father, that soft-headed George Carter,' she says.

Winters politely bids them good-day, crushes the report and throws it in the bin, caring not one jot for people prejudiced about hair of a certain colour, and caring even less for persons who enter his domain and start conversations with, 'Do you know who I am?

An Unquiet Corner

Ennis family home, Henry Street, Quirindi, 1955

ETHEL adjusts a dove-grey felt hat, then flinches as a loud knock reverberates through the house.

A grilling from Lucy about a special school project: 'Your Family History' has unnerved her.

Ethel peeks through the front curtains hoping it's one of the boarders she can dispatch quickly, but it's a uniformed officer. She doesn't need this today. A lunch of lamb and baked veg with Marj Kingston in a quiet corner at the Royal Hotel is a rare treat she doesn't wish to forego.

Answering the door, she accepts a polite invitation to the station to identify a silver hatpin she'd reported missing weeks before.

On arrival, the duty officer sits Ethel in a quiet corner.

She folds gloved hands over her black purse. An inner door swings open. Ethel jolts, hearing Mrs Elisabeth Renshaw thank a constable for his kind assistance. The President of the War Widows Society swishes across the room, and on spying Ethel sitting in that quiet corner, twitches a satisfied smile and pulls her gloves on with a snap.

A flush of heat begins in Ethel's clenched toes and travels to the roots of her hair.

It's a discomfort that lasts long after Ethel greets her friend

Marj and takes a premium seat in a quiet corner of The Royal Hotel where she spreads butter on a dinner roll and introduces the subject of a certain Mrs Elizabeth Renshaw.

'What has that blasted woman against me Marj? I've a good mind to ask her,' Ethel says, alarming her diffident lunch companion into dull silence.

ALEXEI, THE YOUNGEST BARASHEV

Lucy Meredith Carter, Book Of Known Facts, Quirindi, 1955

There wasn't any trouble after I punched Charlotte.
Maybe Sunday School teachers are different.
I don't understand.

THE GRAVEL crunches as I swing the bike into the circular driveway. There's a sign in beautiful script, Montview Lodge, Nursing and Convalescent Home. I hear the voices of children playing. The Barashevs are a large Russian family. They have half a dozen kids who have the run of the place.

There's a large garden at the side of the house. On any given day it's hard to tell the difference between staff, patients or the Barashev kids. I know most of the kids. Alexei, the youngest boy, is in my class at school, but I know Sacha best because she nurses Fliss. She's the second daughter. The eldest, Katya, went away to study physical therapy at some posh place in the city.

THE FRENCH doors to Fliss's room are open.

Sacha is shaking Fliss's braided rag mat, making dust motes dance in the chilly morning air. She waves to me. 'You're early, Lucy,' she calls. 'Your aunt will be ready in a bit. Then you can come and have breakfast with her. There's clotted cream and brown sugar with the porridge today. You will eat with her, yes?'

'Oh, yes please Sacha,' I say.

Sacha heads back inside, calling over her shoulder. 'Alexei is around somewhere.'

Esmeralda flies up to a low branch and settles in, fluffing her white feathers until she looks like a puff of snow. I rest the bike against the mulberry tree and sit down, then lean against the familiar rasp of the knotty old tree. Taking my notebook out of my pocket I open it to where I put the photograph I found at Nanna Ennis's.

There's a word on the back I can't make out, so I slip it back into the book and sigh. I'll ask Fliss.

THE MOUNTAIN mist hangs low, shrouding the bushland. I can't see past the first row of red tomato plants in the garden. The rest of the world has disappeared. I find my Book Of Known Facts and start writing.

'Hey, Lucy.' Alexei flops down beside me. 'Don't you love this fog?'

'No, it's awful. It makes the world look as if it ends just past the vegetable garden. It's creepy.'

'That's dumb. Why would the world end here? What does the encyclopaedia say?'

My cheeks burn. 'Don't tease me about that.'

'Well, you *are* the only girl I know who reads it for fun. I'm not saying you're weird or anything. I like looking up stuff too.' Alexei put his elbows on his knees, resting his head in his hands. He is looking at me with serious brown eyes so I don't think he's making fun of me. 'What's that book?' he asks, pointing at my notebook. 'Are you writing your own encyclopaedia?'

'No, silly,' I say.

He picks a grass stalk, reaches a hand for the book. I decide to trust him. He doesn't snatch things like some of the boys at school. He gets teased too. I pass him the book.

116

'Ah—"Lucy Meredith Carter—Book Of Known Facts". Oh well, why don't you read me something? Anywhere will do.'

Opening the book I read, 'Ewan brought Dad's shears back. He's shy and talks like a telegram.'

Alexei laughs. 'Who's he? Does he work at the Post Office?'

'No. He's one of the Kingston twins. They live across the road from us.'

'I see. What else do you write about?'

I bite my bottom lip. 'Just things I find out, or questions. There's Fliss losing all her words; every single one. It's odd. I mean she has a *voice*, she laughs and hums along to music.'

'Lots of people living here have had strokes. Some speak, some can't. Sacha says it depends which part of the brain has, you know, been damaged.'

'I'm sure the words are in her head, she just can't get them out. I know she understands because she *shows* me, it's a whole language without words.'

Alexei frowns. That means he's concentrating, really listening. Nanna says I get that sort of thing wrong, but Alexei hasn't looked away once.

'It's a magic language, you see,' I tell him, whispering and leaning forward, 'like Esmeralda. She knows stuff too.'

'Who's Esmeralda?' he asks just as Esmeralda lifts her head, fixes him with fierce dark eyes and clucks loudly. She stands and fluffs her feathers like a powder puff.

'That's Esmeralda? You brought a chook!'

'Lucy!' Sacha calls. 'Your aunt's ready. You can have some breakfast with her if you like.'

I scramble up. 'Coming!'

The fog has lifted. I can see through the thick bushland, past the garden, to the valleys and mountains.

The world is back, and I've made a friend.

I wave and say, 'see you later' to Alexei.

I'm so happy!

I, Lucy Meredith Carter, reader of encyclopaedias, collector of important facts, owner of a magic chook, have been understood by the cleverest boy in school.

WOrLD'S END

Ennis family home, Henry Street, Quirindi, 1955

LUCY brushes crumbs off the story stool.

'Uncle Harry, did you know I used to worry that the world went away at night. That everything disappeared in the dark?' She tilts her head, walks to the window, picking up Harry's hat. She doesn't twirl it, or throw it on her head laughing, as she often does.

'Did you, little Lucy? That must have been scary. You must have wondered what was real and what wasn't.'

'Yes. When it was foggy, and mist covered everything I wondered where the world ended. It has to end somewhere. It's weird.'

She taps her forehead. 'Where does the sky begin and where does the world end?'

Harry leans down, placing his hand on the grass.

'Put your hand here, Lucy. This is where the sky and the world meet. Right here. Down here. Not up there.'

Lucy's hand is small beside Harry's.

Turning her hand over, palm up, she makes a fist and says, 'Look, Uncle Harry, I have a handful of sky!'

When Lucy leaves Harry is relieved that there is no story request.

The tale on his mind could not be told to a child.

119

Diggers abroad in Bombay, 1941

HARRY and Lanky were shocked by the Tower of Silence at Malabar Hill where bodies of the dead were laid bare.

On the dusty track back to camp, the men heard wailing up ahead. Then screaming, as if some poor soul was caught in a threshing mill, in agony, only to be thrashed again as stone churned upon stone.

A woman knelt on the ground, sari torn, dishevelled, frantic, careless of time or consequence, reaching for a ragged bundle on the road, her progress barred by a fierce Sikh, his dark blue dastar wound tightly, as black-faced and raging he punched her body, full-fisted at each small inch of her advance to the cloth.

'Nugget! It's a babe!' Lanky tensed, words suspended between moan and whisper.

Harry gripped Lanky's shoulder. 'No, mate. Can't be…'

Lanky crouched beside her. 'It's dead. Poor thing.' He attempted to ward off the crushing blows.

The Sikh curdled a threat, drew a knife. A curved, dangerous affair. Lanky threw a swift, careless punch, caught the Sikh in the throat, a soldier's unforgiving thrust.

The Sikh fell, gargling dust, eyes bulging.

Sari soaked with spent blood, the woman snatched the limp, dusky infant.

The Sikh lurched to his feet, regained his dagger.

Harry yelled warning to Lanky.

The Sikh swung around, bloodshot eyes dark with rage, a new target found. With a warrior's howl he rushed for Harry, robes flaying as feet hammered earth.

Harry fired the Webley.

The sound exploded through the gulley.

The Sikh crumpled like cloth.

Lanky coiled to his feet. 'You stupid prat, Nugget!'

The woman hurled herself at Harry—shrieking, a mad alien sound, arms flailing as she pounded her grief into Harry's body with tiny brown fists; a child herself.

THE MEN ran like madmen.

A soldier's first kill; a damning mistake.

At camp, the Sergeant raved and ranted. 'Christ, ye two, do y'know what ye've done? Ye don't belong here, they do.'

THEY RETURNED with two Indian retainers in tow.

The woman was swaying, holding the dead infant, thumping her chest like the ancient mourners they'd heard about in Sunday School. At the Tower of Silence at Malabar Hill, she lay the babe among the dead. The Indian retainers stood quietly, bowed heads, prayerful hands.

The woman knelt, murmured, then, when she was done with the rituals of death, Lanky gave her a clinking, hessian bag, grimly handed over at camp by the Sergeant; *no insignia*.

Stone-faced, she accepted, with trembling hands. The Indians translated … 'for a life, for a death', or something like that.

Then, leaning on harsh stones at the base of the tower, Harry and Lanky wept as they hadn't since newborn cries.

A Strange New Word

Lucy Meredith Carter, Book Of Known Facts, Quirindi, 1955

Nanna has a Country Women's Association meeting today.

I am going to sneak into her storeroom.

There is a beautiful wooden chest in there.

It has "Lucinda Meredith" on the lid.

It must be mine!!

Maybe there are lost stories inside.

THE CHEST has brass hinges, different than the ones Dad uses, heavier and darker. It's about the size of an orange crate. There's carving on the sides, raised triangles with grooved edges. The timber is yellow-gold and oiled not lacquered. Dad tells me about all that kind of thing. He loves working with wood, he has a woodturning lathe in his shed. The box is beautiful. I wonder who carved it. I wonder if anyone even knows it's there. It was in a corner under some old hessian bags.

It has lots of interesting things in it, old people stuff I don't understand. I haven't had a chance to look at all of it. I found some war medals with striped ribbons on a metal bar. I took them home. Nanna Ennis doesn't know I found the box. I don't want to get into trouble. I creep up the stairs when she is in the garden and look inside. Anyway, Nanna Ennis never goes up to the attic anymore. She says the back steps are enough for an old woman like her.

Yesterday, I shifted the box a bit closer to the light in the window so I could see better and I found a photograph with Mum and Fliss wearing strange hats. I'll be seeing Fliss tomorrow so I can take the photo and ask her about it.

I KNOCK gently on Fliss's door and wait for the answering tap tap of Fliss's walking stick. Fliss is sitting by the large bay windows trying to brush her hair with her good hand. Her eyes light up when she sees me. Sacha is making the bed.

'I'll do that for you Fliss,' I take the brush and sit down. Fliss shakes her head and uses her hand to keep the brush at arm's length.

'You mustn't spoil your aunt, Lucy, it's important for her to do things for herself.' Sacha straightens up and massages her back.

'All right.' I reach into my pocket for my notebook.

'Will you be taking notes today? Perhaps you'd like to interview me.' Sacha thumps a pillow.

'I don't think so. You don't know many interesting facts. Besides, you're always too busy.' I pick up Fliss's brush and drag it through my tangled hair. 'Tsk tsk, tsk tsk!' Fliss takes the brush and awkwardly pulls it through my hair.

Sacha laughs and stands with her hand on her hips. 'Not interesting enough hey?'

'Well, not precisely, I mean...' I frown. 'At least you don't tell me to put my book away because I'm a precocious miss, like Mrs Kingston does.'

'Oh Lucy, really, you're a one-off.'

'Well, don't you think facts are interesting, Sacha? I mean, there are so many mysteries. Like, why Fliss can't talk but she can hum.'

'Oh honey, those kinds of mysteries will do your head in. Who knows why your aunt can make sounds and not words? And you'd have better manners if you called her Auntie Felicity.' Sacha gives me a hard look.

'Rubbish. I've called her Fliss all my life. It's bad enough to have to call people who aren't even related, auntie and uncle just because your parents know them. Fliss is special.'

'There's no telling you, is there Miss Lucy. Well, you two do seem to have your own language.' Sacha smooths the bedspread. 'Okay, I'm off. Breakfast will be here soon.' Giving the room a last squinting scan Sacha leaves, shutting the door with a click.

'Look Fliss, I found a photo. Is it you? And Mum?'

She holds it at arm's length, then nods. 'You're wearing funny hats,' I say. 'You wouldn't wear those to church.'

With a sly smile she flicks her hand back and forth, palm up, palm down, *maybe*.

I turn the photo over to show Fliss the word on the back. Fliss squints. 'It's a weird word, Fliss, too hard for me. Jerr—an… oh darn, Jerry-put-yer-hand-up.'

'Jerranjerup.' Fliss says.

I gasp. 'Fliss! What did you say?'

'Jerranjerup.' Fliss is smiling, even the bad side lifts.

'Can you teach me to say it, Fliss?'

Fliss says Jerranjerup over and over and I repeat it until Fliss claps her hands.

'What does the word mean?' I ask.

She points out the window. 'It's a place?' Nodding eagerly, she flicks her arm as if she's tossing a ball a long way. 'A far, *far* place? Fliss! You have a word! Wait till I tell Dad and Nanna.' Fliss shakes her head. Her eyes are clouded. She slaps the table with her good hand and keeps tapping loudly. Tears fall from her eyes, slow raindrop tears.

'I'm sorry.' I sit back in the chair. 'It's all right, Fliss,' I say, 'we won't tell anyone.'

The tapping stops and Fliss sighs, a great shuddering sound. Then she picks up the hairbrush and pats her knee. I sit on the floor in front of her while she brushes my hair, humming softly.

'You have a beautiful voice, Fliss,' I whisper, putting the photograph back in the book.

I look up at her. She's nodding at someone through the French doors. It's Esmeralda. When I tilt my head and stare at Esmeralda, she pecks at the ground intently. Perhaps she and Fliss share a secret language too.

'Would you like to have this photograph here?' I ask. 'You know, in a nice frame. I could make you one.'

Fliss shakes her head and points at me.

'You want me to have it? Okay. I'd like that.' I wriggle back in the chair, enjoying the soft mountain breeze. 'Do you have any photographs of your fiancé?' I'm not sure if I should have talked about this.

Fliss waves her hand back and forth.

'Somewhere?' I ask. Fliss nods and shrugs. Sometimes her eyes are sad, but not today. There must be happy memories for her, some that don't make her sad. 'Maybe we'll find them one day,' I say, but Fliss's eyes are drifting shut.

Putting the book away in my skirt pocket, I try to understand what just happened. Fliss has a word. It's the strangest, most difficult word I've ever heard. And it's a secret. I've never heard Fliss speak. Her voice is clear. I thought it would sound rusty or raspy, like the bark on the old tree. Lots of the stroke patients have very strange voices, high-pitched or rough—not Fliss.

Pulling my chair close to Fliss, I curl into her sleepy embrace. She strokes my hair as I tell her about my strange dream of swimming in the ocean with Mum. I can't ask her anything more.

SOME THINGS are too hard for questions, especially when you've been trusted with a secret. A really important one. One they can't tell you about because they only have one word.

I can't get the mystery of that word out of my head. A place called Jerranjerup. The encyclopaedias were no help. I guess because it's an Australian place and nothing much has happened here in history. But it's important to me. Fliss was there, and Mum.

Dad's maps are no use. I didn't expect much because I didn't know where to start looking. Australia is a big country. I don't even try the huge maps at school that hang on walls.

THe WorD

Montview Lodge, George Street, Quirindi, 1955

THE RADIO is playing. Someone is singing.

Fliss hums along, wishing the words would come too.

They don't.

She thought that one word, *Jerranjerup*, might be the beginning, that all the words she ever knew and spoke might come tumbling out the next day. Or the next week.

None came.

And of all the words to find voice, why Jerranjerup?

Is it possible to be undone by a word?

LUCY chatters like a little bird as she sits with Fliss. She reads from her notebook. In between her carefully phrased reading, she tells Fliss about the old soldier without a home, mad from the last war, of his escape into the bush, afraid of shadows.

There is a new glow on her face as she talks about Alexei, the Barashev boy her age.

'He's so smart Fliss, he knows about Shakespeare, and you know what?' Lucy grabs Fliss' arm. 'He reads encyclopaedias too! What do you think about that?' Her green eyes wander to gaze out of the window and she sighs.

Fliss wonders if this is Lucy's first crush on a boy. She seems so young. She is growing up and the thought catches Fliss by surprise. The desire to see Lucy become all she can be is so strong Fliss can barely breathe. Will she be around to see?

Lucy seems to remember where she is, and talks about her teacher, Miss Bell, who is helping them solve a mystery, but doesn't know that she is.

Fliss worries that Lucy spends too much time with her, a crippled woman instead of with other children. She is grateful for the balm of Lucy's presence. The day will come when she grows into her own life, a life where there will be less of Fliss, a life where many people will come and go. And one day she will fall in love. One day the world will be a wider place.

Will she be like Sylvia, hungry for it all? Will love come so swiftly and unexpectedly that it will shake her? Or will it come softly?

———

The farm, Jerranjerup, 1945

'SYLVIA!' Fliss called, but her sister didn't hear, or didn't want to.

Sylvia was leaning on the farm truck with her hat tilted back, blinking at the sun's afternoon blaze. She swatted at a fly and still managed to look elegant as she accepted the shy worship of a young farmhand, one of the few men left on the land.

The cooks had begun to serve the evening meal. If Sylvia was late again it would only increase their ire at her aloof separation from the others. Perhaps that's why she did it. She didn't want to come to the farm, wanted nothing to do with farms and animals. She wanted more from joining the Land Army.

In the end, it was Ethel who forced her hand. 'You need to do this for your sister, Sylvia,' she said, 'I'm worried about her state of mind. She's had a breakdown. She walked out of her flat and her job and hasn't gone out the front door of my house. She needs to keep busy. Take her mind off things. Anyway, you're always whining about being bored working at the library, not enough work coming in. I'll take care of your husband. George will be fine.'

Sylvia snorted at that, 'Good old George is always fine.' It was the wrong things to say to Ethel who warned, 'Have a care, girl!' Sylvia paced and spat fire until she saw Fliss cramped within herself. Then she relented with her usual swift mood change, only muttering 'I suppose. I will hate it, you know'.

Fliss didn't care to join the conversation. Fliss didn't care about much at all.

DESPITE her initial bitter remonstrations about the farm, Sylvia had come to life. She radiated a new beauty, with her long golden hair gentled by the scant hot breeze, in shorts and sleeveless shirt, clothes so different from her usual wardrobe. She was all tanned perfection and white teeth.

'Sylvia!' Fliss called again. Sylvia waved. Fliss slumped against the door jamb, too tired to pursue her sister. The summer heat exhausted her but didn't seem to bother Sylvia.

The station owner walked past. It was hard to notice the slight limp where pain gripped his hip, the legacy of shrapnel from a Luftwaffe attack. His tall, lean frame caught Sylvia's eye. She didn't acknowledge him, yet Fliss knew Sylvia had seen him. She was in his company a little too often. Her older sister by four years, Fliss was the only one Sylvia couldn't hide things from, but it wouldn't be long before the other girls noticed.

Suddenly Sylvia ran to Fliss, leaving the young farmhand gaping after her. Back in the shared dormitory Fliss cornered her sister. 'Honestly, Sylvia!'

'Lighten up Felicity. There's a war on.' She laughed. 'A little flirting never hurt anyone.' She reached for a bright neckerchief and tied it with deft fingers.

'Except George,' said Fliss.

Sylvia shot Fliss a sharp look, then opened her makeup bag and grabbed a lipstick, twirling the crimson cylinder. 'Give it a rest, sis!'

'You don't need that, Syl. We're going to eat!'

Sylvia poked her tongue out, smiled and applied the lipstick slowly.

WHEN THE GIRLS arrived at the property Sylvia was furious that she had been allocated farm chores instead of office or indoor work. And yet, she had flourished in the outdoors.

Fliss watched Sylvia lift a sledgehammer high above her head and bring it down deftly on the head of a long metal spike. The metallic clang was ear-splitting and the boss's son, whose job she had commandeered, flinched. He stood to the side sulking, hoping none of the men were witnessing the spectacle of a woman taking over his job to fix the cattle grid near the staff quarters.

Behind Sylvia, the boss leant on a timber post, glinting a smile. He held up a warning finger to his son.

The grid was meant for pedestrian traffic not vehicles. The boss had been furious when the previous setup was bent out of shape by a young farmhand who rode to work on his ex-military motorcycle, a B.S.A. M20. Not only had he punctured a tyre and twisted the wheel of his bike he had wrecked the cattle grid. Then, he'd kicked dirt and jumped on his hat.

Sylvia should have been in the fields with the other Land Girls but she'd claimed boredom with their idle chatter and donned a pair of men's work gloves and tackled the repair of the grid, pushing aside the boss' son. The boy, a budding teenager with none of Sylvia's focus or persistence, shuffled his feet in the dust and shoved his hands in his pockets.

Soon, she was aided in her task by the farm owner and boss, who'd returned from the war with an honourable discharge and German shrapnel in his hip. The boss walked over and knelt on the ground with some difficulty. The shrapnel had shattered his right hip and it had taken several surgeries to remove. The first surgery, conducted in a frantic field hospital in Alexandria had failed.

After Sylvia pounded the last spike, they chatted in quiet voices, their eyes more eloquent than their words, oblivious to the sideways sly glances of the workers.

FLISS had seen Sylvia thrive. 'You love it here, don't you Sylvia?'

'I do, who'd have thought. Up to my elbows in grease and muck, best thing I ever did.' She sighed.

'I hated losing my job. I'd worked so hard for it. I fought to keep it. I had plenty to say to the boss and all I got was the company didn't want someone who would be breeding soon. They wanted "security". I thought I'd be harder to replace with the men leaving for war. I was told there were plenty of women eager to join the workforce. I told the boss I had no intention of becoming pregnant for years, maybe never. He just smiled knowingly and patted my arm as if I'd suddenly lost my intelligence along with my usefulness.'

'I'm sorry Sylvia.'

'You know, I was so angry with George.' Her eyes simmered with rage. 'He could have said something. Stuck up for me. My job. Women shouldn't be disposable.'

Striding ahead, Sylvia pointed at the golden fields with their neat cylinders of hay. 'The boss here stands up for us women. He doesn't replace us when the men come home from war, as if we're second-hand clothes, second best choices.'

Fliss panted heavily, trying to keep up with Sylvia. 'Oh Syl, I'm sorry. I've been caught up in my grief. My fella, he was everything to me, everything, sis.'

Sylvia reached to embrace Fliss, shaking her head. 'And that, my darling big sister,' she said, 'is precisely the heart of the problem. No one should ever be someone's everything.'

WITH THE WAR winding up in Europe, rumours of imminent peace abounded, but the sisters' futures were an uncertain thing.

In spite of Sylvia's furtive attempts to conceal her affair with the boss, Fliss noticed her sister's absence from her bed at night. On Sylvia's bedside table, there was a lease and address.

Sylvia wasn't planning on going home.

THIS IS NOT MY COUNTRY

Lucy Meredith Carter, Book Of Known Facts, Quirindi, 1955

I can't find out where Jerranjerup is on the map.

I can't ask anyone because they will ask, 'where did you hear that?' And it is a secret.

I GATHER a pile of macadamia nuts lying on the ground and shove them into my pocket. I want Alexei to help me crack them open, but he's more interested in his stupid slingshot.

'Sh!' He raises a warning finger, peering into a window of their house. 'Are we hiding from someone?' I ask.

A door slams inside the house. Alexei grabs a brown macadamia and raises his slingshot high. A shadow stretches over us. A hand snatches the slingshot. 'What have we here, Alexei?' It's an unfamiliar voice. A strong accent.

I squint to see, but the sun is behind him and he remains a shadow. 'Who are you? Who is he, Alexei?' I scramble up, yanking hard on Alexei's shirt. He jerks away.

'I'm sorry, *malyshka*,' says the voice, 'I did not see you there.' He moves to the shade. The strange boy has black, straight hair. There's something angry about the angles of his skinny body and the way he stands. Raising his arm he twirls the slingshot around just out of Alexei's reach and says, 'I am Pieter, the cousin of this crazy little *mal'chik* here.' He pinches Alexei's earlobe.

133

I scowl, but it has no effect. 'I didn't know Alexei had any cousins here in Australia,' I say.

The tall boy warns with a flat hand, pushing back our words. 'He didn't. Until today.' He turns cold black eyes to me, pauses then says. 'I came, yes. I came. But this is not my country.'

Alexei steps forward. 'He's an orphan...'

'Tais tois, Alexei. This isn't for you to say. We don't tell our stories. Not to strangers.' The words are sharp, yet his accent is almost musical. Alexei rubs a red ear and I'm angry that he's been hurt. 'I'm not a stranger! I'm his friend,' I tell him, pointing at Alexei.

'Ah, but you are not my friend, *ma petite*.' Long thin fingers pluck a gum leaf. Pieter sniffs it, wrinkling his nose. 'Yuk, is like medicine.' He pats the slingshot. 'This I keep, I think. Is not a thing for children.'

Pieter stares at me. 'You, little Lucia. You never shut up. Is good. One day you will teach me perfect English. Then I will become important man in this miserable country with no history, no snow, trees like medicine, strange animals, and even stranger children.' He quickly fills his pocket with macadamias, then chooses a rock carefully, pocketing it. He bows. 'Now, goodbye.'

He shrugs and leaves. His baggy clothes reveal bony wrists and ankles.

'He's so rude,' I say. 'How come he's here? What language was that, Alexei? Why did he fill his pockets with nuts?'

'He's always picking and plucking, nuts, fruit. All sorts. Mama says it's because he can't forget hunger. He speaks French, Russian. He lived through the war in both countries. He was found on the streets of Moscow, begging and stealing to stay alive.'

'But Alexei, he's just a boy.'

'Papa says there were no boys in Russia during the war, only soldiers, and after the war—orphans.'

Besprizornye, the Unattended

Montview Lodge, George Street, Quirindi, 1955

PIETER FLICKS eucalypt leaves as he walks the moonlit garden, alone with memories of Moscow and Papa. Beggars on the street, cunning in the shadows—where only the cunning eat.

Strolling, head down, back to the orphanage, patting the pocket with black bread and cheese for the children.

Before being reunited with Papa, Pieter had learned silence, to hide in the shadows, to be last in the street to be noticed, looking no one in the eye, first to slip away.

Pieter remembers a ragged cap, always pulled forward, a loose dark coat, carefully stolen from a basement bar with a negligent publican on watch. Not a rich man's coat, better a lowly street vendor—a man whose cries of 'Thief!' will be little heeded by thirsty Russians blunted with post-war weariness, but too shrewd to leave thick winter garments on any coat rack or with a wily publican. They would not be parted from coats with sorrow hardened in every stitch, their only protection from winter's bitter chill. Hands always in pockets, days spent in a slow walk or leaning in broken doorways, appearing to sleep.

Then, a quick snatch, a baker's loaf, an apple, a glove.

Rewarded with a wink from Papa, always watching, a blood-stained rag pressed to his mouth, until Papa was no more.

Pieter was alone.

BARRY JAMES fills the common room with music. He suffered the scourge of polio during the First World War. An accomplished pianist of some renown he played for the troops in the Second. It was, he says smiling, his favourite war. He tells Fliss this, and other things, happy for a nod or smile. He must be lonely. Fliss doesn't remember family visiting, apart from a nephew always eager to leave.

Barry James has struck up a friendship with Pieter, the Barashevs' Russian nephew, a lanky, awkward lad, just sixteen, neither man, nor boy, one who's seen more of war than the wounded diggers at the lodge. Pieter avoids other children, even his cousins.

Barry James, the pianist, and the boy, seem to have little in common, yet Pieter patiently pushes the old man around in a wheelchair, up and down country lanes near Montview, places that the old man wouldn't normally see.

Barry James has listened quietly, piecing together the boy's life story better than anyone. His memory for snippets is as keen as his retrieval of piano pieces.

PIETER had been so silent, so angry, when he arrived, having scavenged for himself for so long. While his father served on the Russian front, Pieter and his mother had gone to France, hoping for better times, seeking shelter with relatives.

After all, Pieter's mother had been born and raised in Paris. But, familial ties were denied. Succour was not forthcoming. Pieter, and his mother, were denounced by relatives wary of a faintly rumoured Jewish connection. They were interred at Saint-Sulpice-la-Poine, a camp for Russian citizens near Toulouse, where Pieter's mother died. Then returning to his father, and the streets of Moscow, they survived in mortared and burnt-out buildings until gas pneumonia strangled Pieter's father's lungs.

BARRY JAMES never expected to outlive his brother, Edward, a Grammar school teacher who excelled at tennis and played violin in a string quartet.

Barry James never expected to receive a bequest of any sort from his brother's estate—a fine violin, not a Stradivarius, but a thing of beauty nonetheless, with an excellent tone.

Barry James never expected the orphaned Russian boy, to be acquainted with, much less play, a violin. The son of a Cossack, the boy touches the violin like a prayer.

Pieter tells Barry James that he played in the streets of Moscow for coins, or black bread, for himself and the urchin-child Nevinka, slipping over the orphanage walls, where he'd once lived before being deemed too old, sent to fend for himself; after Paris, Toulouse and Saint-Sulpice-la-Poine.

Barry James watches music transform Pieter as he plays a solitary Russian ballad, a haunting melody, among the swaying eucalypts at Montview by the garden in the evening while he dances the Hopak like his father and forefathers before him.

I STILL HAVE YOU

Montview Lodge, George Street, Quirindi, 1955

FLISS IS waiting, waiting for Lucy to run down the path—waiting for her to call, 'Fliss, Fliss, you'll never guess!'

Then Lucy will talk about what she found in her encyclopaedias or read to Fliss from her Book Of Known Facts. Last week it was… 'the world was here before we all began'. 'Old Pat, the mad one living in the bush, used to be a soldier. Did y'know?'

FLISS hears Lucy's bicycle, its soft squish as she stops, takes Esmeralda, the magic chook out of the basket, where that imperious bird has been covered with a doll's blanket for the journey.

The hen flies to a low branch of the jacaranda tree where she promptly fluffs her feathers and sleeps.

Lucy skips inside. There is a rectangular shape in her pocket. She has brought her Book of Known Facts, in case she learns something new, or finds someone she would like to interview—a habit that sets her grandmother's teeth on edge.

For that reason alone, Fliss treasures the silk-covered book, along with the wonderful curiosity it represents.

A breathless Lucy rushes through the door.

LUCY SITS in the chair beside Fliss' bed.

'I was there when Mum died, you know,' she says, 'I don't remember much, but I remember Dad picking me up from school in the middle of the day in the old bus he had for taking people to the train station and the bus place. He didn't say anything to the teacher when he came to get me, he just stood at the door and tipped his hat. It was a windy day and his coat was flapping around like wings. I heard the grinding noise of tractors and farm machinery driving through town on their way to the showground for the Jubilee.'

'I still have you, don't I Fliss.'

Fliss nods, reaches her arms to Lucy.

'I can't stay long today, Fliss. I'm off to Nanna's. We're collecting Great-Aunt Bea from the Station.'

GreaT-AUNT Bea

Lucy Meredith Carter, Book Of Known Fact, Quirindi, 1955

We are getting a special visitor today.
Great-Aunt Bea is coming.
She brings juicy yellow peaches from Bathurst. Yum!
She is Nanna's sister.
The only sister she has left.

NANNA'S wisteria is covered in blossoms. Mauve flowers hang like bunches of grapes. 'How odd,' says Nanna. 'They haven't bloomed for years.'

'They have, Nanna. You just haven't seen them. You're usually up with Great-Aunt Bea at this time of year.' I nibble a biscuit slowly to make it last.

Nanna reaches for the cream porcelain bowl sitting on the wide windowsill, covered with a tea-towel, as bread dough rises and stretches. She punches the dough with a square fist. It sighs and shrinks. She covers it with a tea-towel.

'Why did Mum go away?' I ask. 'Charlotte Renshaw said…'

Nanna glares. 'Don't listen to one blasted word from that mean-spirited child.' She thumps the dough. She's done talking.

A horn parps in the street. Nanna looks at her watch.

'Oh my, that's your father already. We best get moving. Bea will be here soon. I'll get my hat and coat.'

GREAT-AUNT BEA is as plump as the ripe yellow peaches she brings every year in waxy brown boxes from Bathurst. Smelling of Lily of the Valley and cigarette smoke from the train, Great-Aunt Bea plants whiskery kisses on my cheeks.

She hands a basket of peaches to the curved-back railway attendant who unloads her cases.

'For your kind self, good sir,' she says.

WITH THE RADIO blaring, pans clattering, Great-Aunt Bea takes over Nanna's kitchen. Glass bottling jars rattle in pots of boiling water. Rich ripe fruit bubbles on the stove. Sweet syrupy smells fill the room. Soon, there's sticky pink and purple juice on aprons, benches and even misted on windowpanes. After cooling, bottles are lined up carefully on shelves Dad built in the outdoor laundry.

Great-Aunt Bea takes me with her to visit Fliss at Montview, choosing a day Nanna has an all-day CWA meeting, where she can gossip all she likes with Marj Kingston, telling her of Billy's vandalism of the school windows, even though I did beg her to say nothing. I should've kept my mouth shut. Nothing good ever comes of confiding in Nanna Ennis. I feel sick at the thought of Billy's revenge.

In spite of her poor dragging leg, Great-Aunt Bea insists on walking to Montview. I'm surprised when Pieter brings a tea tray, setting it down carefully on a small table.

Great-Aunt Bea thanks Pieter as if he is a butler in a palace. He nods formally. Aunt Bea pours the tea, chatting to Fliss as if it's a perfectly normal conversation between two people. 'Now, Fliss— How often do you get out of this place, dear?'

Fliss shrugs. Great-Aunt Bea sighs, 'As I thought.'

She pulls on her gloves and has a quick word with Pieter. A taxi arrives. We're going shopping!

Great-Aunt Bea buys lovely, girly things for Fliss: Pears soap, perfume, nighties and slippers.

While Pieter pushes Fliss' wheelchair, Great-Aunt Bea slips away, reappearing with a brown paper parcel.

ON THE PORCH-swing at our house, while Dad prepares afternoon tea, I read to Great-Aunt Bea from my Book Of Known Facts. 'Your dad told me about this marvellous book,' she says, winking at Dad through the kitchen window.

Esmeralda sits on the swing, pecking at sunflower seeds while we eat biscuits and drink tea. I tell Great-Aunt Bea it's just as well Nanna is away because she can't take to chooks being pampered, magic or not.

Great-Aunt Bea tut-tuts and says, 'It's never been proved which creatures are magic and which aren't, so I'm keeping an open mind on the subject.' She nods at Dad who brings the brown paper parcel. It now has a soft pink bow.

Inside is a large square book that has the thinnest, finest pages I've ever seen. 'What is it?' I ask.

We sit around the kitchen table. Dad brings out a shoe box. Mum's pressed wildflowers are still pretty and bright, still as dainty as butterfly wings.

Great-Aunt Bea's hands aren't steady enough so Dad gets a tiny pair of tweezers and carefully places each flower on a pure white page. It's much harder than it looks when I try, but when we're finished Great-Aunt Bea claps her hands.

She stays for another week, when a wheezing bout of asthma sends her scuttling back to the cool, dry mountain air of Bathurst. When she leaves the ground is covered with fallen wisteria petals.

THE OVERRATED ART OF WALKING

Ennis family home, Henry Street, Quirindi, 1955

LUCY SCATTERS pellets for the hens. Seeing Harry she runs to the hut, tripping on the step as usual. 'You should get that fixed, Uncle Harry,' she says. 'It's an abomination.'

Harry laughs. 'Abomination is it, Missie? That's a big word.'

'Nanna says it all the time.' Lucy tiptoes her fingers along the trinkets on Harry's windowsill, stopping at the clock decorated with bullets. 'This bullet clock. Will it blow up, Uncle Harry?'

'No, No, I scraped the gunpowder out.'

She shivers. 'That must've been dangerous.'

'Trust me little Lucy, that was the least dangerous thing I did.'

Lucy points to her new pair of white canvas shoes. 'I'm getting ready for our cross-country run. Dad bought me new sneakers, thick socks and Band-Aids for blisters.'

Harry groans. 'Prepared for everything, Miss Lucy?'

'Uh huh,' she says, peeling a Band-Aid and sticking it on her knee—'just for practice. My friend Jenny said the teachers let us walk if we get tired. Maybe I'll walk.'

Harry moans. 'My feet have cramps just thinking about that.'

'You must've walked a lot, Uncle Harry.'

'We walked through whole countries, little Lucy.'

'Phewee! So it's a walking story today?'

El Kantara, The Suez Canal, Gaza, 1941

APPROACHING the African coastline, the Rohna moved into the Gulf of Aden. We had neared the coast of Somaliland. There was an increase in escorting war ships that warned us we were entering the battle zone. We were reluctant to go below decks. A thick column of smoke rose, then a burst of flame over the sea some ten miles to the East brought a new solemnity. We later learned an Italian reconnaissance plane had been shot down. It was our first image of war.

At the Suez we anchored near towering sandstone cliffs, baked dry by the sun. We were soon surrounded by small craft, vendors keen to sell their wares, shouting and clamouring for attention, among the "gully gully" men with their strident offers of magic. A slow trip up the canal followed. The other ships, and there were many, seemed to be drifting over the sands, so flat was the land. The waters of the Suez were hidden by the shore. To the East was the Sinai Desert, to the West, fertile agricultural land.

We berthed at El Kantara. The 2/17th had arrived in the Middle East. We were pleasantly surprised by bangers and mash supplied by the Brits. We'd travelled thousands of miles, soldiers without a war. We were soon on the move again. This time, packed and waiting at a railway siding.

We'd travelled thousands of miles, soldiers without a war.

'Crikey, Nugget!' said Lanky. 'Why didn't I join the goddamned air force?' He reached for his boot and had it partly off when one of the officers noticed.

'There's no time for playing with yer feet, digger. We've a train to board. It'll be here any minute now.'

Lanky smacked the boot back on firmly and watched the officer stride along the narrow siding. I sat beside him, crossed my arms and legs and brought my hat down over my eyes, took a quick glance to check that the officer was out of earshot. 'We've a train to board, he says, as if we didn't know that. This place might not be much as far as stations go but the rail tracks do give it away a bit.'

'The army mightn't tell us much but they sure take us places. For those young blokes that wanted to see the world, I think they've got their money's worth, but for me, my feet are in a permanent state of agony and we haven't even seen any action. Not that I'm hanging out for it.'

'I think you've got the worst feet in the battalion, Lanky.'

His, 'Shut up, Nugget' was interrupted by swarms of Arab children begging for food or money, their language broken by crude English obscenities.

'Good grief, Lanky, did you hear the swearing on that little bugger? They haven't picked up much English but they've sure learned how to cuss.'

'Like troopers?' said Lanky with a wink.

'Ah, I see your point.'

Once on the train Lanky took off his boots and fell asleep.

A bleak desert highway travelled beside us. There was the occasional oasis of date palms, and even the comfort of seeing a few gum trees. I was between home and history in a mystical land, a land portrayed in Bible stories, the land of sandal-footed disciples, of the ancient kings of Israel, of Solomon. I was taken aback by the spirituality of the place. It was also a land of accustomed to bitter conflict. We passed through scenes of grim wilderness that had heard the pounding footsteps of many an army intent on conquering or defence. Near Gaza, the train hissed to a halt with the metallic screech of wheels on steel tracks.

In the tented camp we slept on bamboo beds that had to be staked securely to prevent us landing on the ground when we rolled over in our sleep. A medic took a look at Lanky's feet and informed him that his boots were a size too small. He returned with some Murlex Foot Powder and a pair of boots a size larger.

'Where'd you get these beauties? I asked, but the medic tapped the side of his nose. Don't ask.

Lanky didn't care. After a few days of his new footwear he even declared he was a new man.

'JEEPERS, I wonder if I have enough Band-Aids.' Lucy sets them out in rows to count them. 'Perhaps I need Murlex whatsit.'

Harry tweaks a smile in a corner of his mouth, wondering how many more stories he will yet tell the child, wondering how much time he has left.

Fire Begun with Weak Straws[1]

Quirindi, 1955

OLD PAT stirs in his humpy in the bush, then sits upright, vigilant.

The planes, with their wild hum, they're upon him, to do their lethal turn, to level him to dust, to maim, to claim. Or is it trench fever? This war, this war with its diseases and distempers that rule, ravage and surpass the terrors of machinery, artillery or even the hand-to-hand rage of enemies.

To lie weak and delirious, heedless of masters or might, of patriotism or surrender, not because of battle with its incumbent agonies, but because of an influenza so potent and so wrathful that men are dying, without the distinction of heroic deeds.

Smoke circles around Old Pat.

The canvas flap is on fire. But not just that, the camp, all of it, and there—the enemy. Strange shadows in the full moonlight. Slender, crouching, crowing their victory, like hyenas prowling, laughing. Counting his loss, their gain.

He lopes crookedly into the eucalypt-scented scrub. His ragged coat flaps back and forth, the only movement in the bushland.

Even children perched on crackling seats of the rattling school bus talk of it, the inferno.

---

[1] "Those that with haste will make a mighty fire/Begin it with weak straws". Shakespeare, W 2010, *Julius Caesar*, Oxford University Press, New York, p.19.

Lean and Hungry Men

Lucy Meredith Carter, Book Of Known Facts, Quirindi, 1955

Alexei can be stubborn.
I told him we must do something about Old Pat.
The old man's humpy has burnt down to the ground.
It's just ash now.
Someone has to care.

ALEXEI stops dragging his stick along the dirt path long enough to give me a discouraging look. 'What can we do, Lucy? We're just kids. Anyway, It's just a humpy. He'll build another one.'

'It was his home! It was all he had.' I'm angry.

Alexei draws a circle in the dirt. He looks bored. 'All right then.' I reach into my pocket. 'Not that blasted notebook again!' Alexei blurts, then looks down, scraping his shoe along the dirt track. 'Sorry, it's just, well, it's probably best to write stuff down after.'

'After what?' I ask, hoping that means he has an idea.

'After … well, after we talk to the police.' Alexei smiles as if he just invented the wheel.

'The cops already know, and they did nothing.'

'Yeah, but they might be able to tell us what to do, or somethin'. They like talking to kids, improving community relationships, you know. They can't always act on everything.

There's the issue of manpower … and stuff.'

'You're talking like a politician,' I say.

'How would you know?' Alexei swats a fly. 'Come on, let's go to the station.'

A UNIFORMED policeman is sitting at the desk, working his teeth over with a toothpick. I cringe.

'Hello Sergeant,' says Alexei, looking over the desk. I stand beside him. It might be good to let him do the talking.

'What can I do for you kids?' The officer breaks the toothpick and throws it in the bin.

'Lucy is … I mean, we are worried about Old Pat's … ah, fire.'

'What d'ya mean? He always has a fire.'

I jump in. Alexei isn't getting it right. 'Yes, er, but see this time someone else started the fire. They burnt his house down.'

The sergeant lifts his bulk out of the chair and comes around the desk. He's smirking a bit.

I press on anyway. 'Must be an arsonist.' I remember to keep things concise. Dad says I ramble on. 'Never know what they'll do next.' That's straight out of Nanna Ennis' mouth and it gets the sergeant's attention. 'Could start a bushfire…'

Alexei jabs me with his elbow.

'Well, there is that,' murmurs the sergeant. 'Hey Blue!' he calls out, 'do y'know anything about this lot?' He turns to us. 'Blue's off duty, just hanging 'round the place, he'll help ya.'

When "Blue" into the room and I recognise him as Peter Winters, Dad's friend, whose hair is redder than mine. 'What lot?' asks Blue, smiling.

'Old Pat,' I say.

'Ah,' says Blue. 'Now there's a story. He's been on the wallaby since the twenties, from what I can make out.'

'On the what?' Alexei asks.

'The wallaby. It's an old expression for a swaggie.'

Alexei frowns. 'I thought a swaggie was a bag.'

'No, that's a swag. A swaggie is a wanderer, roams the highways. The old fella wasn't always homeless.'

The word homeless chills me.

'I don't know where he came from originally, he's been around for years. He's too old and confused to wander now. He fought in the First World War—as an infantry soldier. Came home with shellshock. Couldn't abide noise, cried like a babe at loud noises. Just couldn't handle any sort of job.'

Alexei pipes up. 'He yells at us kids.'

'He's harmless,' Blue says, 'he's more afraid of losin' his stuff. He's afraid of the whole world, poor bloke.'

My throat tightens. 'He ran away this time. There's just burnt rags near his humpy. We don't know where he is. I mean...'

Blue taps the side of his cheek with long tobacco-stained fingers. 'He usually hides out under the old Wakefield Bridge when he feels under threat. Let's go check there. He knows me, doesn't run away at least.'

ALEXEI and I squash in beside Blue in his Ute. He's such a big bloke and there isn't much room for us. While he drives along the creek on the rough trail, he tells us about swaggies. 'They used to be able to get food rations from the police stations at one time,' he says, 'my dad remembers handing those out. He was a copper too. That helped the poor blokes keep body and soul together. Doesn't happen anymore of course. Shame really. For some of those fellas their only crime was to come back broken after serving their country.'

The Ute jerks on the uneven dirt road, rutted by the rain.

'Wattle's out early,' says Blue, waving his arm out of the window.

He slows down as we pass Old Pat's humpy.

Old, blackened fruit tins with wire handles are scattered on the ground, left behind in the old man's hurry to escape whatever frightened him.

Burned-black strips of canvas hang limply. There's part of a number on one of the strips.

'Hmm,' says Blue, 'see what you mean.'

The stringybark trees are shedding bark like tired old snakeskins. The road becomes a dirt track with deep cracks and potholes. Dust swirls into the truck.

Alexei and I cough, but it doesn't bother Blue Winters.

We don't find Old Pat.

ALEXEI thinks I'm being silly.

Nanna says it's time something was done to get rid of the old vagrant, leaving his rubbish all about the place and scaring people minding their own business.

Dad told me not to cry for the whole world.

But Old Pat's bush humpy has burned down.

Everyone is talking about it. Some of the kids saw him run wildly though town, screaming about murderers and thieves.

I wonder where he'll live now. But as long as there hasn't really been an important crime, no one seems to care about an old man's lean-to.

It took me ages to talk Alexei into it, but now we're looking for Old Pat ourselves, now that Blue Peters couldn't find him.

We walk through the scrub, upsetting a wombat that bares its teeth and runs into its burrow spraying dirt. We hear the creek gurgling 'round the next bend.

Smoke curls up through the paperbark trees. Creeping closer to the creek, we see Old Pat squatting, dragging his billy back and forth through the water of the creek.

'He's washing his dishes like soldiers did,' I say, 'with ash and sand. Uncle Harry told me about it. He was in the war.'

'Uncle Harry?'

'He's not my real uncle, I just call him uncle, like you do with all your parents' friends, you know. He's been here for 39 months.'

'How come you know exactly?'

'He came the same time my mum died, so … I remember.'

'Don't know him. Where's he live?'

'He's a boarder at Nanna Ennis's. He lives in the hut at the back.'

'I thought there was nothing in that hut except old junk,' says Alexei, 'this Uncle Harry person, does he tell you stuff about the war?'

Alexei is mad keen on anything to do with the war.

'Of course not! Why are boys so dumb about war? He tells me ordinary things, not killing and that. He was injured, he has a bad leg and a big red scar on his neck that runs down his chest. He tries to hide it, it's hard to see. I think he has other wounds. I'm not sure, I don't ask him. Nanna Ennis says I'm enough of a nosy parker without bothering her boarders. Nanna is pretty bossy.'

'I could tell you a thing or two about bossy, Lucy Carter. With six brothers and sisters my place is a zoo. It'll be worse soon, because Katya's coming home and she's the bossiest of all.'

'I like Katya, that's great.'

'You don't have to live with her.'

WE RUN back to the police station to tell them where we found Old Pat. He turns wild eyes as he hears the crunch of footsteps as Blue Winters arrives, sits quietly and watches the old man.

There's dry food on the old man's beard. He tugs at the long white strands with shaking hands.

Blue takes a few steps, walking slowly, then stops when the old man raises a hand and whimpers, 'Don't hurt me', then lets out a weak cry, like a bleating lamb. Blue sits quietly on a rock not far from the old man and reaches into his pocket for his tobacco pouch.

Old Pat is startled by the match flaring, then he returns to mumbling.

'It's me, Pat, Blue Winters. Y'know me, don't ya. What happened Pat?' He drags on the cigarette and blows a lazy cloud upwards with pursed lips.

Old Pat tugged at mud-hardened trouser hems. His ankles were spotted with red swollen weals. He tore at them with filthy fingers, making them bleed.

'Damn sandflies 'ave been at him.' Blue shakes his head. 'Pat, let me take you to the nurse. Get y'somethin' for the bites.'

'Double vision, sir. Double vision. Saw them, saw them. Cassius has a lean and hungry look, lean and hungry. Dangerous men. Double vision. Dangerous, dangerous men, sir, lean and hungry. Watch out!'

'He's quoting Shakespeare,' Alexei whispers, then flushes, 'or somethin'...'

Blue smiles. 'Thought your lot was Russian.'

Alexei shrugs. 'My sister Sacha was in a school play. She was Portia, or somethin'...'

The old man ignores the conversation.

'Damn sandflies 'ave been at him.' Blue shakes his head. 'Pat, let me take you to the nurse. Get y'somethin' for the bites.'

'No sir. Double vision. Dangerous.' Old Pat looks up. His eyes are a brilliant blue. He rubs his face. There are burns on his fingers.

'Double vision, sir. Saw them, the enemy, lean and hungry men, sir, lean and hungry. Burnt me out, sir. Took my kitbag; the enemy. Did m'best, sir.'

Blue sighs and walks back to the Ute. Lifting the flap to the tray he pulls out a tarpaulin, a metal flask and a grey blanket. 'Look in the glove box, son,' he says to Alexei. 'There's a cake of Solvol in there, I use it to keep the missus happy. Can't wander in the house with greasy paws. Women don't like that sort of thing. That's it son, that grey lump of soap. Thanks.'

Blue manages this rambling conversation with the cigarette dangling from his mouth. He walks towards the old man and places the items at his feet. 'For you, Pat. Right? I'll bring you back some ointment for those bites, okay? Look after yourself.'

'Yes, sir.' Old Pat scrambles to his feet, grabs the bundle, tucking it under his long brown coat. Throwing Blue a brief glance, he turns and flees into the bush. His ragged coat flaps back and forth, the only movement in the heat-drenched landscape.

AFTER SCHOOL Alexei and I wait to talk to our teacher, Miss Bell, about what Old Pat said. I told Alexei we should wait until school finished. That bothered him, he's always keen to bolt home. 'Thanks a bunch, Lucy.' Alexei mutters under his breath, shuffling his feet. 'We might miss the bus. I don't wanna walk home.'

I tap his arm to make him be quiet and keep my eyes on Miss Bell. She sees us waiting and smiles, with her eyes all shiny as if she's pleased to answer questions after the home bell has rung. 'What did you want to know, children?'

'What did Shakespeare mean when he talked about men with lean and hungry looks?' I reach into my pocket for my notebook.

Alexei gives me a hard stare to remind me that I'm not allowed to write in it in front of people, but Miss Bell is a teacher. She'd like that sort of thing.

'How marvellous,' she says, 'you're interested in Shakespeare.'

'Alexei thought of it,' I say, nudging him in encouragement. Alexei shrugs, looking embarrassed.

Miss Bell begins. 'It's from a play Shakespeare wrote called Julius Caesar. It's based on a time in history.'

I write Julius Caesar and put a star next to it to remind me to look it up in the encyclopaedia at home.

Alexei looks confused. 'My aunt said she had a Caesar for her fourth baby.'

'Oh, that's different,' says Miss Bell, 'that's a caesarean section, an operation to deliver babies when they can't be born naturally.'

'Really,' says Alexei, leaning forward and brushing his hair out of his eyes. 'An operation?'

Miss Bell blushes and hesitates for a moment. 'It's called a caesarean—after Julius Caesar actually, because mythology suggests he was, er, delivered, er, born that way. Um.'

'Mythology?' Alexei is really interested now, but Miss Bell clears her throat and starts talking about Shakespeare again. She tells us Julius Caesar was the head of the Roman Empire, sort of like a king. 'They were a bloodthirsty lot, forever overthrowing their own rulers, knives in the back, never mind fighting other nations.'

'Shame someone didn't bump Hitler off,' says Alexei.

Miss Bell continues. Her voice is musical and quiet. She recites,

> '"Let me have men about me that are fat, sleek-headed men and such as sleep a-nights. Yond Cassius has a lean and hungry look, he thinks too much; such men are dangerous".'

'Yikes,' says Alexei, 'so it's poetry.'

Miss Bell smiles. 'In this case it's talking about men hungry for power.'

Miss Bell tells us that just like skinny men are hungry for food, men who want to rule over others are hungry for power and that makes them dangerous.

I want to write the quote down but Alexei interrupts, 'We gotta go now. We'll miss the bus. Thanks, Miss Bell.'

We race to the front of the school and see it drive off. 'Bother,' says Alexei. It's a long walk home through the scrub. Alexei moans and picks up my school bag. The handle squeaks as Alexei swings it beside him. 'What the heck have you got in here, Lucy?'

'Books.'

'Feels like the whole Encyclopaedia.'

Alexei throws it over his shoulder onto his back and holds it with both hands behind his head. It thumps as we walk.

'That's a good trick,' I say, grateful for his help.

'S'alright.'

Esmeralda's Magic

Lucy Meredith Carter, Book Of Known Facts, Quirindi, 1955

Esmeralda keeps pecking at the window.
I don't now how, but she IS magic.
Esmeralda is only allowed in my room for a little while.
Dad says Esmeralda doesn't have inside manners.
It's good to have her with me while Dad visits Nanna.
Now she can stay for my "little while" and not Dad's.

ESMERALDA fluffs her feathers anxiously and looks at me with fierce black eyes, nearly turning her head upside down.

Across the road, the Kingston twins are playing cricket in their front yard, laughing and yelling at each other.

The clang of the tennis ball on the metal bin they're using as stumps disrupts the quiet street. It's a Sunday afternoon kind of quiet. Lawns have been mown, while some families went to church, and many enjoyed their Sunday roast dinner.

'Howzat,' yells Billy as the ball hits the bin.

Ewan is out. He protests, waving his gangly arms like a windmill.

I can't get it out of my head that the twins might have burned down Old Pat's humpy, taunted him and taken some of his stuff. It's not easy to tell them apart, especially for a confused old man. 'Double vision,' Old Pat said. When Barry James said he was seeing double with the Barashev girls, something clicked.

And I can't make it unclick.

Esmeralda is pecking at the window again, more insistently, then flies to the floor. Her claws make a clip-sliding sound as she minces to the doorway and turns to look at me and clucks, 'Begerk!' Maybe she wants a ride in the bike basket.

I'm supposed to be "holding the fort"—something Dad says when he has things to talk about and doesn't want me tagging along and sticking my nose in. I'm not supposed to leave home, a few turns up and down the street past our house won't hurt.

It's four in the afternoon. The southerly breeze that relieves the day is trembling the treetops. Soon it will gust and blow. There's a smell of rain in the air. Esmeralda's feathers flutter as I glide down the road. Instead of scrunching down, she's alert, her eyes fixed on the Kingston's place.

Suddenly she is all wings and fluster, 'Begerk, begerk!' She flies right into the Kingston's shed. It's piled high with stuff.

Ewan and Billy go wild—yelling and waving their arms at Esmeralda. 'Shoo! Shooo! Stupid chook! Get outta there! We'll make chicken soup out of you!'

I drop the bike and start screaming, running as fast as I can. 'Don't you touch Esmeralda, you horrible boys! I'll tell Blue Winters! Call the police! Help!'

The twins run towards the shed. I get there first. Esmeralda has flown up to a high shelf and is settling onto a hessian bag. It has stencilled white lettering like Old Pat's burned canvas. Now I'm excited and start shrieking, 'They're the ones! They burned down Old Pat's humpy! They're firebugs and thieves!'

Mrs Kingston pelts around the corner, her arms flapping. She looks messy, half of her hair is in curlers. She stops in front of the boys, red-faced and puffing. Billy throws the tennis ball at Esmeralda but she doesn't flinch, just glares at him.

'What is wrong with you two!' Mrs Kingston yells.

Then she turns and sees me. 'Ah. Lucy.' She droops and reaches to touch her hair. 'I should have known.'

Mr Price, the retired bank manager from next door to the Kingstons' wanders over to see what all the commotion is about. It's that kind of street. 'What seems to be the trouble boys?' He calmly tucks his singlet in.

I'm pleased Mr Price is talking to the boys. I take the chance to sneak into the shed while the twins yabber over the top of each other.

'I'm so sorry, Ted.' Mrs Kingston flushes a dark red. 'What the heck were you thinking Billy?'

'Oh, it's always my fault isn't it? It's not fair.' Billy put his hands in his pockets and curls his lip.

'I'll box your ears, see if I don't,' says Mrs Kingston. Ewan is hanging his head, but Billy is watching me with slitted eyes, warning.

Esmeralda stretches, flaps her wings with another 'Begerk!'

'Is that your chook, Lucy?' asks Mr Price, ignoring the Kingstons who are all shouting now.

'Yes, Mr Price.' I hop from one foot to the other, unsure of what to say next. With a harrumph Mr Price saunters into the shed, grabs a stepladder and eyes Esmeralda warily. 'Fierce chook you've got there young Lucy,' he says.

'Yes Mr Price.'

With a crooked smile, he pats a rung of the ladder. 'Why don't you scamper up there Lucy, grab your chook and take her home, there's a good girl.' He walks back to the others. 'Snuff it, you two,' he says to the boys. 'Your mother has enough to worry about without you lot acting like hooligans.'

It doesn't take me long to clamber up the few steps on the ladder. Esmeralda hops into my arms as if nothing has happened.

She turns to peck at the hessian bag, so I nab it, shoving it under my other arm and running home, leaving the ruckus behind, just as Dad swings into the driveway.

DAD IS A bit distracted over teatime. Dinner is a pretty quiet affair and it suits us both. Normally I'd ask Dad a million questions about his visit with Nanna Ennis, but I'm relieved he didn't pay any attention to the commotion across the road. He didn't even notice me race over to bring my bike home.

Dad cooks tea. He apologises that it's tinned Baked Beans again. I don't mind. I'd rather have beans than another tuna casserole.

I stowed the bag under my bed when I got home and I can't wait to look at it. I was worried the boys might come for it. Maybe I had everything wrong? But there was no tap on the door, nothing. They'd have come if it was theirs, sneaking past their mother's ear-boxing threats, one keeping her attention while the other escapes. I've seen them do that a lot.

Their house is quiet, with the usual evening lights on, so I'm relieved.

Dad doesn't read the paper after tucking me in. He puts a record on the gramophone instead.

The music is soft and low. I hear Dad singing along with Patsy Clyne. I smile. It's been a long time.

Sliding my door till it's nearly shut, I drag the bag out. I fold back the damp sticky sacking, it smells awful. Inside, there's an old biscuit tin. That opens easily, as if it's been used a lot. By Old Pat? How will I know if it's his? It might be some old stuff that belonged to Mrs Kingston's late husband. Then how will I get it back to the shed?

The box smells funny, musty. There's a whiff of eucalyptus that stings my nose and makes me sneeze. There's another tin, a circular one, like the one Mum used for her dressmaking pins. It's a dull grey colour with most of the words rubbed off. It's hard to read in the semi-dark and the words are blurred with age and use. I think it says "TINCTURE OF" something and it has "BALM" on the side. There's a broken thing that looks like part of a broach. It has a sharp end; the other part is missing. It has bits that stick out like spokes on a bike. There's a symbol on it, but I can't read it. I don't know what colour it used to be. It's smudged with black, and silver looking.

There are some folded papers, yellowed, worn and grimy with fingerprints. I open one carefully, worried it might fall apart but it's stiff and stronger than it looks. It crackles as I fold it open. I hold my breath, my heart is thumping. There's a name, "Private Patrick Warren Calloway", and a number that matches the stencilled white number on the bag.

It's Old Pat's.

A KITBag

BLUE WINTERS sits at the Station desk, watching Lucy Carter and the Barashev kid head into the station with a canvas bag.

Lucy stumbles, calls him Mr Blue, begins a rambling tale, interrupted by Alexei, who tells her, 'It's "Constable Winters".' She sighs and starts again.

'It's like this, *Constable*,' she says. 'Remember what Old Pat said when his humpy burned down? Stuff about double vision and lean, hungry men? Here's the thing. The Kingston twins are identical! And skinny. Mrs Kingston says they're always hungry. So you see? Double vision, lean and hungry, get it?'

Lucy hands over a smelly hessian bag.

Inside the bag, there are grimy papers for one Private Patrick W. Calloway, service number, address, Next of Kin.

After they leave, Blue phones, gets the son, Franklin P. Calloway, a man delighted to find his father, missing these past twenty years.

After he hangs up Blue Winters sighs. Be careful what you wish for, mate.

Old Pat has been assessed by the Hospital Mental Health Team when he was found stealing dressings so his days as a wanderer are numbered. In fact, the old man had been transferred to Montview Lodge, after a brief scuffle and prudent sedation.

Love Should Save a Man

Lucy Meredith Carter, Book Of Known Facts, Quirindi, 1955

I took Old Pat's bag to the police station.

Blue Winters gave me a book on war insignia and other facts.

There's information about Old Pat's badge.

The badge is called the Third Pattern Rising Sun Badge.

THE BADGE has a scroll inscribed with the words 'Australian Commonwealth Military Forces' and it was worn by soldiers in both World Wars. Blue cut a picture out of the book for me. I think it's beautiful. Old Pat's is worn and grubby. He was so happy to see it he cried and shook Blue's hand. Blue says that the war never ended for Old Pat.

The police searched the shed at the Kingstons'. They didn't find anything else. Nothing happened to the twins because they're underage. The sergeant says he put the wind up the pair of them. He said it was more a prank than a serious attempt at a criminal career. He made them "volunteer" at the local garage, cleaning parts for Blue Winters' father. Billy was cranky and hated it, but Ewan worked hard. He asked if he could leave school to be a mechanic.

Mrs Kingston doesn't go out much anymore. She hasn't been to church for weeks. I overheard her telling Nanna Ennis, 'I could just crawl up a hollow log. Those two boys will be the death of me. Billy is uncontrollable and Ewan wants to drop out of school', then Nanna said, 'Let the boy leave school and make something of himself with Stan Winters in the joinery before it's too late'. Mrs Kingston marched up to the school and took Ewan out that day. Now he's going to Tech.

AT NANNA'S I wander down to the hut.

'Uncle Harry, do you have a copy of the "Noter Dame" book about the crooked man, the wonky church and Esmeralda, the gypsy girl? Maybe you have the book at your other house. The one with your mum. Is your mum still there? Do you have another house, Uncle Harry?'

Uncle Harry shakes his head. 'You're making my head spin. That's too many questions for this hour of the day.'

I told him about Esmeralda and her heroic actions in finding the stolen kitbag of the old wandering man gone mad from the war.

'It's lucky Esmeralda is magic,' I say. 'She can fly, you know. I mean not just flapping up to the perch, she can really fly.'

I pick two ripe mandarins from her Nanna's tree and hand one to Harry.

'Esmeralda has other adventures, y'know. At night when no one's watching. She flies all over the town and looks down on everyone.'

'It's a great life for magic chooks then,' he says.

I coo softly to Esmeralda and she curves into the my neck. She gives me the comfort of a creature with no secrets, no mysteries or lies.

TO FAIL AT THE BRINK

Gaza, 1941

A TIGHTLY packed train of hard, fit soldiers left Gaza. Violent windstorms battered. Thick sand and dust filled the carriages, leaving no escape.

Respirators were brought out to deter the choking sediment.

Icy desert rains pounded the earth at Mersa Matruh.

Chaos reigned as the men scrambled for equipment.

Ominous smoke clouds were near, too near—inescapable signs of war. Debris of combat was everywhere: artillery pocked earth, bullet-spotted squat buildings, clutter of captured weaponry, roofless, battered barracks.

A GENEROUS supply of rum brought swift sleep as the men slumped on ravaged cots half-open to the sky.

Harry dreamed, drifting back to the Tower of Silence. He dreamed of the woman and the dead babe, of the Sikh, first lying dead in the dust, then running toward Harry, his flesh falling along the road, and always the sound of that young mother…

THE MEN woke to a hot midday sun that seared, no longer soldiers without a war.

Nightmares clung to Harry's every movement as trembling hands jerked at straps and buckles.

Spilt out of the truck onto hard earth, smoke clawed their lungs as the troops ran to the fray. Harry stood paralysed, his rifle loose and useless by his side.

Something pinged his ear. He reached up. His hand was wet.

There was screaming, 'get back!'

Sarge dragged men to the truck.

Someone yelled, 'the driver's down'.

Harry sprinted, jumped into the driver's seat.

'Thank Christ, Nugget.' Sarge leapt to the sideboard, then hung out the door yelling instructions as the men scrambled aboard.

BACK AT CAMP a medic bandaged Harry's ear while the men slapped him on the back.

'I'm not a hero, Lanky,' Harry confided later. 'I froze like a loon. This gun hasn't fired a shot—Anyone could see, looking down this barrel. I failed under fire, mate, failed!'

Lanky quietly took Harry's gun, walked out of camp, fired off a few rounds, told the others he was shooting at rats raiding the food-tent, then told Harry to sit down, shut up and clean his weapon like everyone else.

STaN HaLL

Lucy Meredith Carter, Book Of Known Facts   Quirindi, 1955

Old Pat is in hospital now. He won't wander any more.
Or have his humpy burnt down.
Constable Winters said Old Pat's son is coming for him.
I guess that's the end of his story.
But I still feel sad.

ALEXEI watches a small brown gecko's quick race across the bush track. 'Hey, do y'wanna go and get a fruit ice from Stan Hall's garage. He's got a new freezer. And Dad gave me a shillin' for my chores.'

'Okay. Just wait till I tuck Esmeralda in.'

'Crikey,' says Alexei, 'I always forget about that chook. I dunno how she sits there so quiet and happy.'

Esmeralda answers with a satisfied bergerk and ducks her head under the doll's blanket.

The track widens and the thought of a cold treat has us both jumping back onto our bikes.

We hear the rattle of another bike coming down the track, someone riding quickly so we move to the side.

It's Billy Kingston and he looks mad. His eyes are slits below his blonde fringe, his jaw is pushed forward, his mouth is pressed tight.

I move a little further off the track and hold my breath. I feel my heart thudding.

Billy's coming fast, heading straight for me. He skids and rams the front wheel of my bike. I'm thrown backwards, but I hold the handlebars tight and start screaming.

'Lucy Carter, you're a dobber and a sneaky pest,' Billy sneers as he gets off his bike and comes towards me. Alexei yells something in Russian as he makes fists, then stands between me and Billy.

I put my hands in front of my face just as I see Esmeralda fly out of the basket. She flies at Billy again and again, managing to get a few sharp pecks in.

'Call off yer bloody crazy chook!' Billy yells, trying to hit her, but he misses and rides off in a hurry.

Alexei is gaping.

'I told you Esmeralda is magic,' I say, as Esmeralda hops back in the basket as if nothing happened. 'Believe me now?'

'Wow, she's some kind of chook. She can move in with our hens and fight off the foxes any time she likes!'

'She's not that kind of magic. She does other stuff.'

Alexei lines his bike up ready to clamber on and says, 'Well, let's get out of here anyway, in case Billy comes back. We might need more than a magic chook next time.'

My hands tremble and my mouth is dry. 'Alexei.' It's only a whisper, but he hears me.

'You okay, Luce?' He flicks his bike around. The movement raises a cloud of dust.

'I ... do you think Billy will come back?'

Alexei shrugs as if he's already forgotten about it.

'Can we walk the bikes for a bit?' I say. I feel a bit dizzy but don't want to tell him.

'Sure,' Alexei spins a pedal with his foot. 'It's not far anyway.'

WE LEAVE the dirt track with its bush sounds behind.

Our tyres make a softer sound on the smooth tarred road.

The morning feels different now. The happiness I felt for an autumn day that seemed like summer has disappeared.

I try and get excited with Alexei as he chatters on about which fruit ice he might have. I know he'd love to climb on his bike and race down the tarred road, but he doesn't. He licks his lips as the road curves.

Stan Hall's Garage is up ahead.

A tin sign with faded blue letters says:

HALL'S GARAGE.

Underneath, there's Stan's crooked handwriting:

NOT RELATED TO THE BUSHRANGER BEN HALL.

One of his two sons has added UNFORTUNATELY in large letters and red paint has dripped down the sign.

I STOP at the side of the road, shielding my eyes from the blazing sun. Heat shimmers off the sticky tar road. It's a busy intersection. I look left then right.

'Hurry up, Lucy,' Alexei mutters, 'there's no cars for miles.'

'Your little friend is just being careful,' says a voice. I jerk. It's Pieter, swinging the keys for the Barashev station wagon.

There's a man in a pale blue shirt like Dad's in the office, but the window is too grimy for me to tell if it is Dad. He often stops and chats with Stan Hall if the place is quiet. One of Stan's sons wheels a car tyre into the back workshop.

There's a car at the bowser, a rundown Ute, its wheel guard held on with thick silver tape.

Stan Hall has just filled the tank. He yanks on a strap of his navy bibbed-overalls, pulling it back over his shoulder and smiles at the customer, a man in dark grey.

There's a bang, like a penny bunger, a car backfiring. Something snaps in the air.

There's a metal clang as someone drops a tyre iron or a crowbar. I can't see much.

Hundreds of sparrows flutter straight up.

A man is lying on the ground twisting and groaning. A slow red pool spreads thickly beside him. Dad's hat is lying on the ground. I start calling, 'Daddy! My Daddy!' then someone falls on top of me, holding me down, their hot breath in my ear. The bike under me cuts into my leg. I try to look up but a hand presses me down.

I hear screaming so loud and close it burns my ears. I'm cold, shivering. There are other sounds, so far away I hardly recognise them. Noises I don't understand. Feet running, sirens, cars, voices. There's no breath left in me.

I push my hands into the ground. They sting, but I'm almost up now, on one knee, arms pushing. Something holds me back. I put my hands over my ears, there are too many voices. A strange feeling burns through my body. I need to throw up.

I WAKE UP and wait for Dad to pick me up and tell me I've been dreaming, but he doesn't. Here's not anywhere.

I'm lying in a white bed in a bright room that is much too busy and loud for heaven or dreams.

Someone is stroking my forehead and telling me everything's going to be alright. A pain shoots up my arm. There's a pumping sound as a band on my arm gets tighter.

'It's okay, sweat pea, you fainted,' Katya says, stroking my arm.

I whimper—'But Daddy...'

'Your Dad's okay. He wasn't there.'

I believe her because Katya is always in trouble for telling the truth.

'Someone kept screaming, Katya.'

'That was you, sweet pea. You maybe went a little crazy because you thought your dad was hurt.'

The nurse takes the pumping thing off my arm. 'Everything's fine. Her observations are good,' she says to Katya, then turns to me again. 'You're a lucky young lady that your mother was just across the road shopping,' she adds.

My tongue is thick. I try to speak, but the words seem stretched and strange. 'Oh... I, she...' I say, but Katya pinches my arm.

'Yes, isn't she!' Katya is talking very fast and her face is red. I don't say anything. My mouth won't cooperate anyway, and I'm trying to work out what's going on.

'Who knows what would have happened to my poor little sweet pea if I hadn't been there.' Katya looks at me, hesitates, then leaps off again. 'How awful it would have been for her to come here without her darling mother by her side. All alone. I can't bear to think about it.' Katya smiles widely at the nurse and puts her hand over her heart.

I open my mouth, astonished.

'I do understand,' Katya winks at me. 'Only relatives can accompany patients in here. Of course, you can't let just anyone ... in.' Katya's arm waves to take in the room. I catch on and giggle. It's a strange sound and the phlegm in my mouth makes me have a coughing fit.

Katya pats my back a little too hard, then she slumps into the chair when the nurse leaves. 'Gosh, sweet pea, I thought you'd tip me in it then.'

'Alexei said you never tell lies.'

'Well, there's a first time for everything,' Katya says, using a sheet of paper to fan herself. 'How did I do?'

I give her the thumbs up, then hear Dad's voice in the corridor. Katya turns pale.

'WHAT THE HELL'S going on here! I was told my daughter was here with her mother.'

The curtain is thrown back. Dad is standing there. His face is white. Katya starts mumbling something in Russian and Dad is glaring at her with the angriest face I've ever seen.

'You?' he says. 'You can't possibly know how shocked I am. Deeply, truly shocked!'

The nurse starts telling Dad about me, how the doctor's given me a sedative and other medical stuff about being okay to go home. It's all too confusing so I close my eyes. It's just as bad on the way home in the car. Dad has to give Katya a lift because Pieter had taken us to the hospital in the Barashev station wagon and had to get back to Montview.

That set Dad off all over again. He started banging on about Katya having something called unmitigated gall.

I've never heard Dad talk so much, ever. He asks how old Pieter is, does he have a license? Why did Katya lie, such a terrible lie? Does she have any idea how he felt being told his daughter *and wife* had gone to the hospital?

He'd nearly lost his mind.

My head is thick and fuzzy.

I'm getting really annoyed. I'm just about to tell them I had a splitting headache when Katya says very quietly, 'I'm sorry you lost your friend Stan'.

Dad clears his throat and that's all I remember.

THE NEEDLE the doctor gave me to calm down must have had strange medicine in it because I had the weirdest dream that night. Dad and Katya were arguing in the hall.

Dad was saying that Katya was the stubbornest woman he'd ever met, that she didn't have to walk back to Montview. He could have dropped her home if she hadn't such a monumental amount of pride, that she needn't put on the martyred act with him, if she wanted to walk home at night with God knows who about, then he wasn't to blame.

Katya, who could yell louder than her brothers in the non-dream world, was speaking quietly and clearly, but mainly saying nothing. She told Dad he might be in shock, and perhaps should have a cup of tea.

Dad said people who gave unsolicited advice really got his goat and Katya said she was Russian and asked what that meant, did he really have a goat, then he laughed.

That was when the strangest thing of all happened.

Dad put his hands on both sides of Katya's face and pulled her roughly to him and kissed her. Right on the lips. For a long time.

Then Katya slapped him and his hat fell off.

IN THE MORNING I creep into the hall.

Dad's hat is hanging on the hat peg by the back door where it always hangs so I know for sure it was a dream.

I don't say a word about the dream when Dad brings me breakfast in bed.

He tells me how worried he'd been.

I don't go to school. I ask Dad to shut the window because it's too bright.

I don't want my favourite book to read.

I don't want lunch and only want biscuits and milk. I don't even want my Book of Known Facts.

I'VE SEEN a man shot dead with a gun. He died where his blood poured out of his chest and stained the ground.

Nothing will ever be the same again.

Catching a Murderer

Quirindi Police Station, Henry Street, 1955

CONSTABLE Peter "Blue" Winters descended from a long line of law enforcement officers.

Not that he bandies that titbit about the pubs in this part of the country, better known for its support of Messrs. Ben Hall, Thunderbolt, and bushrangers of their ilk, where housewives once hung red blankets as warnings and white sheets for all clear.

He and Constable Bain apprehend Stan Hall's killer only a stone's throw from the shooting.

The ignorant offender had stopped for a pint, a mere four miles from the scene.

It had been almost too easy.

TOO MUCH

Montview Lodge, George Street, Quirindi, 1955

FLISS JERKS. Her head pounds. There's a mechanical scraping inside her skull. Too much, too much of everything.

Fliss do this, Fliss try that.

YESTERDAY was the happiest in a long time.

Yesterday she thought she could do anything.

Yesterday, music played.

Yesterday, there was song.

YESTERDAY, her dreams were vivid, but he did not come to her with smiles and love tokens. Instead, her head buzzed with pain and memories of Jerranjerup.

Those tight hot days and taut fears. With Sylvia's grim comfort and cloying concern.

Transient dream joy visited with his soft lips, burning out in malicious splendour.

Yesterday is a million miles away.

Katya has brought large flashcards and discipline, bringing words that refuse to be arranged, refuse to obey.

Katya has brought words. Large black print on pristine white cards. Fliss glares at the cards Katya left behind, stacked in neat precision. The pile taunts her.

One word on each card. In Katya's bold hand. Words. Fliss

knew them all, and yet she couldn't say one after hours of pointing, nodding and smiling.

Turning the cards over, one by one, Fliss grows angrier. Door, table, window, mat—words for a child. Things in her room. But she is not a child. Soap, towel, paper, pen. She is still young. Her skin is soft. Umbrella, serviette, spoon, fork. Words with distinct careful meanings that require elaborate games of charades to convey. Piano, chair, floor—things in the lounge room. Hall, slippers, comb, teeth.

Fliss swipes at the cards and they skid across the smooth table. Several fall to the floor like an inevitable waterfall. Cheese, bacon, eggs.

Ethel came that afternoon, still mourning, still pitying. A lifetime of sorrowful looks and sighs, of everyone picking things up, moving things aside for poor Felicity. Cloying acts of kindness that have become a memorial to her helplessness.

Fliss longs to batter the table into useless shards—a parody of what it once was. As she is. Her vision blurs, angry tears follow. A decade of them, falling in torrents, heedless of the years.

THE DOOR to the kitchen slams open.

It's Maria Barashev. She holds a sheet of paper and is checking the table settings as she mutters to herself. 'Those girls. Where is…?' Seeing Fliss, she stalls. 'Oh Bozhe!' she calls, 'She weeps! Katya!'

Fliss sweeps the rest of the word cards to the floor. Now even her tears will be picked up and taken away.

Katya comes. She sits with her pale strong hands folded in her lap. 'It will get better,' she says. Her calm infuriates Fliss. *'Not, not. Not, not!'* Fliss glares as Katya smiles.

What is wrong with Katya? Fliss thumps the table. The crystal vase rattles. *'Not, not!'*

Katya stands, kisses Fliss on the head, then laughs. She's gone mad. Fliss pushes away and sobs.

'Cry,' Katya says, hugging Fliss, 'cry all you want.'

But Fliss stares with angry eyes. 'Not, not.' And then, she hears the words—not thoughts, but sounds. 'Not, not,' she says.

She touches her lips. She has spoken out loud.

They're both crying now, and Sacha arrives. Sacha says Fliss has had too much excitement for one day, that Katya is a brutal task master, but she's smiling.

LUCY ARRIVES and reads from her Book Of Known Facts.

Reading what she found out in her encyclopaedias about pressing wildflowers.

'Is that Pieter wheeling Barry James?' Lucy asks Fliss.

Fliss looks and nods.

'Goodness, he's very kind to the old man.' Lucy watches Pieter attending to Barry James, adjusting the walking stick across his lap as he prepares for a ramble around the grounds. 'I'm glad he likes *somebody*.'

DUGOUTS AnD DUST

Ennis family home, Henry Street, Quirindi, 1955

'UNCLE HARRY, I met a cousin of Alexei's, Pieter. One minute he speaks French, then Russian, then English. He doesn't speak to us kids unless it's to tell us to get out of the way. He's impossible!'

'Ah, Europeans speak any number of languages. Confusing for Aussies that haven't ventured from their own backyards. You should've heard the rabble in the bazaars and streets.'

'But he's in Australia now. The others speak English.'

'Ah Lucy, maybe for him, forgetting his language would be like you losing your Book Of Known Facts.'

'But, he's not even trying, he's angry all the time.'

'So you'll weep your pretty tears for an old vagrant broken by war, but not a skinny orphan? You can't judge someone until you know their story. His story isn't in words. It's in the care he takes with an old man. It's in his thin body, his slouched shoulders, his badly-fitting clothes, and his need to hold on to all his languages. And he's much more than those small things.'

'How do you know all that, Uncle Harry?'

Harry thinks of Lucy, confined beneath Pieter's protection, not knowing it was he who sheltered her, her heart thundering as she watched a hat like her father's, roll away from a dying man. When Lucy begs a story, He says, 'It's about a desert with only one tree.'

Tobruk, Libya, 1941

'STREWTH, HARRY, what are y'doin? Still clearing away the cooking gear?' Lanky Calloway leant on his shovel and eyed me through the sweat and grime that was oozing down his face in spite of the kerchief he'd tied around his head.

Lanky's cheeks were sunken. Low rations had done him no favours. He'd been digging in the hard earth for hours. His previous dugout had been blown to hell by the Stukas. He was cursing the bloody Gerries, the war and the flies as the sun slowly merged with the treeless horizon. Lanky sighed. 'I dunno why you're bothering, Harry. Every meal has sand in it no matter what we do.' His lazy baritone rumbled with exhaustion.

'It doesn't help with you chucking filth everywhere.'

'Yeah righto. Tedious job this. Feel like I'm digging my own grave.'

'Don't worry,' I said, tossing him a strap of beef jerky. 'You won't have to dig your own grave. We'll fix you right up. Dig halfway to China for a fine upstanding whinger like you, we would.'

'Leave off. We're not all blue collar schmucks like you. Some of us had jobs we actually liked before this flaming war interrupted everything.' Lanky dragged the handkerchief off his forehead and mopped his face.

'What are y'talking about Lanky. I liked my job.'

'Driving trucks?'

'Why not?'

Lanky groaned. 'I should've known. You drive like a mad man.'

'Don't knock it. My driving has saved your bacon a few times on night patrols.'

'Fair enough.' Throwing down the shovel he lowered himself into the dugout.

'Oh, for fuck's sake. It's still a foot short.' His scrawny knees protruded. 'Hey, Harry old mate, I could bunk in with you. That thing's big enough for a fecking Panzer.' He pointed the shovel at my dugout. 'At least you've still got your tarp to keep out the cold. Mine's shredded.'

I threw him the shirt he'd hung on a stake in the ground. 'This'll keep you warm, princess.'

DAWN ARRIVED with the threat of a sandstorm, so we covered everything and ate under our blankets. The sand slithered through the camp but didn't rise above our waists so by midday we were hard at it again, checking and cleaning equipment.

In the desert, haze and dust ruled the landscape and windswept tussocks were rare signs of vegetation. The bleached sand was always on the move, whispering and sighing between us as we passed decaying remains of the dead, or lime pits for hasty burials.

Few of us wore shirts through the day. With our helmets unbuckled, shorts rolled up, we looked more like a construction crew than an infantry battalion. What a sight we must have been? What would they have thought at home? A shirtless army, who'd have thought. But then the cinema films and posters showed spic-and-span soldiers smiling beside perfect rows of tents.

WE MARCHED into the desert near Tobruk, haze and dust—our first tyrants. Our unit was a bush artillery in a bleak land. Our dugouts were grim resting places or bleak refuge from attack.

Open knotted camouflage, like fishing nets, was spread precariously over our equipment and work areas, with randomly placed corrugated iron sheets added for cover. In most places, we could see straight through to the dull blue of the sky by day and the unfamiliar stars at night. From the air the place must have looked like a rubbish tip. With any luck, the Luftwaffe was thrown off by its ramshackle presence. We took comfort from that, comfort being a scarce commodity in our lives.

Sometimes we didn't know we were under attack from the skies until the strafing of the Stukas exploded the sand and dirt in front of us. However, most of the time we heard the scream of hell, the "Jericho-Trompeten"—the sadistic dive sirens designed by the Germans to induce fear. And fear is what it delivered. And when it wasn't the Gerries, the Italians with their field guns sent 75 mm. shells our way. A shout went up when we captured one of those! It was time for photographs and victory cries then.

The only tree in sight was at the entrance to the underground Aid Post.

WHEN SANDSTORMS hit, we covered everything, retreated to our dugouts and ate under blankets.

On a recon mission late one night Lanky and I met with a group of loose-robed Bedouins at an Arab encampment. They welcomed us. We sat over an open fire near goatskin tents. They gave us thick strong coffee, soft, delicious dates and seasoned rice while they spoke of an Italian retreat. An artillery gun had been left behind, a good find.

After we left Lanky said, 'We're as dark-skinned as the locals. The Gerries won't be able to tell the difference. No one will know us when we get home.'

'What will you do when this is over, Lanky?' I asked. 'Go back to the law?'

Lanky paused so long I thought he'd gone to sleep in the passenger seat of the Bren Gun Carrier we used for scouting around. Lanky was renowned for sleeping through mortar fire. 'Just get us safely back to camp, will ya mate? If the Gerries don't finish us off, your driving will.'

THERE'S a loud clap as Lucy brings her hands together.

'Thanks Uncle Harry, I love your stories. They're much better than History lessons.'

She wriggles off the story stool. 'Did you really drive like a maniac, Uncle Harry?'

'Did I say that? Good heavens!…'

prinyatiye party

Lucy Meredith Carter, Book Of Known Facts, Quirindi, 1955

There's a party at Montview today.

Katya is home!! I hope she lets me help with teaching Fliss. Fliss might get some more words.

Perhaps Fliss will share the word with Katya. Then she can help me solve the mystery of Jerranjerup.

I can't actually ask Katya.

I'm no good at hinting. That never works.

Not for me.

SOME THINGS are too hard for questions, especially when someone has trusted you with a secret. An important one. One they can't tell you about because they only have one word. I can't get the mystery of Fliss's word out of my head. A place called Jerranjerup. I wish there was someone I could ask. I've never had trouble asking questions before, but I don't know how to go about finding stuff out when I'm not supposed to be poking around.

'We're going to see Fliss today, Esmeralda.' I pat her as I tuck her into the basket.

AT MONTVIEW, after a few soothing sounds to Esmeralda, I set her on the ground and slip in the door leading to the kitchen.

Mrs Maria Barashev stirs a huge pot of spicy stew. 'Ah Lucy, you are early, *kroshka*. You have come to the party?'

There are platters of pan-fried potatoes sausages, and Lucy's favourite Russian treats, golden ponchiki and honey pryaniki.

'Today we celebrate *prinyatiye*,' she says. 'Adoption. Today Pieter is our son.'

Mr Barashev waves a document and spins.

'Where's Pieter, Alexei?' I ask. He points to an open window. Pieter is outside, smoking and pacing around the courtyard.

'Is okay,' says Maria, 'Pieter is happy.'

Mr Barashev winks. 'Yes, like all good Russians, he is. Happy on the inside.'

Barry James crosses the room to Dad. 'Fancy a piano duet, George?'

Dad does a soft shoe shuffle and bows. 'What's your pleasure, Barry? No high-falutin classics though, you know I'm a dance hall man myself.' He joins Barry at the piano and they play "A Bicycle Built For Two".

Music fills the room as everyone joins in, then Barry throws up his hands when the song is over and bows to Dad. Dad smiles, sliding effortless fingers over the keys. I recognise the opening chords to Tennessee Waltz. Someone pushes Katya forward and her voice is sweet and low as they harmonise.

WHEN THE party's over, I help Fliss to her room.

Nanna Ennis, Dad and Katya are there. They stop talking. Dad's arms are folded. Nanna's eyes are red.

Katya is pacing like a panther. 'We'll start later in the week.'

'Start what?' I ask.

'Physical therapy.' Katya touches Fliss's hair gently.

Dad turns to Nanna. 'Sylvia didn't ... Are you sure about this Ethel?'

Katya jumps in. 'You must have your own thoughts, George.'

Her eyes ask questions I don't understand.

'George hasn't exercised his own opinion since 1916,' Nanna says, her voice tight.

Dad blushes. 'I was *born* in 1916, Ethel.'

'I know.' Nanna gives Dad a hard look.

'Give it a chance, George.' Katya walks to the window and stares at the garden.

'It's just that I worry...' Dad tries again.

Nanna jumps in. 'No one is expecting miracles George.' She stands behind Fliss, a hand on her chair. 'She's my daughter,' says Nanna. Dad's voice is low as he says, 'I worry about false hope, that's all.'

'Tsk tsk, tsk tsk,' Fliss taps the table.

'You're right, Felicity,' Dad says. 'It's your choice.'

Fliss sobs. I run to her.

There's something in the air holding everyone apart and I don't understand it.

DAD TELLS ME to wait in the hallway.

I'm angry. I wish I knew what was going on. Grownups speaking but saying nothing. I lean against the wall of the long wide corridor and stare at the shifting light from the stained-glass windows in the doors at the front entrance.

I move closer. To the doors. To the office, where all the records are kept, a small, cramped room full of answers.

Just inside the door, on the edge of a wide desk is a pile of mail. And on top with beautifully crafted writing is a cream envelope for "Miss Felicity Ennis", postmarked *Jerranjerup*.

I look down the hallway. Even the kitchen sounds have stilled.

I grab the letter, stuff it into my pocket, and run.

THE SPACE between Dad and me is different over tea. I wash the dishes and Dad gets a tea towel. He takes such care with each plate. There's a lump in my throat thinking that's how he is with me. I want things to be comfortable again, so I tell him the story of Old Pat. He listens with a frown.

'You can't fix people, Lucy.'

'Is that what you tried to do with Mum? Fix her?'

Dad sighs. When he speaks his voice is low. 'Yes.'

'I don't want to fix Old Pat. I just want to fix one thing for him.'

'That's a fine sentiment Lucy, but you're not to go near him alone. Do you understand that?'

'I don't want to Dad. He frightens me a little; he seems to be out of himself, so wild and confused, and yet so lost as well.'

'Okay, just keep that promise and don't interfere. There are proper authorities for that sort of thing.'

I tackle the saucepan, scrubbing it with the steel wool soap pad the way Mum used to. 'Dad, why are you fighting Katya about Fliss having therapy?'

'It's … well, it's complicated. We shouldn't have talked about it … today. There are some things grownups need to discuss.'

'Without children around.' I thump the saucepan onto the draining tray. I don't want to look at him.

'Buttons.' His voice is pleading.

Guilt over the letter in my pocket burns me up, but I'm angry. 'Maybe grownups should get better at saying nothing then. If you're not going to tell us anything maybe you should take better care to hide stuff you don't want kids to know instead of saying half-things! We're just kids, right?'

'You'll understand one day.' Dad looks sadder than I've seen him for ages.

'Really!' I'm yelling now and I know my face is red. 'One day? Which day, Dad. Which birthday brings that? Is it like the tooth fairy? Santa? Or should I say the story of them—the lie. Do I wake up one day and just understand? Is that how it is?'

Dad sighs and takes the dishcloth from my hand. 'Sit down Buttons.'

I fold my arms and sit stiffly on the edge of the chair.

'The thing with strokes is that part of the brain has died, there was too much damage. It … happened so quickly. She's lucky to be still with us. If there's improvement it won't be much.'

'Mum said you're a pessimist.'

Dad rolls his eyes. 'Yes, she did, didn't she.'

'Katya just wants to see if she can improve things for Fliss.'

'Yes, and that's a fine thing. As long as we don't expect too much … it's understandable to want the best for someone you love. Especially for Nanna Ennis, she's had so much sorrow. A son, your Uncle David killed in France in the war, and then your mother to-ing and fro-ing, then dying of cancer, so quickly gone. Your aunt Felicity is the only child she has left. I just want you to understand that Fliss is never going to walk freely. The doctors have gone into all that. And she'll never be able to speak.'

'How can you know for sure?' I look away quickly. I can't tell Dad that Fliss has a word and one word has to mean something.

GEORGE'S FAMILY DILEMMA

Montview, Quirindi, 1955

LUCY STANDS by the bay window in Fliss' room. She's not an elegant child. Her red hair spills in tousled ringlets. It has depths and layers of colour. Fliss hopes one day the child will realise it's one of her best features, along with her green eyes and pale skin.

Lucy finds voice. 'Dad doesn't understand. I wish he'd … fight for … for you, for family.'

Fliss wishes Lucy understood the unique heroism of her father.

Lucy's finger traces the raindrops as they creep down the window. It's too blustery to go outside today. She turns, her eyes burning.

If Fliss could, she would tell her Lucy about her father's quiet control and forcefulness when he insisted on packing Fliss' things to move her into Montview after he realised how much she had suffered with the Ingram sisters.

Fliss would tell how her father stood up to his own sisters when it was the right thing to do.

She would sit Lucy on her knee and begin with—'Let me tell you a story about your father'.

The Carter farm, Black Mountain, 1944

PRIVATE David Ennis died on the 19th of August 1944, three weeks before his 18th birthday, as he was crossing the River Seine after the Normandy Victory. The Ennis women floundered. Ethel fell into herself. Fliss and Sylvia feared she would never recover. It was the week Sylvia accepted George's proposal.

It was also the week that George's two older sisters summoned him to sort out the family property at Black Mountain. He'd delayed his actions as executor of his father's will by a year, to give the three girls time to recover, but the oldest two, Lydia and Claire were anxious for things to be settled. They felt he'd had long enough. He was malleable enough. The older sisters didn't foresee any difficulties once George could be reminded of his responsibilities to the family.

Sylvia was frantic with wedding plans and asked Fliss to go with George. Fliss knew the girls a little. She felt a strange venturing into George's family affairs, but the war had changed the way things were done. Families were struggling with bigger issues than ever before. Rules about conducting everyday life were being rewritten in every home and business. People who were expected to step up, crumbled, and some who were expected to fall to pieces, shone.

Lydia and Claire sat—poised, at the blunt table in the old family home. Sly glances spoke of synchronised undertones—sisters dominating the room as they once did as teens. Both had married up, and remained there, leaving Black Mountain and the life they shared as children far behind.

Apart from a brief greeting to Fliss, they ignored her.

Susan, the youngest, was living in the family house while her wounded husband ran the farm. She faltered as she placed cups of tea on the table in front of the others.

'Will this take long?' Lydia stirred the tea vigorously, spilling some into the saucer.

'Is something wrong with the tea?' Susan asked.

'The tea's fine.' Lydia slopped the tea from the saucer into the cup. The gesture confused Susan. She was too young to remember the running hostilities between Lydia and their mother, too young to remember Claire's aloofness and embarrassment at having a simple country mother with work roughened hands.

'Well, George. You have the floor. Anytime you're ready.' Lydia swirled her tea.

Feigned airs of the past had become practised elegances.

Claire registered her disdain by merely sipping. She briefly touched Susan's hand. Susan leaked a smile, hungry for the affection the gesture promised, but cold eyes failed to deliver.

Lydia and Claire were so confident of the outcome they'd left their upwardly-mobile spouses behind, secure in the belief George would serve their interests, as he once did.

George was taking his time and it grated.

'The house won't be sold,' he said, the words dropping like stones. 'Susan and Eric and the boys will continue on here. The house is theirs. After all, they cared for both parents and kept the farm going. We've all shared in the profits.'

Claire gasped, gripping her Glomesh purse with white knuckled fingers.

Lydia, white-angered, blanched. 'What the hell!'

Susan sobbed into a serviette—crushed shapeless by pale hands.

'Ken will have something to say,' Lydia said.

'We'll get a solicitor.' Claire found her voice.

'It will do you no good.' George leaned back in the chair. 'I signed the bank papers a week ago. Let that be an end to it. But if not, then go ahead. With or without your husbands.'

Lydia removed a slender gold cylinder from her purse and twisted it, revealing blood red lipstick. One hand held the gold mirror as she applied it with care, stretching thin lips, *ooh, aah,* with slow precise movements.

War had been declared.

Mail from Home

Tobruk, Libya, 1942

AT NIGHT, somewhere between wide-eyed vigilance and dreamless sleep Harry imagined the women at home crafting the camouflage nets, knotting and chatting; feeling useful—his mother, his sister perhaps. He didn't know for sure what they were doing for the war effort apart from knitting socks and helping with Red Cross Comfort packages. They had to be careful what they wrote, but not as careful as Harry when he wrote. Harry slipped the letters from his beloved between those from his mother and sister. It was her letters he ached for. And her letters he feared.

When the mail arrived the men stood with mock nonchalance in courteous queues. Then they scattered and tore open the envelopes and parcels like hungry animals while flinging carefree jokes that fooled no one. They masked their anxieties. Mail from home also brought fear. The men worried about bad news— illness, death, estrangement. Some of the men received letters from girlfriends, fiancés and wives, begging forgiveness for finding new love.

Tiggy Greenwood, a stretcher-bearer, and a fine fellow, fell to his knees after a year of fighting, pale as a ghost. The men thought someone had died. His fiancé had broken it off. Tiggy would have taken that on the chin, but it was the white feather falling out of the envelope that finished him. His girl had been going to meetings where the men who refused to carry guns were considered cowards, even if they were serving. The soldiers had heard women were handing out white feathers as a symbol of cowardice to any man in the city not wearing a uniform. One officer had been approached when he was in civvies after an injury.

Tiggy slipped out that night into the darkness. The men heard a single shot. Tiggy Greenwood had finally carried a gun. That hit the men hard. They passed the next day in mute solidarity, stopping only to eat and share cigarettes, talking only to relay orders. One day, and their grief had to be pushed aside.

MEN'S MINDS came undone in an instant over there. Like their bodies. It was as if they became machines in battle, putting their thoughts aside, setting them down carefully. Then later, when the air was clear and pure, and the threat far away, they fell. Squeaky Taylor was found weeping like a babe in the corner of the only structure out there, the underground El Adem Aid Post. Strands of hair were prised from his fingers. It took three months in the war neurosis clinic set up in Tobruk before he was right again, but that was better than some.

It was both easier and harder having a lover, so far away. mortality was a fragile thing. The vulnerability of family, wives and lovers was never far from our minds.

Harry might have left with greater ease with only his mother and sister to worry over, knowing they would cling together, giving each other strength.

But then, in those last days before leaving, Harry met her, with her shimmering hair, slim glamour, confident walk and utterly joyful smile. He spoke of her to no one except Lanky. Perhaps fearing she would disappear as quickly as she'd come into his life.

Yet, every evening as dusk ended the tasks of the day it was her face, her smile that rose to inhabit the tossings and turnings of the night.

For Harry, the war was now a different beast, a vengeful Zeus with callous barbs to wound his mortal flesh, flesh that desired nothing more than to return to her and live. Some of the men never spoke of loved ones but others shared photos of their sweethearts, talking of them until the rest of the men begged them to lay off.

'Can't stick me missus next to me 'eart anymore,' moaned Knobby Burns, pulling a box of fags from his shorts pocket, 'don't 'ave a breast pocket. Here we are, a bare-chested battalion in this stinkin' heat. Jeez, if me missus could see me now.'

'Yeah, she'd tell you to have a wash and air your blanket,' said one of the men.

The mention of blanket-airing caused a great deal of hilarity and backslapping. A recent order from above to pay diligent attention to the airing of blankets seemed incongruous in that treeless land of dust and sand.

The men lined up at twilight on the night they received the directive and shook their blankets in unison until one of the officers wandered out, fag in mouth and shouted. 'Cut that out, you idiots! You're chucking dust everywhere. There'll be hell to pay if it gets in the machinery.'

They went to their dugouts that night with well-aired blankets to cover from the night's chill. It took a while for the dust to settle; the night air was thick with it. Another odour to endure, but at least familiar. It still smelt better than the animal stalls at the Hordern Pavilion in Sydney where the men were first billeted after enlisting.

It wasn't just the new sounds of a foreign land that pushed a man awake at night with their strangeness. It was the absence of the everyday sounds of home, a dripping tap, the sound of leaves clattering as gum trees swayed, the creak of a door, the postman's whistle. And most of all, the sounds of a woman, a whispering sigh, the tinkle of female laughter.

NO STOrY TODaY

Ennis family home, Henry Street, Quirindi, 1955

THROUGH the grimy window of the hut Harry sees that Lucy has forgotten to wind the hose up. It lies across the yard like a careless serpent enjoying the morning sun.

Lucy settles on the stool in Harry's hut with Esmeralda. She reaches into her bulging pocket, bringing out her Book Of Known Facts. 'I was in the hospital,' she says, 'but I was okay. I … oh.' She hiccups on a sob.

Harry taps the book. 'Why don't you read it to me.'

'Okay. "I don't want to talk about war anymore. A man shot Stan Hall dead because he didn't want to pay for a lousy gallon of petrol. It was the most awful thing". So, you see, Uncle Harry, I don't have any more questions about war. Awful things don't have words.'

Lucy tilts her head to the chook, as if listening to a secret. Then, covering her hand, she whispers to the hen. 'No, I can't tell Uncle Harry … shsh Esmeralda … It was only a letter.'

'A letter?' Harry says.

'What if someone had a letter that wasn't theirs, but might have answers that are important? Never mind…'

Closing the book, Lucy wanders up the long yard rocking Esmeralda in her arms.

There is no request for a story today.

THE LETTER

Lucy Meredith Carter, Book Of Known Facts, Quirindi, 1955

I FEEL SO BAD for taking Fliss's letter.

I just wanted to know about Jerranjerup.

I'll have to take it back but - I'm afraid it will be lost or thrown out. Then I'll never know about the place behind the secret word. The place where Mum and Fliss wore strange hats and smiled into the sun.

Nanna Ennis says curiosity is a curse and I'm more cursed than most.

I WATCH Alexei throwing feed for the chickens.

'You're rubbish at that, Alexei.' I grab the bag of feed. 'Watch me.' Bending over each hen, I pat them and murmur soft words.

'They'll starve while you're gabbing to them.' Alexei steps out of the pen and flops down, cross legged against the thick timber steps. Thick black hair falls over his face.

'They won't lay eggs if they're not happy.' I scatter the feed quickly.

'You're grumpy today. What's up?' With his head resting in his hands I can't see his mouth but I know he's smiling. I can tell by his eyes. In the shadows they are as dark as his hair.

'Nothin',' I say. He's watching me carefully. I don't think he believes me. I sit next to him on the bottom step, staring past him.

My throat feels like I've swallowed sand. 'That wisteria has a mind of its own. It only ever flowers while Nanna Ennis is away visiting her sister in Bathurst. It happens every September. When she comes home and sees there's no flowers she'll curse it and threaten to dig it up, like she does every year.'

'Nanna Ennis won't really dig up the wisteria.' Alexei pats my head, the way I've seen him comfort his sisters.

'I hope not. It's so beautiful. It's just a shame Nanna Ennis never gets to see it flower. I wish it grew outside my window.'

We sit quietly. Alexei brings out an apple from a calico bag. 'Do you want some?'

I nod and he breaks the apple in half with a twist of his hands.

'Neat trick.' I bite into the apple, eating slowly.

'So what's bugging you?'

'Is it wrong to take a letter? One that isn't *specifically* yours?'

'You know the answer to that, Luce, or you wouldn't even ask.'

'It's complicated.' I chew my lip. 'What if it has an answer to a mystery? A very important one. One the person can't tell you. It's not as if Fl … she can read it herself.' Apple juice drips down my chin. 'She can't read anything!'

Alexei grins. 'Maybe Fliss would let you read it to her if you asked nicely.' He throws the core into the chook pen and wipes his mouth on a sleeve. 'I'll wait for you.'

AS I TURN the corner of Montview towards the patio outside Fliss's room I hear the gardener muttering as he tends the plants. It's a slow hazy kind of day. I'm in no hurry, I'm not sure how to talk to Fliss about the letter so I sit against the stone wall where I can look in the room, but not be seen. A tiny bunch of sweet peas sits in a crystal vase on the table inside the door. Fliss caresses the petals with distracted tenderness.

Katya is singing softly, a Russian ballad, something sweet and low. Fliss hums along, not quite in time, but she's in harmony. Katya is brushing Fliss's hair, lifting the thick waves with one slim hand while the other drags a brush with rhythmic strokes.

'Ow, ow,' Fliss complains.

'Your hair is too long, Miss Felicity. When was it last cut? Decades ago?'

'Not, not.' Fliss taps the table.

'Da! Yes, Yes!' says Katya, waving the brush with teasing menace. 'Something must be done I think…'

The gauze curtains flutter a slow dance out the door, as if they are enjoying the last days of autumn. I watch the two women: Katya, dressed in a flowery skirt and white blouse, scowling with her hands on her hips; Fliss with her lip curled like a huffy child.

Katya produces a slim pair of scissors from a large pocket and stands in front of Fliss, threading her fingers through the thick unruly hair. 'Hmm. It's not good, Miss Felicity. Not good at all.' Fliss waves her arms. 'Tsk, tsk.' Katya ignores her pleas and circles her.

I shade my eyes. Ramius, the Barashev cat, a fabulous mouser, is asleep at my feet, his whiskery eyebrows twitch as he dreams. Maria, the cook, is arguing with a delivery man at the back door, accusing him loudly of 'a *terrrible mistake*' with pots and pans. Alexei is chasing a younger brother down the worn dirt rows between the vegetable beds in the garden, offering to clobber him if he doesn't return his tiger's eye marble.

The gardener calls for them to leave off the nonsense, and turns the sprinklers on. The two boys leap around in the cooling spray, their tongues stretched out to receive the droplets, their fight forgotten.

'Ratbags!' says the old gardener.

I hear the metallic clip of the scissors as Katya tackles Fliss's hair.

I slip into the room and curl up on the window seat.

'Ah, good morning Lucy. I'm trying to rescue your aunt.' Katya looks up, sweat trickling down her face.

Fliss wriggles to see me.

'Keep still, Miss Felicity! Ah! You're behaving like a child.'

'Tsk, not, tsk.' Tap tap on the table.

'Bah! You can get around the others with your tapping and slapping of tables, but that doesn't wash with me. I'm Russian.' Katya brandishes the scissors in a warlike pose.

Fliss sighs, an exaggerated sound, then giggles.

'That's better.' Katya sets to work again, her face creased with concentration as the lifts small sections of hair aloft and snips. 'Oh my, there is so much grey. Hmm. Next, we dye it.'

Fliss growls.

'Oh no, do not argue. You look like a wild gypsy, uncared for. This is not good enough. Time to join the living.'

Katya moves to attend to the back of Fliss's hair.

Fliss sniffles.

'Don't cry. I'll cut your ear if you jerk around like that. Ah, don't give me that look "Shame, shame, Katya – she has no pity for me". That's right. No. None. Keep still.'

THE WRITING is careful, with a backward slant, as if it's leaning into yesterday. I smile at Fliss, grateful she wants me to read it to her. My heart is beating like a hummingbird, tapping in my chest.

"I hope this letter finds you well and happy." I read. 'Why does everyone say that?'

Fliss nudges me.

"Summer has been harsh this year, nearly as bad as when you were here with us. I can't believe nearly a dozen years has passed. So many winters and summers have come and gone.

"I wonder if you are wearing those wonderful cotton dresses

200

your sister made from the material you bought here. Have you used all the fabric? You bought so many bolts of it. That's what we women do, fill our cupboards, worrying if everything on earth will run out. The heartaches of war remain, some seen, some unseen. Those little anxieties, anticipations. The uncertainty of it all.

"Do write to us, dear, if you can spare the time. We couldn't find out about you after that dreadful day. Sylvia came back a few times. Of course, she stayed in town, a good many miles from the farm. Naturally we never saw her, not the way things were. But I'm sure you know all about that. She did have a soft spot for our farm manager, but enough said about that. He was lucky to come home from the war, and whole, just a gammy leg from a stray bullet. Only served a few months early in the thing. I won't go on, it must be all forgotten now, or should be. He's back with his wife and family, and nothing said.

"Glenda—you remember the cook? She wanted to call and ask Sylvia about you, but I told her to leave well enough alone. She's the only one of the original girls here now. She married one of the roustabouts. He came after your time.

"Anyway, my dear, I'm glad we finally found you. Glenda went for surgery at the Mater in Brisbane and one of the nurses said you were transferred to The Montview in Quirindi. It sounds like a wonderfully posh place. I can just see you as the mistress of a large country estate with children at your feet…"

'Oh Fliss, don't cry.'

SACHA comes and cares for Fliss. 'Why don't you go and visit with Alexei while your aunt has a quick nap, Lucy?'

'Okay.' I don't want to leave Fliss, but she needs a rest. 'I'll be back soon, Fliss.'

Alexei is waiting for me when I leave the room. 'Wanna come for a walk?' he asks. 'I have to water the veggie patch.'

'Whatever,' I say, looking down. *My mother had an affair.*

'You all right, Luce?'

'Sure! Why wouldn't I be?' My voice is gruff. *My mother had an affair. She left us to visit her lover.*

'What's y'beef? We got answers. I thought you'd be pleased. You found Old Pat's bag.'

'Oh yeah, there are answers. Yep! Be careful what you wish for.' *My mother had an affair. She left us to visit her lover. Then she came home to die.*

'What the heck does that mean, Lucy? I don't get it.'

'Be grateful,' I say, scraping my shoes. 'Be grateful you *don't* get it, and pray you keep *not* getting it, because once you've got it, you're stuck with it.' Angry tears sting my eyes, but I won't let them come. Alexei touches my shoulder. His eyes are clouded with confusion. I nearly cry. I look at him and I can't be angry with him. He's so very kind.

We walk along the garden. Alexei doesn't try to talk me out of the mood, he just lets things be as he adjusts the watering system. Then we sit and watch the spray.

I wonder if Dad knew. I think of all the things Nanna Ennis said, and I'm pretty sure she knew. *My mother had an affair.*

With a man who belonged to someone else, belonged with some other family, some other sons or daughters. A soldier who came back from the war when so many others didn't. When the man Fliss loved was shot to hell and buried overseas, far from home. Life isn't fair.

WE HEAR a siren. An ambulance pulls up at the side of Montview. Alexei and I wander over to see, but Mr Barashev spouts something in Russian to us. I ask Alexei what it means. He scratches his head before he answers.

'It means to buzz off.'

Avant ça (Before This)

Montview Lodge, Quirindi, 1955

'BASTARD bastard bitch bastard.' The stream of abuse sounds like one word, uncommon at Montview.

Fliss jolts upright in the armchair in her room.

'You bastard, you bitch bastard.' The voice is coming closer. The hullabaloo is outside on the patio, outside Fliss' room. Looking through the French doors, Fliss is surprised to see Maria and Sergei Barashev standing at the back of an ambulance that has just disgorged the foul-mouthed woman intent on abusing the world.

Pushing herself to her feet, Fliss moves slowly towards the doors. This is a drama she had seen many times in her nursing days. Perhaps not with such inexperienced players, but the temptation to eavesdrop is tantalising.

Sergei Barashev's voice is strained. 'Why you let this woman come here Maria?'

'Is just for tonight, Sergei. Be patient. Her sister beg me. "No room at hospital". But this woman, she thrash wild like windmill. Her sister did not tell me this.'

AN AMBULANCE officer addresses Maria. 'You'd better find her a bed, love. It's starting to spit. It'll be pouring soon.'

Sergei steps back. 'Take her, then,' he says. 'Just take the mad thing away. Back where she came from.'

The officer taps on a clipboard. 'We have regulations. Besides we'll never get her back into the ambulance throwing herself round like this, mate.'

'Then how you get her out?' asks Sergei, his arms raised in desperation.

'She was sedated.'

'Then give her more. Lots, lots more.' Sergei suggests reasonably, then adds, 'And then take her. We don't have this sort here. They go to the, how you say, nuthouse?'

Maria eyes the woman. 'Oi, oi, oi. This one is psikh, I get Sacha.' She turns. 'Sacha!'

'Radi boga, Maria!' says Sergei, 'enough yelling already. We wake all the patients.'

There's the sound of scuffling feet as Sacha flies through Fliss' door and out to the courtyard. 'Sorry, Miss Felicity.'

Fliss hears Sacha's low voice as she conducts a mumbled conversation with the officers while rain arrives in vicious sheets.

Shielding her face Sacha points at Fliss' doors. Swinging both doors wide open, Sacha and the men pull the trolley into Fliss' room. The woman on the trolley is shaken by the sudden movement. The abuse, thrashing and kicking stop for a moment.

'You can't bring her in Miss Felicity's room. What you thinking, Sacha?' Maria rushes into the room to Fliss, apologising profusely in a mixture of Russian and English.

Fliss waves her words aside with a smile.

'It's alright, Mum. Miss Felicity was a nursing sister. And this is a big room. Remember it used to be a double room. It's not the only room that can take two patients but it's the best option.' Sacha turns to Fliss. 'Just while we work things out?'

Fliss nods and retreats to the armchair by the bed. Sacha presses the call bell. It buzzes through the corridors.

The woman grabs Maria's arm. Maria screams. 'She bit me! Pouchon! Where is Pieter, he could help with this.'

'Pieter is never around,' says Sergei. 'Pieter wanders. That's what he does.' Sergei stands back and scratches his bald pate. 'Ah, what we do to deserve this, Maria?'

'How she not fall off the trolley?' asks Maria, returning her attention to the men. 'Is amazing.'

The ambulance officer speaks. 'She's had a stroke. She can't move her left side.'

'Bastard bastard bitch bastard. Bastard bitch bastard.'

'The mouth she can move,' observes Sergei.

THE EVENING sister arrives. After a quick whispered conversation with ambulance officers they deftly lift the woman along with the sheet under her, to one of the Montview's trolleys and leave. The screaming and abuse continues.

'I'll phone the doctor. You stay and watch her, Sacha.' The sister hurries off.

The woman throws her head back and forth, her greying brown hair as wild as she. It's all Fliss can see of her.

Pieter's lanky frame looms in the inner doorway. He gives the woman a cursory glance. He has seen worse. He smiles weakly at his aunt and enters the room.

'Peter can help,' says Sacha touching his arm. He flinches.

'Pieter is not nurse.' Sergei's eyes grow round.

Maria pulls her shoulders back. 'He is now. He's been helping all over. Is how all our children started. Why not?'

Pieter shrugs. 'One day I might be orderly, even doctor.'

'Tsk, tsk.' Fliss waves the call bell cord and nods vigorously.

A wild scream, then angry guttural growling rises from deep within. The abusive words continue, louder, with renewed venom.

It's decided. The mute patient who once was a nurse and the

angry Russian boy will watch over the mad woman.

Pieter brings a straight-backed chair, places it carefully near Fliss and sits, compressed. Fliss clutches the call bell.

The Sister returns. She moves with speed and stealth, jabbing a needle deep into the woman's thigh through her nightgown emptying the syringe quickly.

Fliss watches as the abuse and thrashing slows. The woman winds down like a clockwork doll. Her words slur, lengthen. There's brief panic in her eyes, which turns to murky glass. Her face slackens and turns. Fliss puts her specs back on, leans closer, recoils.

It's Ernestine Ingram. She claps a hand over her mouth.

'You know this one?' Pieter asks.

Fliss nods. The boy leans towards Fliss. 'You were a nurse, avant ça?' Fliss nods again, remembering her high school French. Avant ça, before this. So much meaning in those two words, before this. All of her life, her past joys, *before this*.

'Ah. A nurse. She will sleep, da?'

Fliss nods. Ernestine snores. It's a rough and drowning sound. Pieter closes his eyes and leans back, arms folded.

THEY SIT. The lean angry boy who speaks three languages fluently, but has little use for words, bequeathing them with sparse indifference. And the wordless patient yearning for speech. No hospital would have such strange night staff, but ad hoc systems were the rule rather than the exception in nursing homes converted from houses or hotels.

Peter is strangely calm. Fliss didn't expect this. Outside he paces the grounds with restless energy resisting kindness, unable to adjust to the alien beauty around him. Fliss dozes, figuring they'll probably have six hours of peace.

Ernestine Ingram wakes in four, and hell returns.

ROMANCE AND RUNNING

Ennis family home, Henry Street, Quirindi, 1955

LUCY frowns and looks around the room. 'Uncle Harry? Are you still in the Army? I s'pose they still need soldiers, even broken ones.'

Harry laughs. 'You're helpful, answering your own questions.'

'Are you on leave?'

'Something like that,' Harry says. It's time to steer her away from talk of soldiers and war. 'I saw you spinning around in the garden. Don't you get dizzy?'

'Oh no, I'm awfully good at it. Nanna says it makes her sick to watch me.' She giggles, then becomes thoughtful. 'I'm going to see Fliss today. I'm wearing my best dress, one Mum made for me. She was a great dressmaker. I miss her.'

She sits on the story chair and pouts prettily. 'A story? Please.'

'Okay then. Let's see. This one's about the three Rs, romance, running races and running away.'

'OOhwee,' she says. 'All that, in the middle of war?'

'Nope, Atherton and other places.'

'Where's Atherton?' Lucy asks. 'In Australia?'

'Yes, up north in Queensland. Lucky for us, we had leave to visit family. I got to see Lanky's family too.'

'Oh good, the skinny cardboard man.'

Those three words, Leichardt, Sydney, 1943

BACK IN SYDNEY it was great to meet Lanky's missus, and his little tike, a deep voiced little bruiser of a toddler with the vocabulary of a barrister. But I guess that's what you'd expect from any kid of Lanky's. His wife, Shirley, was a tall, curvy smile-on-legs with chocolate brown hair. She worked at the war neuroses clinic in Macquarie Street.

'You'd think working in a place like that would be depressing,' she said, as she poured gravy over Lanky's meat. 'But it's rewarding.'

'Hang about Shirl, I can serve my own food, you know.' Lanky held his hand over his plate.

She laughed, a warm rich sound. 'Sorry darl, I'm so used to doing it for Davey.'

Davey heard his name and rushed into the dining room. 'G'day, Nugget, how y'doin'?' He charged off on chubby legs to the sideboard, rattled around in a drawer and brought me a pen and piece of paper. 'Jus fill in dis form please.' He scowled and tapped the pen on the page.

'Just like his mother,' said Lanky, putting his hand over his face in embarrassment. 'When are you going to teach the kid some manners, Shirl?'

She ignored the question and glared at Lanky as he scraped the gravy to the side. 'I take him in to work with me sometimes. Seems he's picked up some of my spiel.'

'And that bossy look,' said Lanky. 'That's pure Shirl, that is.'

'You've been gone to long, Mister,' she said. 'Now eat your peas or you'll get no desert.'

'There aren't any peas. What are you talking about?' Lanky moved his food around the plate searching for hidden vegetables.

'There's no dessert either.' Shirl laughed and winked at me. 'So, Harry.' She gave me what my mother would have called a speaking look and asked, 'What about you? Got a girl to look up?'

The question took me off guard and I stammered. 'Well, that's … um, we'll see.'

Lanky shook his head and moaned.

'Getting him to talk about his love life is like pulling teeth. Give a bloke a break.

I grinned and made a great to-do over mopping up my gravy. 'You'll keep,' said Shirl, taking the plate from me and heading for the kitchen.

But how could I tell Shirl, or anyone else for that matter, that I was buzzing with nervous anticipation over meeting up with a woman I'd only seen a few times, had exchanged letters with for a year or more, but said no words of love.

WE WALKED the rain-slicked streets of Leichardt, hand in hand, heedless that the trees were still splatting soft cool droplets on us after the deluge had stopped. I'd rehearsed a thousand speeches, but found no need for words. Neither of us wanted to traverse the terrain of "next". We diggers were headed to the Atherton, and then possibly for the Pacific arena, we'd been told that much. After jungle training in northern Queensland, still a thousand miles apart, or so it seemed.

Outside her flat, I kissed the raindrops from her face and held her so close I heard her heart quicken.

Back home with her in my arms there was no hiding between the pages of a letter—in reports of weather or everyday activities stretched into sentences. Just a man and a woman on an ordinary night, ready to say the words they'd hidden in a hundred worn, re-read and re-folded pages that had crossed oceans and deserts.

The words were written in our eyes, and on our lips. I caressed her ear with worshiping fingers and gently blew warm breath there, hoping to convey all the love I'd found in her. A light came on in a neighbour's window. Someone called for Fred to let the cat out. A dustbin rattled, and I told her I loved her.

'I don't want to leave you.' I pulled her closer.

'Then don't,' she said, trembling into my neck.

Watten Siding, Jungle Training Camp, 1943

'THE ATHERTON is a reprieve.' That's what the higher-ups told us. And God knows we wanted to believe them.

Back on home soil after more than two years abroad, in Egypt, Syria, Alexandria, there was no stutter of machine guns, no artillery fire, no screaming bombs. Yet peace was illusive.

I got another bout of malaria, but got no sympathy from Lanky. 'Don't fuss over him, mate. He's a nuggety little bastard. The mozzies thrive on him. Keeps them away from the rest of us.'

Disease was a far more familiar friend. Even though the Tablelands were officially a malaria free area, plenty of the boys were suffering from the disease. The men who laid lowest were sent to one of the camp hospitals at Rocky Creek. It was no fancy affair, but it had operating theatres. It was amazing how many patients the staff cared for. Most of the soldiers came from New Guinea through Cairns, but at times some of our lot ended up there.

Men were dying in the hospitals. I'm guessing that wouldn't take up too many pages in the history books. I imagine a list of enemies, Gerries, the Ities, the Japs and millions of infernal breeds of insect, as well as all the usual medical complaints like piles, constipation and asthma that don't let up just because there's a war on.

"Swilly" Babcock had malaria pretty bad most of the time and reckoned the god-damned mozzies followed him home from New Guinea. He couldn't have been too bad because he kept joking that the army should import some of those mosquito-eating fish from Moresby. He said the worst thing was being back on the base between hospital visits because he was too knackered to do a runner like the others.

A lot more of the boys were going AWL. Absent Without Leave. Sarge said it was 'a bloody epidemic'. Family was no longer far away. Suffering of loved ones at home was harder to ignore. Taking off for hearth and home was a strong temptation with transport close at hand. All they needed was a train ticket, a long walk to the station and railway staff that didn't care who had leave and who didn't. One private took off because his sister had attempted suicide, cut her wrists. Another soldier bolted when he heard his mother was poorly with nerves. Lots of the boys had lost family members at home as well as in the battlefield.

With more reliable mail deliveries from family, there was a greater abundance of newspapers. Sometimes when I read articles about the war I wondered if they were writing about the same war, but others told what the journos were doing, slogging it out side by side with our diggers. Telling our stories, taking our histories and telling their own stories.

There was a story in the national paper about Kent Hughes who served in both world wars and competed in the 1920 Olympics. He's quite a legend, especially as he admitted to nicking an Olympic flag from the stadium. I think that got him as much admiration as the rest. A champion in the hurdle races. I reckon the papers got that account right at least.

Some men were still making trench art. Lanky reckoned the war helped them find their creative side. Many more were writing journals. Maybe they wanted their stories to survive if they didn't.

I didn't write much. It felt like a jinx to put pen to paper, never knowing who'd see it or what they'd think. Maybe if I'd had kids like some of the guys I'd have felt differently.

The tender regard of the officers was focused on keeping us busy. That was Lanky's opinion on the subject, a speech he delivered with tongue firmly in cheek as we lined up for cross country runs and stretching exercises that made us look like a bunch of would-be marathon runners.

I told Lanky they were getting us ready for the next flaming Olympics. Mind you, some of the men were honest-to-god athletes. The foot races at the 88 Sports Ground in Ravenshoe proved that over and over again.

It was exciting to watch the men compete. We cheered during all of the races, but were rowdiest during the 1 mile race. But we knew we were being prepared for the next stage, the next hell— the tropics; and for the 2/17th that meant our first stint in Papua New Guinea.

Lanky shoved a pair of socks in his kitbag. 'Neither the Japs or Hitler will win this round, Nugget. This round will go to the bloody mosquito.'

Harry jerks as Lucy says, 'I hate bloody mosquitoes.'

It's easy to forget where he is.

BaDge

Lucy Meredith Carter, Book Of Known Facts, Quirindi, 1955

Fliss is having a word lesson with Katya.
I'm taking notes about it.
No one here at Montview minds me writing in my book.

IN A QUIET corner of the large dining area, the murmur of their voices soothes me. One of the elderly patients, Miss Elvira Bertram, comes into the room and buzzes from table to table, stuffing things into a big black velvet purse.

'What's Miss Bertram doing Katya?' I ask.

'Who?' asks Katya. She's watching Fliss. Fliss has tired of the word cards and is idly turning them over in front of her.

'Miss Bertram.'

'Oh dear,' says Katya, focusing on the old woman. 'She's at it again.' Katya sighs. 'I'd better keep an eye on her. She's a bower bird, picks up anything the other patients leave behind.'

'Look Katya, she's collecting dirty serviettes.'

'I know, she thinks they're ration cards. She has dementia. I'd better check her purse. Goodness knows what's in there.'

Katya slips to her feet. 'Emily sweetheart, come here pet.'

Miss Bertram clips her purse shut quickly and glares at Katya, but Katya just beckons her over. The old woman moves quickly across the room to our table. She is wearing a muddy rose felt hat

213

with a huge pearl hat pin. A fur stole hangs loosely over her shoulders. As she comes closer the eyes of the fox seem to look me in the eye. I shudder.

'Put that down Miss Emily. Let me get you a cup of tea.' Katya reaches for the purse. Miss Bertram grips it with gnarled fingers. 'Oh dear, Miss Elvira. Your fingers look so sore. Let me rub them for you.'

Miss Bertram smiles and sits. There's nothing she likes more than attention from the nurses. Katya rubs the old woman's fingers gently and eyes the black purse.

'Let me do that,' I say, patting the old woman's arm. She lets me massage the arthritic swellings. Montview is always full of children helping out so she accepts this with a satisfied sigh.

'What lovely little warm hands you have,' she sighs. 'It's this dashed war. It's made everything so hard. We'd just got over the Great War, then the Depression, now another one.'

'But Miss Bertram, it's over…' I say. 'Long ago.'

Katya shakes her head, warning me. 'It's not that long really.'

'It's a lifetime, Katya,' I say, leaning forward.

'For you,' she says, quietly tipping Miss Bertram's purse upside down. She slides a few items behind the vase of flowers, then returns the rest to the purse.

Miss Bertram's eyes fix on the cards in Fliss's hands. She makes a grab for them.

'Not not!' cries Fliss, 'not not!' She crushes a card in her hand.

'Emily!' Katya's voice is firm. She stands and towers over the old woman, who straightens up and glares. 'Those aren't yours, Emily. Leave them alone please.'

'But Mother doesn't have any dripping and sugar left, only powdered eggs and maggoty flour. She has to sift the maggots out before she uses it.' The old woman's voice falters.

Katya points to the open door. 'Look Emily, can you see the

214

garden? There is plenty of food here. There is everything we need. Even fresh eggs and milk.'

'Oh, Mother will be pleased.' The old woman sighs.

'Perhaps a little rest before lunch, Miss Emily?' Katya hands the old woman her purse.

'I might do that.' The old woman flicks the fox stole higher on her shoulder and pats Katya's hand. 'I'll be all right dear.'

'That's sad,' I say. 'It's like Old Pat Callaway.' I tell Katya about Old Pat, his burned-out humpy, his stolen bag.

'The war isn't over for so many people, Lucy.' Katya sorts through the pile of things she found in Miss Bertram's purse, spreading them in front of her.

'Is that a badge?' I ask, peering closer. 'Nice nice, nice nice.' Fliss bends over the table.

Katya sighs. 'Oh dear, that's Nurse Cathy's badge for her Woman's Army uniform hat. She wears it on her nurses' apron. Cathy loves that badge. She says her time with the Woman's Land Army was the best of her life.'

I look closer. 'Fliss, look! That's like the badge on … your hat.' I bite my lip, worried that I've said too much, but Fliss is nodding happily. Her face is flushed.

'Are you all right, Miss Felicity?' Katya asks.

'Nice nice.' Fliss is excited, and points at the badge.

'There's a photo of Fliss … and … well she was wearing a hat with a badge just like that,' I say, watching Fliss carefully.

'Were you in the Women's Land Army, Miss Felicity?' Katya is smiling. Fliss nods with excitement.

'Oh my,' Katya says, 'the stories you must have.' She sighs. 'I wish you could tell them all.'

FLISS' HAND is clenched tight. Katya reaches across the table and gently prises her hand open. 'What have you got there, pet?'

215

It's a card with the word "home".

Katya turns to me. 'Lucy, has your aunt been back to the house?'

'What house?'

'The Ennis place, you know. The family home. Where you all lived.'

'All of us? Dad and I never did … we didn't.'

I look at Fliss. She's nodding.

'I'm surprised you don't remember, Lucy?' Katya asks. 'You and your Mum and Dad lived there for a few years.'

I struggle to remember. Fliss is staring out of the window.

'I think Nanna wishes we lived with her now.'

'I know she didn't want your family to leave.' Katya caresses Fliss's hand. 'Fancy Miss Felicity being in the Women's Land Army.'

THE BACK door squeaks open. Dad aims carefully and throws his hat. It arcs through the air and lands on the hat stand.

'I'm getting good at that,' he says, ruffling my hair. 'Get your stuff. We're off to Nanna's for tea. Hurry up!' Dad grabs a thick cake of grey, gritty Solvol and scrubs his hands with a nail brush.

I use prayer hands. 'Dad, can I please take…?'

'No! You're not taking Esmeralda tonight!'

'How did you know what I was going to ask?

'Ha. I'm your father. I can read your mind.'

FLISS is there, at Nanna's. I wonder if Katya said something to Nanna about having Fliss at the house. Fliss smiles. I cover her face with kisses. We have tea, a Sunday roast.

Nanna sends me out to check on the hens. When I get back I hear Dad say—'it's time for the truth, Ethel'.

When I walk in Nanna starts talking really fast about how

much ironing she has to do.

Fliss isn't there. Dad must have taken her back to Montview while I was outside.

I didn't get to say goodbye.

Another's Utopia

Montview Lodge, George Street, Quirindi, 1955

'OH MISS FELICITY,' says a voice, 'how wonderful that you were in the Land Army.' It's Cathy, the cleaner, holding her badge, the one Elvira Bertram filched.

She pats Fliss' hand and sits, takes out a cigarette, waving a hand towards the smoke, as if by that simple gesture she can move the noxious smell outside.

Fliss sneezes, but Cathy doesn't notice. Her face is slack with pleasure, she's lost in memories of yesterday. 'The best days of my life, they were …'

It's late afternoon and the cleaner's chatter full of utopian memories grates on Fliss.

It's growing cool in the dining room.

Fliss looks look around for a passing nurse to take her to her room, but there isn't one and they haven't left her a bell.

Through the windows she sees Pieter wheeling Barry James around the orchard. One of the other patients is walking beside them.

Cathy is still rambling.

Why doesn't anyone understand that their joyful tales and life stories only serve to highlight Fliss' own piteous state? And yet, so many treat her as a willing recipient of their pleasures and pains, heedless of the effect.

Fliss longs for night, and sleep.

Nights are her retreat, the sliding into her former self into a world of dream where words flow freely from her lips, where she can find all she has lost, where she can be all she once was, running, twirling, loving.

Where she can find him, with untorn sinew and laughing smile, untouched by war.

OF MEN AND MADNESS

Ennis family home, Henry Street, Quirindi, 1955

LUCY LEAPS off the bike with a skip, letting it drop. 'Did you see that, Uncle Harry? I've been practising.' Her face is alight as she jumps back on the bike to show Harry her new manoeuvre to dismount. 'See, I can slide right off before the bike stops!'

'Heck Lucy, don't throw your bike around like that. What's the use of new tricks if you just chuck it anywhere?'

'Alexei taught me.'

'Well, I'll un-teach you. What else is going on in your fascinating life, Lucy.'

'I'm helping Katya with physical therapy. I love working with her.' Lucy wears a grown-up frown. 'But it's slow going. Katya has flashcards with words. They're supposed to help people remember the shape of words. Katya learned a lot of stuff at University, then at some fancy hospital in the city.'

'Ugh!' Harry shudders. 'Don't talk to me about hospitals, Miss Lucy.'

'Why? Don't you like pretty nurses fussing over you?'

'Ah Lucy. Not all hospitals have pretty nurses.'

Lucy hops from foot to foot, runs to her bike and brings back a large square book. Opening it dramatically, she shows Harry delicate wildflowers, pressed and placed carefully between translucent pages, as butterfly-thin as the flowers themselves.

'Great-Aunt Bea did this for me. For Mum's flowers.'

Harry wonders about her other book, but as she turns pages and chatters about her Great Aunt's visit and all the interesting things they did, the bottling, the kitten, Pieter's company on the shopping trip, he relaxes. Lucy has far too much to talk about to bring up the daunting subject of war.

HARRY'S wartime memories are now gentler, kinder things, like the early morning light that delivers the soft truth of present safety to night-time terrors. Those night terrors, those mirrors to the reality of war, they were not visions of nameless fears, of things that never existed, but memories of things that once existed, but did no more. Memories of a time when all men had gone mad.

Some of them returned from madness, became a kind of sane once more. They often envied those who embraced insanity as one would a seductive mistress, until they saw the agony, the juddering, shivering horror of a world of fear.

The child would ask more of Harry than he can tell. Just as he cannot tell her of the horror, neither can he tell her why its memory is a softer thing. Why he is a luckier man than most.

Why he is here.

AFTER LUCY leaves, Harry sinks his head onto his knees.

What could he tell a child about war?

How could he keep that hasty promise to explain war to her? How could he speak of the intolerable assault on the senses? or the cherished ordinary comforts they dreamed of, made precious by their scarcity? How could he tell her that man himself is the chief instrument of death? How could he tell her of war, its half-alive, half-dead state when all men had gone mad?

How could he tell her of his own madness?

Lae, Papua New Guinea, 1943

AFTER THREE years in Africa, and months of jungle training at the Atherton the battalion was shipped out to Papua New Guinea where there was no time to set up camp or check supplies.

Death had preceded their arrival at Lae. As soon as boots hit earth—the men faced a burial detail like no other.

Slain soldiers lay bloated and torn at water's edge, in gullies, in the river, amid the debris of digger's hats, guns, kitbags, first aid kits and mess supplies.

Some of the dead had morphine syrettes pinned on their collars, but many had fallen and died so quickly they wore an open-eyed stare of surprise. Eyes, still luminous like gemstones that refused to dim.

The men exchanged wordless glances, then set to, gathering, bagging, burying, toiling in numb silence.

If any of them found a soldier they knew, they didn't look up from their funereal task. Nothing prepared them for that. All the jungle training on earth couldn't begin to capture the effect of the carnage, or their leaden responsibility to their fallen diggers. They'd all done grave duty, here and there. Germans, Italians, and of course their own.

But the numbers! It was unthinkable, impossible.

The stench of death was brutal. Trying to dull the odour with handkerchiefs or shirts wrapped around their faces only served to conceal their grief. Day after day the men returned to camp, decimated from the god-awful, endless parade of death and decay.

KNEE-DEEP in mud, Harry's body burned as he rolled the next corpse over, a young digger with black hair like his.

Familiarity clenched his gut.

It's me, I'm dead.

HARRY HEARD screaming, the sound searing the silence.

Thick, dark sludge of the riverbank pulled him down into the muddy water. He grasped the body of the soldier.

'What's wrong, Nugget?' a voice yelled.

Harry stared at the corpse. Half its face was missing.

It's me, thought Harry, half my face is missing.

I'm dead.

HARRY'S MIND divided, circled his body, rising and falling. Birds above screeched.

He saw his father, Harry called to him, wanting to see him, make him speak. Harry wanted to ask more of him, but wounds on his father's chest opened and blood poured down his shirt onto the ground.

'I'm dead now too!'

HARRY'S CLOTHES were torn off by quick, brown hands as tender as a mother's touch.

Wrapped in damp, white cloth, Harry tried to tell them it was too late, that he was already dead, his father had come for him.

But he had no voice.

His throat felt crammed with dry sand that gouged and burned. A voice spoke.

To him? Harry didn't know.

Where am I in this death state?

HARRY DRIFTED between a cold, angry heaven and a simmering hell.

His mind wavered between staying and leaving, living and dying, sane and stark raving mad.

Terrified they'd find him out, test his death, see his madness.

Is that my father? Running here and there?

A LARGE, dripping tree with benevolent leaves covered him. He drank from its leaves.

Mud reached with soft, slippery fingers.

He lay down.

A Jap passed, so close Harry could have touched him.

The Jap's bayonet was ready.

It was of no use.

I am already dead.

A Few More Words

Lucy Meredith Carter, Book Of Known Facts, Quirindi, 1955

Mum and Fliss were in the Australian Women's Land Army!!! I would like to know more about that!

I am going to Nanna's today. If I am really good maybe she will tell me what she knows.

I can take Esmeralda even though she is not allowed inside. She can peck around outside, where she used to live.

She can say hello to the other chooks.

I SIT ON the kitchen floor at Nanna Ennis's. She has given me "something to do". I thought I might talk to her, or ask some questions about Mum going away, but she's distracted. The letter I read to Fliss has upset me, but I can't talk about that with Nanna.

Along with running a boarding house, that 'isn't a boarding house', as she constantly tells me—'just a home with a few rooms to rent', Nanna Ennis takes in ironing. A few of the townspeople drop off baskets of crumpled clean clothes for Nanna to turn into crease-free perfection. She hangs them carefully in the huge wardrobe in the guest room that overlooks the front garden, tying the metal hangers with white tape. Then she pins a label to the tape with their name and the amount they owe.

It's my job to dampen the clothes, sprinkling water on them so they are easier to iron and starch. A different amount according to the fabric and use. More for linen and tablecloths. Every time I do it for her, Nanna shows me how it's done, again, 'Don't just plop it on, Lucy, you need a quick wrist,' she says, flicking water from a bowl into a fine spray across the clothes.

She lets me iron the handkerchiefs and anything that isn't starched even though I iron everything at home. I once said it seemed like a waste of time.

'Starching is important, Lucy. Lots of people bring me their clothes just for that. There's a real knack to it. If you get the damping right, it makes my job so much easier.' She says this with a sideways look that tells me she's checking everything I do.

After I've sprinkled the clothes I roll them up tightly and put them back in the big cane basket for Nanna to iron.

Today she is staring out of the window. The iron is face down and there's a smell of burning.

'Look out Nanna! The iron!' I scramble to my feet. It worries me when she does this.

'Oh dear,' she says, standing the iron up. 'I should be used to it being electric by now. I'm slipping back to when my mother put that old cast iron one on the stove to heat up. It was important to keep it hot...' Nanna frowns.

She's told me this many times, but today she looks pale and worn out. 'Thank goodness it was the ironing board cover and not a business shirt or...'

'Are you okay, Nanna?'

'I have a bit of a headache. I might lie down for a bit.' Her forehead shines with sweat. She dabs it with the corner of her apron. 'Leave that, Lucy. Do it another time.'

'But Nanna, the clothing, the damping...' I point at the basket. It's not like Nanna to leave a job unfinished. She waves me aside.

'I'll go and see Fliss then.'

'That's a good idea, pet. Can you please ask Katya for some of that herbal tea? I haven't been sleeping well. That must be why I'm so tired.'

'The factory girls won't disturb you, will they?' I hesitate, reluctant to leave. Nanna often complains they annoy her with their giggling and chatter.

'No pet, they're both working afternoon shift today.'

I put the cane basket on the kitchen table, take a quick look to see that Nanna has turned the iron off, then slip quietly out the door, grab my bike and try to ride to Montview with no-hands. I'm not as good as Alexei but I'm practising lots.

KATYA tells me about Fliss, the things that are improving. I'm glad she is taking the time. Nanna doesn't tell me anything.

Fliss has a few more words. She says 'good', 'right' and 'terrible', often repeating whatever word she says. he brain specialist said it isn't likely she'll get very many more words back. He said Fliss understands nearly everything that's said, she just can't form sentences. It's like they're all there trapped in her head.

Katya's exercise and physical therapy have helped Fliss's walking. She even walks around Montview on her own now with a walking stick. Katya thought Fliss might need spectacles because eyesight is often affected by brain accidents. The eye test showed Fliss has bad eyesight, especially her right eye, which is on her bad side. Katya said Nanna Ennis cried the day Fliss got her new glasses and said. 'Why didn't we think of that?'

Turns out Fliss can read. I think about all the times Fliss has opened books with her good hand, all the times she's leant over books, a newspaper or magazine with words blurred like fog on the page. I think about how she tried to tell us and couldn't.

So much was lost for so long, and I wonder how much there is still locked inside. She's the only person who would tell me the things I want to know, but she's the only one who can't.

Nanna Ennis is the worst for answering questions. I've tried. There are so many things I want to talk to Nanna about. The letter I read to Fliss has upset me, stirred up all kinds of ideas. And worries.

Memories keep popping into my head that I don't understand, making me wonder if they're real, or things I dreamed. I'd like to talk about how I don't fit at school. It's like someone gave me the wrong size coat as a hand-me-down. It seems to fit in all the right places, but it's uncomfortable somehow, in ways I can't explain.

I want to ask if the stumbling man found her house, the one looking for the Ennis place.

The man who knew my name.

DAD'S BEEN acting kind of weird lately. Humming around the house a lot more. He acts even weirder around Katya. They smile a lot at each other, the kind of smile people have when they've forgotten everyone else in the room.

I don't know how they went from arguing about things to sitting and talking for ages, and laughing for no particular reason.

Dad and Katya take Fliss home to Nanna Ennis' on Sundays for lunch and Nanna Ennis fusses over us all.

Dad, Katya, Fliss and I went to the cinema together. We watched a musical 'A Star is Born'.

Fliss leaned forward as if she didn't want to miss a word or a note of music.

When I reached for the popcorn I saw Dad holding Katya's hand. I think they missed some of the show, looking at each other without saying anything. They whispered once or twice and that made Fliss start 'tsk tsking' so they stopped.

Dad slumped down in the seat and pulled his hat over his eyes and Katya started giggling.

I'm kind of hoping that Katya will want to be his girlfriend, but

Dad's a bit old for that sort of thing. Sacha said one of the gardeners at Montview just got himself a second wife and he's older than Dad, so maybe things will happen. I don't think Nanna has noticed anything.

But then grownups don't tell you much.

Wanting, Waiting

Montview, Quirindi, 1955

AS GEORGE turns the corner of Montview towards the patio outside Fliss's room he hears the gardener muttering as he tends the plants.

George sits in a deck chair on the patio. It's unusual for him to wait, but today is different. He takes off his hat and spins it in his hands. It's a slow hazy kind of day.

The French doors to Fliss' room are ajar. Katya is brushing Fliss' hair, lifting thick waves with one hand while the other wields the brush with rhythmic strokes.

George smiles as he watches them through the gauze curtains that are fluttering a slow dance in the breeze, as if they too are seduced by winter's last days.

'Ow, ow,' Fliss complains.

'Your hair is too long, Miss Felicity. When was it last cut? Years ago?'

'Not, not.' Fliss taps the table.

'Da! Yes. Yes!' says Katya, waving the brush with teasing menace. 'Something must be done I think … It's time we cut your hair.'

George hears the metallic snip-snip of the scissors as Katya cuts Fliss' hair. 'Keep still, Miss Felicity! You can get around the others with your tapping and slapping, but that doesn't wash with me. I'm Russian.'

George peeks through the curtains to see Katya brandishing the scissors in a warlike pose.

Katya sings softly, a Russian ballad, sweet and low. Fliss hums along, not quite in sync, but melodic. 'Miss Felicity,' she says. 'your brother-in-law. *George*. Will he come today?'

George tenses at the sound of his name. Does she suspect? He checks his pocket for the small square royal blue box.

'He's a handsome man. Not in the usual way, mind. But … a kind man must always become handsome, don't you think? Ah, and those thoughtful intelligent eyes.' Fliss giggles. 'I see you approve, Miss Felicity,' Katya says, tweaking Fliss' check.

GEORGE sees a flash of movement and shrinks back in the chair, noisily sliding his feet under the table.

The French doors swing open, and there she stands, her dark beauty overshadowing the day.

Katya laughs. 'Oh my. George. How long have you been there?'

Leaping to his feet, George causes the chair to topple, jettisoning his hat at Katya's feet.

With supple elegance, Katya retrieves the hat and twirls it in her hands. Her black eyes are solemn, laid bare.

George's heart leaps—does she care?

Katya smiles and looks down at the hat. 'In Russia…' she says.

'In Russia?' He leans towards her.

'If a man throws his hat at woman's feet…'

'I love you, Katya,' George confesses, out of patience with his dawdling tongue and awkward words.

Katya comes to him, with willing steps and soft eyes that shine. He reaches for her and she snakes her arms around his neck, lips pressed against his skin.

'Tell me,' he says, the words a thick rasp.

Katya looks up, her eyes teasing. 'But I've already told you once before … on our kitchen stoop.' She twists her lips. 'You gave me a broken biscuit. It was one of Mum's…'

'…*Pryaniki*,' he says, softly. 'You called me "milk boy".'

'You remember?' She feels the curious bulk in his pocket and finds the box hidden there. She squeaks a reward, then drags her lips slowly across the stubble on his chin.

'A man never forgets his first declaration of love—you called out for all the world to hear.' George draws her closer, hovering so near to her lips, but waiting.

'I love you, George Carter. I always have.'

'So, you'll ear my ring? Marry me?'

'Only if we have the wedding here.'

'Ah, so you want a circus, not a wedding.' George nibbles Katya's pink ear.

'Yes, a circus. And, do you think your mother-in law will come?'

I'll speak to her tonight.' George kisses the top of Katya's head. 'Wish me luck.'

Yes, Ennis family home, Quirindi, 1955

THE SUN streams in the kitchen window. George concentrates on sharpening Ethel's knives. 'I never thought I'd be rattling around this old house all alone.' Ethel avoids George's eyes as she speaks.

It's a familiar line, a common theme.

'What about the scissors?' he asks, holding the wet stone. 'Next time,' she says, wiping down the benches for the second time.

George smiles. Towards the end of any list of chores, Ethel invariably says 'next time' as if she fears he won't return without a task. She's lonely, but she won't admit it. Wiping her hands on her apron she eyes the chair in front of George. 'Sit down, George. Take the load off. Have a cuppa with me.'

She eases into the chair opposite, her calloused hands resting on the table. She tells George about the factory girls, their chatter and gaiety, how the noise of it all grates on her nerves. How she worries about Garnett, the young man going to Tafe, riding his bike everywhere but never eating enough, trailing into the house at all hours of the night.

George's eyes follow hers to the open door, to the cumbersome old black iron. It is coal fired, cast iron. Ethel used it for ironing until a few years ago. 'I still think that iron did a better job,' she says. She retells the story of her mother's big square hands, deftly handling the iron's weight, knowing when to place it on the wood stove to reheat, then on the windowsill to cool. It stands like a guardian of Ethel's history, a testament to hard work and the pioneering backbone—part of her Irish heritage. Like the woman, it sits proud and resolute. George has sanded and painted over the burn marks, but still the dimpled scars remain. He often watched Ethel as she pounded and thumped away at the ironing, lost in the rhythm, her face flushed with pride.

Sylvia had loathed the old iron along with the stoic stories that came with it, but it held a strange fascination for George. For him, it was the centrepiece of a simple hard life, a humble tool of trade. Even though Ethel now possessed a newer, electric version, the old iron still occupied pride of place, albeit as a hazardous door stop.

Ethel's eyes are cloudy.

'I was sweet on your father once, George. Did you know that?'

'No, I didn't, Ethel.' He tries to picture her as a romantic young woman, but fails. For George this is new, softer territory. Ethel has become more introspective of late.

She seems as surprised as George by the change.

George rolls up his tool belt, clears his throat. 'I best be getting on home now.'

Ethel stands, rubs her hands nervously. 'George, there's something I want to ask you.' She stares out of the open door, her toe touching the old iron. She wipes her eyes with her apron. 'You and the therapy girl? Katya?'

'I've asked her to marry me—she said yes.'

'As she should, George. As she should. You're a good man. I always say as much.'

'Does that mean you'll dance at our wedding, Ethel?'

'Get out with you, George Carter. You know very well I didn't dance at my own wedding.' She flicks his arm with the back of her hand, a gesture often used on her son. She retreats.

'A man can hope.' George says, patting the top of her head as he would Lucy. He looks back when he reaches the gate.

Ethel has her back to the side window.

Her shoulders jerk as she weeps for Sylvia, and the life she had hoped for, for her daughter and George.

REUNION

Lucy, Montview Lodge, George Street, Quirindi, 1955

FLISS TAPS the table loudly. The sound startles Lucy from staring at the tea leaves in her cup. She and Fliss have been sitting and listening to the radio.

'Oh Fliss, are you all right?' Lucy asks, but she is looking past Lucy to the open French doors.

Two men are standing in the doorway talking to Sacha. One is Blue Peters, in his constable uniform. The other man before is very tall and thin, smartly dressed in a brown suit with a bright white shirt. His fawn fedora has a shiny black band. He is listening carefully, nodding occasionally. Fliss watches intently. Lucy strains to hear them. Sacha says, 'I'll get Alexei for you.'

The man in the brown suits turns towards the room, scanning it with sharp eyes. One of his sleeves is pinned up. He's lost an arm. Another returned soldier?

'Good good.' Fliss's voice is excited.

He shades his eyes with a hand and sees Fliss. 'Oh my God! Felicity? Is that you?' he says, striding across the room. He clasps Fliss's hand. 'Well, I never. It is you.'

'You know my Aunt Fliss?' Lucy asks.

'I'll say.' The man smiles. 'I was at the wedding.' He pats Fliss's hand. 'As I live and breathe. Felicity. Our very own Felicity. I wondered what happened to you. We all did.'

'Happy happy, good good.' Fliss is glowing.

The man sits next to Fliss, shaking his head. He has brown eyes and tanned skin, weathered by the sun.

'She had a stroke,' Lucy says. 'You know, a brain accident. She can't speak. I mean, she has some words, but not many. She says good, not and…' Lucy stops, realising she is talking too much.

The man caresses Fliss' hand. 'So that's what happened to her. So long, so long ago.' His voice is low and thick as if the words were having trouble being said. He looks down at the hand he holds, then up at her. 'Still beautiful,' he says. 'Always. And that gorgeous hair. I'd know it anywhere.'

BLUE WINTERS clears his throat, bringing everyone back from where they'd been. He takes off his cap and fumbled with it. 'Well, this is … unexpected.'

'Hey there.' Alexei skids to a stop in front of the constable. 'Hey Blue. Er, Constable Winters, sir. How are things at the station?'

Blue scratches his chin. 'Busier than Pitt Street and just as confusing,' he says. 'Heck. Okay everyone, this is Frank Callaway. Old Pat Callaway's boy.'

'His son, d'ya mean?' Alexei's eyes are wide. 'Jeepers.'

Frank answers. 'Yes, I'm his son. Dad went missing years ago. We'd given up finding him until Blue phoned us and told us a couple of kids had found Dad's kit bag with his army papers and his details. So here I am.'

'Where'd he live? Old Pat? Before he became a swaggie?'

'Alexei!' Katya whacks Alexei in the back of the head.

'In Sydney.' Frank Callaway takes his hat off, 'before he went to war, that is.'

'Jeepers!' Alexei says.

'And Fliss was at your wedding?' Lucy hasn't forgotten his earlier remark.

'Heck no kiddo!' Frank chuckles. 'That's a laugh. It was your aunt's wedding. I introduced them.' There's mischief in his eyes. 'Whatever made you think that. It was your aunt's wedding. Remember Fliss? Your aunt Fliss was a beautiful bride, kiddo.'

Lucy gulps. There's been some sort of mistake. She looks at Fliss, waiting for her to protest, but she's smiling. A wedding! Fliss was married and this smart man was there.

'Remember Fliss?' Frank leans towards her. 'Then off we went to war, and the last I heard of you, you'd joined the Land Army with your sister and were both off to Jerranjerup.'

'Jerranjerup,' says Fliss, as if it's a word she uses every day.

ETHEL ENNIS snorts at George's careful tale. Fliss married, the very idea! It's time to meet this Mr Frank Calloway. What's his game? Some of those soldiers … Sly-groggers, SP bookies, street brawlers with their Victory Girls. Her Bill's mates, a fine example. Drunks and liars, pilferers and schemers, womanisers the lot.

George chats with Frank on the porch, shows him in, offers tea? coffee? while Ethel's narrowed eyes glare at Frank Calloway's back as he hangs his hat and coat on her coatrack with his right arm—the left is missing. The pleats on his trousers are so sharp she'd be proud to lay claim to having ironed them. George makes a tardy introduction.

Frank shakes her hand. 'Nice to meet you, Mrs Ennis. Lovely home.'

She sits back down in her dining chair, deflated. This man is no good-time Charlie, no time-wasting chancer. Ethel Ennis would have bet her life on the cut of his jib, his Florsheim shoes, and his wholly cultured good manners.

The men lean across the table with steaming cups of tea, in cheap mismatched china supplied by Ethel, a choice now regretted. Frank talks of his father, Old Pat Calloway.

'A cop phoned. Decent sort. Came soon as. A shock for sure. I'd not have known him. Sad. Fine actor in his day. Shakespearean. Mind's gone now. Rambling lines from old plays. Been roaming all over. At that Montview place at present where Fliss lives. Sent there from the hospital. Been in a spot of bother from all accounts. Bit drowsy when I saw him. Sedated, I imagine. I'll see how the old boy is in the morning.'

IT'S TIME for a sherry. Ethel's best this time.

There's mention of a fellow digger.

Ethel's eyes flit between the men. She'd hoped for clarification, explanation, but this nonsense, this rambling, this Frank talks too fast, this half-sentence blathering as if he assumes they know— have always known about Fliss' marriage, her supposed husband. As if he'd met the family and was known to all. Worst of all, it doesn't seem to be bothering George in the least.

Ethel yawns.

Frank pats her arm, checks his watch, apologises for maudlin reminiscing. 'Must be off. I'll come again.' He lets himself out. Clack.

'But ....' Ethel grips George's arm. 'He didn't say anything about ... the ... the wedding. I couldn't make out the half of what that man said.'

She's surprised to find her sherry glass empty.

'Wait until I see Felicity,' says Ethel. A headache threatens. She massages a temple. 'It's a galling thing, George, when a woman feels like a spectator in her own home!'

238

To Sleep, To Dream

Montview Lodge, George Street, Quirindi, 1955

ETHEL VISITS, full of ire, anger directed at Fliss. 'Why didn't you tell us, girl? Do you know how much trouble this secret marriage of yours has caused? Do you have any idea what this has done to me?' Ignoring Fliss, Ethel berates her daughter. Then sits out of breath, huffing and puffing, mopping her damp forehead with an old handkerchief. 'Everything falls back on me,' she says.

Fliss grips her walking stick and thumps the floor, louder and louder until her mother leaves, an act that may be her first rebellion. Fliss longs for peace. On other days she allows the nurses to open every door and window, accepting the diversion to diminish the tedium of her cramped days, the dull routines in the place of the broken. When she feels soft breezes or chill winds she knows she is alive, at least in part. She hears the children's chatter, arguments between the Barashevs, conversations of patients.

Sounds she usually enjoys. But not today. She tries to read. The print hurts her eyes. The words march to their own pace, errant ants across the page, bringing a dull ache to her temples. Fliss remembers many of the words, however some have simply slipped away—blurred hieroglyphics. She weeps torrents of tears that she cannot stop. Cannot contain any longer.

The sister brings a sedative. As Fliss drifts she remembers....

A honeymoon, Stanthorpe, 1944

FLISS made him put his digger's hat in the cupboard of the hotel room. She didn't want to talk of war, to think of it, to reside in the shadow of evil, even for a moment.

Fliss couldn't have enough of him, or he of her.

He undid her apron strings and laughed. She hadn't heard his soft footfall. It was his favourite trick. It always caught her off-guard. She squealed, then feigned annoyance as she attempted to fry bacon and eggs, rations saved for the honeymoon. Those brief days.

Fliss' neck tingled with his soft kisses as his arms encircled her, rocking her sideways as he hummed the tune to 'Only you, can make my dreams come true…'

'Only you.' Fliss sighed.

He turned her towards him, taking the greasy egg lifter from her hand and returning it to the pan, giving him free rein to deepen the kiss. The bacon sizzled. Fliss shook free reluctantly. 'Let me get on with this. I don't want to burn our first breakfast.'

He leant against the pantry, his fingers reaching for a crisp bacon strip. 'We could have told your mother,' he says.

Fliss' eyes warned him. They'd had that conversation many times. Fliss didn't want to talk of how bitterly her mother was grieving the loss of David, her only son, "killed in action"—those dreaded words.

Thirty six hours leave and a chapel wedding left no time for that other world, that other life.

'Your eyes are bossy,' he said.

'I didn't say a word.' Fliss turned back to the stove.

'Your eyes are bossier than your words. They say everything so much louder.' His voice rose with each word. Fliss kissed him into silence. She wanted all of the last three-days of his leave. He had already visited his family.

'And don't dare say that I'm ashamed of you, you know that's not true. 'Sh,' said Fliss, 'we only have one more day.'

Breakfast was overcooked. They ate on a red-checked tablecloth by the open fire, each mouthful interrupted by passion. He turned to Fliss with sadness in his eyes. 'Are you disappointed you didn't have a proper wedding dress?'

Fliss slapped his arm. 'How dare you call my dress improper! My sister made it. She's a fine seamstress.'

'She didn't know we were getting married?' He looked perplexed.

'I told her, I told her it was for a special dinner with your friends.'

'That's a stretch.' He frowned. Fliss looked away. 'Anyway. It was a wedding dress, it just wasn't a bridal gown.'

'Don't expect us blokes to know the difference.' He drew Fliss to him and she relished the surrender. 'It's a beautiful dress, gown, whatever.' He pulled her into a formal dance position and laughed. 'You must wear it every anniversary. In fact, you can wear it for me now.'

'You like it that much?'.

'I want to take it off. Slowly.'

FLISS had spurned his offers of overtures to her family, claiming their obstinate devotion to church and ceremony. As it was, things had been terribly rushed.

There had been no time for wedding finery or tense family dinners. He didn't know how bitterly her mother would have opposed the marriage, had she known of it. He didn't know of her brother, David's death in France and the family's devastation. She would not speak of it, not when he was shipping out in days.

TO DREAM

Montview Lodge, George Street, Quirindi, 1955

AT NIGHT, sleep hurls Fliss like an ocean rip.

She dreams of rooms.

Crowded railway station rooms, a rented room in a small hotel with an open fire.

The cramped confines of a chapel, the room of her childhood, the hospital.

Her heart thunders as her feet run.

Floors shift, windows fly open, curtains flounder, wet with rain.

The furniture morphs, photos crash from mantels, paintings fall from walls.

Fliss dreams of every room she ever entered, but not as they were.

She dreams of all those rooms, except the room she lives in at Montview, that prison of comfort and care.

Fliss rushes about, eager for all of them, expecting to find him, waiting for her, as she wait for him.

She dreams of rooms, sparse and ornate, connected only by their familiarity.

Here, there, everywhere.

She stands alone in a chapel. The last room?

He's not standing there at the front, waiting in uniform, hat tilted down, smiling.

Fliss looks down.

Her silk wedding dress turns to rags, grey and shredded.

She weeps.

Solemn faceless men dressed in sharp black suits enter.

They march down the aisle. They don't see Fliss. They carry a coffin.

Fliss screams for them to leave. They don't belong in her dream.

They walk through her, past her, and on.

A bugle plays.

Heads down, they shoulder the weight of the plain timber box.

The chapel doors open by unseen hands, slowly, silently.

The sun shines brightly, yet Fliss shivers.

They are leaving. Fliss cries for them to return, but they do not heed her.

She asks the wind where he is, but there is no answer.

She wakes, and remembers.

They buried him on foreign soil.

There are no more rooms.

eavesdropping

Lucy Meredith Carter, Book Of Known Facts, Quirindi, 1955

Nanna would not believe the story about Fliss's wedding.
She wanted to meet Frank Callaway straight away.
She was sure it was a silly prank.
Then she met him. A tall smart man. A solicitor.
Nanna knew then that the story must be true, all of it.

MR FRANK CALLOWAY has a lot of things to sort out for his father, Old Pat. He's transferring the old man to the city where he lives. But he has promised to help with legal things for Fliss.

Dad and I go over there when Mr Calloway visits again.

He has thought of a war pension. He says Fliss should be registered with Veteran's Affairs. He got Nanna Ennis to sign to get a copy of Fliss's marriage licence, and he wrote a letter to Legacy to find out about assistance for Fliss as a war widow.

It's a busy night around the table. Mr Callaway talking of forms and benefits.

Nanna Ennis is very pale and Dad makes her some hot strong tea.

'You'd better hop it to bed, Buttons,' he says.

'Here?' I ask, playing for time.

Dad frowns. 'But Lucy. You like staying here at Nanna's.'

I pout. 'But Dad. I want to be with you.

244

He pats my head. 'I'm staying too, Buttons. I need to talk to your Nanna.'

'Will you tell me about Jerranjerup, Dad? And Mum? All of it?' I beg.

'Yes, Buttons, but not tonight. It's late.'

I moan and complain, thumping down the hall so they think I've gone to bed, before sneaking back and peeking around the corner. Nanna is sitting like a statue at the kitchen table, holding a cup of tea with both hands, staring into it.

Dad reaches across the table. 'This does change everything, Ethel. There can't be any more secrets. Not now.'

'We'll see,' Nanna's voice is tired.

They move into the lounge room, their voices mingling in low murmurs.

I creep back to bed. Tomorrow seems like a long time away. I don't think I'll ever fall asleep. Then Dad crumples on the other bed in the guest room and I hear his gentle snoring, a sound that comforts me.

DAD WAKES ME. The sun is hardly up.

I hear voices. 'Who's here?' I ask.

Dad sighs and kneels on the floor beside my bed. 'The doctor. Your Nanna died in her sleep. Her heart was tired.' Dad takes me home. I run to the corner of our house. I hide in the grevilleas. They have grown and choked Mum's May bush.

Everything has changed.

CHANGE

Ennis family home, Henry Street, Quirindi, 1955

THE SUN glows pink below the eucalypts, spreading purple hues across the yard, leaving Harry's hut in shadows.

The sun's yellow orb hangs between the lush branches of the old mulberry tree, where the birds are singing their first trill.

'Uncle Harry.' Lucy hesitates at the door. 'There were strange people in the house this morning, men in dark suits and black ties, whispering and nodding. Nanna died in her sleep. Just last night. Everything has changed.'

Harry pulls up a stool. 'I know, Lucy. It's awful when things change, but everything has to change. Sometime.'

Lucy sits quietly, fiddling with the hem of her dress. 'Dad and I are moving into Nanna Ennis' house,' she says.

Harry sits quietly as Lucy takes a long, slow breath, then starts a rapid-fire conversation.

'Uncle Harry. Do you know about trees? Can you can dig up a May bush and plant it somewhere else? It was Mum's favourite. I'd really like to bring it here. To remind me of her. I love May bushes. They have these sweet tiny little flowers.'

'Maybe you can get a new one.'

'But … I don't want to leave Mum's tree behind.' Lucy sighs. 'It's like I'm leaving her behind.'

Belait River, Borneo, 1945

THE ARMY told the battalion that the tide of war had shifted, that things had changed, that they'd probably only do reconnaissance, that the war was as good as over, that they were lucky, and in turn, the men pretended to believe them.

The 2/17th had only been in Borneo a few days yet Brunei rain continued to leak from the sky in an endless drift.

IN THE MESS tent Lanky accepted his meal. 'Why did we ever long for trees?' Lanky accepted his meal. A leafy monsteria slapped dark lush leaves on the mess window.

'We've had every kind,' Harry said, hoping this wouldn't lead to talk of their incredible luck in surviving the Middle East campaigns and Finschhafen. Harry was in no mood to talk of war. Every bullet that misses meant the one that might hit is closer.

'Nearly to the end Harry, old son,' Lanky said, as their metal trays hit the laminate tables.

Harry's response was little more than a grunt. He was in no mood to talk of war. Every bullet that missed meant the one that might hit was closer.

They ate in silence, then retired to their huts, sinking in mud underfoot.

THE RAIN had gone in the morning, leaving an indifferent sun and soggy ground.

Lanky's hat was pushed back, his hands casually at rest in his pockets. Smithy wandered past. His arms were filled with parcels and mail. 'That's a nice little lot Smithy. Can hardly see you over the top,' said Lanky.

Harry admired Lanky's eternal good humour.

As they walked along the Belait River, Lanky watched Harry closely. 'All right mate? You look like shit.'

'Didn't sleep.' Harry shrugged. 'It's alright for you, mate. You snored like a sick camel through mortar fire at Tobruk. Sorry mate, I'm a pain in the arse today.'

'Just today?' Lanky laughed. 'I noticed you were weird around the Sarge when I mentioned your wedding. What's with that?'

Harry shrugged. Lanky grabbed Harry's shoulder. 'Oh no. Don't tell me. You didn't get permission to marry. Even you're not that stupid, Nugget.'

'Fraid I am, Lanky. I just want to get home, to her.'

'Cheer up mate, we're only here to usher the Japs home, y'know. This thing's all but over. The Gerries are scuttled. It's just a matter of time.'

'I dunno, Lanky. Japs are a different breed, fierce to the end. They take some getting used to. Especially after the Italians starving and ready to surrender, risking bullets for biscuits.'

'Ha, those Ities, they sure knew how to throw in the towel.' Lanky takes out his tobacco bag and begins the ritual of packing the dark leaves with brown calloused hands. 'We've run out of rationed cigarette packets,' he says. 'This would be a beautiful place any other time. When we're not shredding it. Do you think we'll see the Japs off all the way to Tokyo?'

'Hope not, Lanky, I've seen enough countries to last a lifetime. And I'm over this place, the river's too muddy, the whole place is too chaotic with life. This has nothing on Atherton. I'd like to go back there. A man could find peace there.'

'Look, the Dyaks are ready.' Lanky crushes his cigarette, instantly alert. He waved to the Malay guides.

THE LONG narrow canoes were low in the water.

The two Dyaks stood smiling as the men stowed their gear and weapons. Murmured voices blended with lapping long oars. Tangled mangrove roots crowded riverbanks. Sleek Macaque monkeys scrambled in tall, scrubby treetops. Dark green casuarinas towered over clustered sea hibiscus that exuded lemon-yellow cheer. It was a slow trip, a floating dream, free of enemies. The men held their guns loosely. On their return they thanked the Dyaks.

Another day over. Another day alive.

MEMORIES and images of Harry's Lae madness lingered, unnerving and intrusive. Army records noted "malarial complications", but Harry wondered, and doubted.

Yet, in spite of the shadows of his mental fragility, sleep drifted in that slow, warm slide he had once known as peace. Until flares of light seared his closed eyes as the night exploded. Lightning? Thunder? Tropical storms put on quite a show. The Atherton months were punctuated with many displays of nature's power. War seemed far away there.

HARRY smelled battle. The stench and roar of it all. His heart pounded, thick and fast. He saw the sky. The hut roof was gone.

Jagged ruins of the walls smouldered. Smoke tensed his nostrils and congealed the air. Flames reached for the stars.

The bloody Japs! How they loved their night assaults! Sarge shouted, boots thudded, men yelled. Harry heard rapid return gunfire, mortar rounds. Shrapnel joined flying debris.

Crouching where the door once stood, Harry shielded his head. His hip burned and he fell. Light flashed. Lanky's pale face was beside him.

Blood spread, black in the indigo night.

Harry's voice failed as he reached for Lanky.

The world flared brighter than day, then faded.

SILENCE OF THE SODDEN EARTH

Quirindi Cemetery, Russell Street, 1955

A DELUGE of Biblical proportions hampers the grave diggers, then, on the day of Ethel Ennis' funeral, simpering grey rain falls in shifting sheets on the black-hatted, umbrella-wielding mourners.

In a glass display case, a Last Will & Testament is found, used as a bookmark in a dog-eared copy of *The Australian Women's Weekly* opposite an article on the cultivation of wisteria. Contrary to general supposition, Ethel Ennis had never claimed, much less received a war widow's Pension.

George is the last mourner at the graveside.

He tosses a white lily onto the coffin and watches raindrops slope down the pristine flower like tears.

Silence is buried with Ethel Ennis, sunk in the sucking mud.

In the warmth of Bea's sedan, Lucy watches him.

'Dad said there's important stuff ... to talk about.'

Bea draws the child closer. 'All in good time. Your father will tell you. All in good time.'

AFTER the funeral, George takes two leather-strapped tan suitcases; suitcases that are worn and battered, suitcases that have left and returned, brought joy and pain.

He burns them in his mother-in-law's incinerator.

THE WAKE

Ennis family home, Henry Street, Quirindi, 1955

GEORGE is quiet during the wake. He says nothing about why he was late, last to leave the graveside. He makes sure that Lucy is all right and that Fliss is comfortable. Then he moves slowly around the guests.

To Fliss, the old house on Henry Street seems empty with Ethel. It was the place she longed to leave when she was young and ready for life. It was the place she ached to return to after the stroke, after losing so much—love, hope and a thousand tomorrows.

It's not empty at all of course. The house is crammed with people offering their condolences, adding to the abundance of food on the tables. Honouring the dead.

And yet, Fliss doesn't want to stay, not now. Every squeeze of the hand from a friend of the family, every embrace and touch of sympathy burns. Every carefully phrased 'the town won't be the same without your mother' fails to console. Most of these people haven't visited Fliss in all the years at the Ingrams or Montview.

Aunt Bea stops beside Fliss with a light hand on her shoulder. It's a gesture that holds more comfort than all the other words, all the other gestures. She beckons to George.

'I think you should take Felicity back … to that place, George.' Bea squeezes Fliss' shoulder. 'I'll stay on here, at the house, for a few days, see to the boarders. Then it's over to you, George. You're the executor. I'll not say much, but I think you should live here. And if it's possible, bring Felicity back home where she belongs. At least for some of the time. It's up to you.' Bea squats down tuck a rug around Fliss, then casually says, 'I hear tell you're stepping out with the older Barashev girl. Katya, isn't it?'

BACK AT MONTVIEW Fliss' head throbs with hope after Bea's words, but Elvira Bertram is on the move again, zig-zagging through the dining room into the lounge area. Fliss reaches for her walking stick. It's hard to avoid Elvira when she's like this. She's wearing a mud pink velvet dress that probably turned heads a few decades ago years, when she was a younger, slimmer woman.

It's too late to escape. She plops down on the settee beside Fliss and pats her knee with a gnarled hand.

'You're too thin, Elsie,' she says, looking sadly into Fliss' eyes. 'I've always said so.'

'Not...' Fliss' voice rasps. She clears her throat and tries again. 'Not, not.' Fliss puts on her sternest face, hoping the eloquence of the spoken word can be replaced with sharpness of gaze. It's no good, Elvira is staring into the distance, lost in the past, with Elsie, whoever she is. She scrabbles around in her large black purse.

'Oh darn. I can never find what I want.' She grunts a sigh that shudders her jelly bosom. The scent of lavender escapes the purse, making Fliss sneeze over and over. Fliss loses her grip on the stick and it falls.

'Terrible, terrible,' she says, reaching for it, but Elvira bends awkwardly to retrieve it as her joints creak in protest.

Delving back into the purse Elvira removes a small bottle of perfume. She flaps her hands in distress and drags a small side table in front of the two of them, crashing it into Fliss' shins as she lets out a satisfied harrumph.

Fliss rubs her shins. Elvira doesn't notice.

'Here Elsie, you hold that.' Elvira hands Fliss a coin purse and sorts through the items on the table. 'Now, where's the lid for that perfume?'

She turns some of the papers over and Fliss realises one is a photograph of a younger Elvira, arm in arm with another woman with an uncanny likeness. Elsie?

Elvira's attention is caught. She traces the photograph with trembling fingers. Fliss sighs, trapped in the moment with her, a moment when they both remember that they once had other lives.

Elvira's eyes are soft and the palest blue as she looks at Fliss. Perhaps she is in the present for a rare instant. She laughs, 'Two old spinster sisters. My twin. Elsie. Gone now, of course.' She wipes a tear and the moment passes as her eyes cloud with confusion and she scoops the scattered items, returning them to the big black bag. She jumps to her feet and scurries off.

GEORGE COMES, touches Fliss' cheek. 'Things will change.'

Fliss jerks forward, leans in to catch his next words.

'You're coming home, Fliss.'

THE STRANGE SUBSTANCE OF DREAMS

Lucy Meredith Carter, Book Of Known Facts, Quirindi, 1955

Nanna's wake was fussy and busy.

She had so many friends.

All the women from the CWA brought food.

When Dad and I got home I was so tired I fell asleep on the lounge.

IN A FOGGY place where the grass is white and spiky I call out, but no one hears. There are shadows everywhere, but they're light, white, not dark, they're moving.

I run. The road is hard under my feet, smooth as glass.

White, feathery trees sway and whisper.

There are people beside me, lined up along the road, peering at the other side.

Pieter is here. 'What are you waiting for? I ask.

'Everything, and everyone,' he says, staring across the road.

The fog shreds apart.

Cloud shapes appear on the other side. The shapes look like people, but not real. Statue people, like old photographs glued to cardboard then whitewashed. The whitewash drips, down, off. Colour leaks through the watery paint.

The cloud people whisper to each other. They look across the road and see us. Both sides rush to the middle. They hug and cry, like people at train stations.

I see Fliss, straight and tall. She walks toward me. 'Hush Lucy, everything's alright.' Her voice is smooth and soft.

She puts her arms around me and stares. I try to see where she's looking, but the cloud is gathering, growing thicker.

Then everyone is gone.

IT'S SUCH a strange dream that I don't know what is real in the morning when I wake up. Dad isn't here. He has left a note to say he won't be long. Esmeralda isn't in my room. I go out to the front yard to look for her.

Mrs Kingston across the road is raking leaves and dry grass after Ewan has mowed their lawn. She keeps looking over at our place. I guess Dad asked her to keep an eye on me while he does errands up the street.

Late afternoon shadows move across the slats of our front verandah. Lightning flashes. I jump off the bench swing so quickly the chains holding it rattle and run to avoid Mrs Kingston's *cooee*.

Thunder clouds are rolling like bonfire smoke right across the sky until it's as dark as night.

There's a brown paper parcel by the front door. It must be a late birthday present. I tear it open.

There are photos, badges, funny little trinkets, a yellow paper—maybe it's a gift certificate, so I can choose something for myself.

I start reading…

Lucinda Meredith Carter, born: 9:30 am, Wednesday, August 15th, 1945, Brisbane Mater Misericordiae Hospital.

Mother: Felicity Anne Ennis, occupation: nurse.

Father: H. W. Meredith, occupation: soldier, (dec).

I check the brown paper for a label. It's addressed to George Carter.

THINGS START buzzing in my head. Who am I? Is Fliss my mother?

I remember Nanna's whispers and sideways looks with her friends at the store, whispers that ended when I arrived. I remember the night of my birthday and the night Nanna died— the funny talk with Dad when he said, 'It's time for the truth.'

My stomach cramps. There's less air in the room.

They thought it was time for the truth.

All that means is there was a right time to lie, and I'll never be able to tell the difference ever again.

THE STORM has arrived. It feels good—the sky is as angry as me, purple and black and wild. Air crackles, lightning flashes.

I hear Dad's truck. I can't face him.

I run outside.

Soon my dress is so wet it's like another skin. A tight skin that has grown on me.

I RUN.

I run and keep running.

I want to go where they'll never find me.

Where they can never lie to me again.

AT THE CEMETERY I crouch down between the graves of *Sylvia Jane Carter*, its white marble shiny with rain, and *Ethel Jane Ennis*.

Its new pile of dirt is muddy. The flowers have drooped but haven't had time to die.

SHeLTer

Ennis family home, Henry Street, Quirindi, 1955

A FULL MOON lights the hut where Harry paces restlessly as lightning slashes across the yard, punishing the earth and dragging a brutal wind behind it that shudders the grass. Haunted by shadows, Harry can't sleep. Then he knows why he's wakeful.

Lucy is running, slapping muddy squelches with bare feet, beside the house, past his door and down the path by the fence-line. She holds her soaked dress up so she can run faster, as wet hair swings wildly, whipping her flushed face.

She doesn't see Harry.

She doesn't see anything. Harry finds her at the cemetery and throws his army coat over her shivering shoulders. 'I don't know where to go,' she says, hiccupping tears.

'Yes,' Harry says, 'you do.'

The kitchen door at Montview is never locked. Lucy knows Fliss' room so well she could find it if there was no light left in the world.

THE DOOR to Fliss' room creaks open. Lucy pads quietly in, peeks to see if Fliss is awake, kisses her forehead. Fliss smiles, then shakes her head. 'Tsk, tsk.' *It's late.* Fliss reaches to flick the night light on. The child is soaked through, hair dripping. Fliss points at the white towel hanging on the rail.

Dropping her dress to the floor, Lucy dries herself quickly. Fliss pulls back the bedclothes. Lucy slides in beside her, curving into Fliss' warm body, before soft sighs become surrender to sleep. Tears fill Fliss' eyes as she gazes at her daughter, cradled in her arms.

The moon is hidden behind storm clouds that have leaked and thundered across a sky that has roared and hailed icy bullets.

AN ELASTIC shadow slants at the French doors. The shadow drips in the torrent outside, removes a hat, enters the room and bids Fliss silent. Seeing Lucy, George smiles crookedly, returns to latch the French doors with a slow clack, shrugs his dripping coat into the basin, then lowers himself into a corner chair. He hardly moves but Fliss sees the soft shine of his eyes in the dark.

Fliss remembers a promise made a decade ago as she lay mute and fragile, 'when the child is old enough—*then*'. Fliss wishes she could tell Lucy of the child's father, of her love for him, of how after he died her grief was all. In the early months, struggling against despair Fliss hadn't known she was carrying a child, then, during a Queensland midnight storm she felt the baby move, becoming Fliss' second secret, as precious and protected as the first.

The day Lucy was born, Fliss' speech died in a slow slur. She watched Sylvia hold her child, surrendering her freedoms to become a mother, to stand in the place of Fliss' shredded body. While George made that infinite leap to loving fatherhood in the stead of a dead soldier he'd never met.

THAT BIRTH-DAY

Jerranjerup, Queensland, 1945

THE HEAT and humidity was hell, even in the evening. It was suffocating. There was no breeze to ruffle the dormitory screens.

Fliss fought dizziness. Pressure was building in her head, screeching like a runaway train on steel rails. She slumped in Sylvia's arms, her eyes filled with alarm. 'I'm so sorry Syl,' Fliss babbled. 'Syl, Syl, my baby sister, Syl, Syl,' the words were coming from somewhere else, somewhere far away and slow.

Fliss' eyes struggled to stay open. 'Syl.'

There was so much Fliss needed to tell her sister, but her voice became a strange instrument, no longer at her command.

Sylvia shouted for help, her voice thick with fear.

The Land Girls flashed and blurred with shocked faces. In a low voice Sylvia told them what to do. They ran to obey her.

Fliss concentrated on the ceiling fans, staring at the whirring blades. The sound hurt her ears. The thrum grew louder, faster, and yet the room was airless. Faces floated in front of her, around her. She beckoned to Sylvia, 'Tell ... tell, tell,' she began. her throat cramped as Sylvia became a blurred silhouette.

Fliss tried to lift an arm to point to the old Bible beside her bed, where her papers were cramped between its pages, but her arm lay dormant.

The words faded, and Fliss with them.

Sylvia murmured. 'She tried to tell me something. I didn't catch it.'

WHEN THE mist that shredded Fliss' days eased, she realised she was at the Mater Hospital in Brisbane, wondering how many days had passed. Testing her body she found that her left side responded, but her right arm and leg were leaden. The light returned so bright it blinded. Words wouldn't come. The temptation to drift into unconsciousness was seductive, but she fought it. Would this body be her prison?

Her mother hovered at her side, anxiety tugging at her face. She stroked Fliss' right hand. Her touch hurt.

Ethel sobbed. Fliss felt the presence of others and tried to focus. A nurse stood in a corner of the room, holding a wriggling bundle.

Fliss' heart leapt. She lifted a hand towards the nurse but found she wasn't moving at all, only dreaming of movement.

George was talking to the bundle. His voice was tender.

A baby cried. Fliss' breasts pinged.

A nurse was holding her baby.

George smiled and reached for the babe. The pink blanket fell away as he cradled the child, rocking her gently. He crossed the room to Fliss. 'Felicity,' he said, as he peeled back the blanket edge. Fliss saw the face of her baby. Her tiny mewling face was out of focus, but Fliss felt the joy the poets write about.

'Meet your daughter,' George said, finally giving words with meaning, as he placed the babe near Fliss' face while still cradling her gently in his large hands. Tears fell.

With a crooked, drawn face, mouth skewed to the side, Fliss smiled her gratitude. She remembered seeing George as a teen pacing the front veranda with his youngest sister in his arms, rocking and shushing, and she knew that while George Carter lived her child would be safe.

THE CLOUD PEOPLE

Lucy Meredith Carter, Book Of Known Facts, Quirindi, 1955

Who am I?

IT'S MURKY and grey in the sea.

The storm under the ocean blows sand through the coral breaking it into pieces.

Fish are rushing about, sobbing.

An eel retreats backwards into his watery cave, snarling at a bright yellow puffer fish seeking refuge from the stinging sand.

Mum is the only still thing in the angry sea. 'Shush, Lucy.' she says, 'can you see them?'

'Who?'

'The cloud people of course.'

'From the long white road?'

'Yes, mustn't miss them.'

I remember the lies. 'Why didn't you tell me, Mum?'

She pouts at a yellow clown fish. 'Tell you what, pet?'

'*You know, Mum!*'

'Your answers are too hard, Lucy.'

'Don't you mean *questions!*' I scream.

'Oh no,' she says, 'it's answers that are difficult. Your father was always better at that...' Her voice grows softer as she glides around me, making me dizzy.

'But he's not my father!' I yell.

The cloud people from the long white road come and take her away.

The seaweed becomes grass, cutty grass that slices my legs as I run, away, away.

Away from long whispering shadows.

A VOICE startles me. 'Everything's okay, Buttons.' Dad is kneeling by Fliss' bed. His hair is sticking up, his clothes are crumpled.

They smell of damp wool, Brylcream, and Dad. I throw my arms around his neck, remembering how hard he fought to tell me things. He pulls me out of bed, hushing me.

'Oh Daddy, I'm sorry.' I cry fat wet tears on his neck. 'You came and found me, and waited. You waited for me like we waited for the cloud people.'

Dad frowns. 'The who?'

'Never mind, Dad. In my dream there was a long white road, Mum, and a blustering storm under the sea.'

Dad makes a gruff noise. 'Then you're okay, Buttons?'

I see his coat in the sink, his ruined hat.

'Uh huh.'

I nod and squeeze his neck. 'Dad, I always wondered, wondered why I didn't have a story; a being-born story like the other kids. All I have is a radio speech, a celebration and the day the war ended. But, Daddy, I know you wanted to tell me, tried to tell me.'

Dad puts my head on his shoulders.

Then he tells me all of it while magpies warm up their early morning voices.

A Being-Born Story

Montview Lodge, Quirindi, 1955

SACHA leaves the French doors open. The clouds are clinging to earth as if they are too tired to ascend to the sky.

Fliss slept indifferently, apprehension gnawing. At morning light, panic grows. Somewhere, George is talking to Lucy, *her* Lucy, *her* child. Her daughter will finally know, but will Lucy understand? If only she could tell Lucy of her father. To convey how precious his child would have been to him? Even if she had speech, how could she explain the secrecy of her love? How impossible it felt?

After, when he died, she could not bear to speak of him. He was gone, torn asunder by shrapnel in a foreign land. What did it matter? What did living matter? All Fliss wished was to lie beside him, join him in that burial place.

Until Lucy. Fliss hadn't known she was pregnant. With the weight loss from grieving, her monthly cycle had disappeared. Then everyone put her weight gain down to farm life at Jerranjerup. Even Fliss believed it for a time. But then, during a tropical Queensland midnight storm Fliss felt a fluttering, felt the babe move. Her child. Then the babe became her second secret. As precious and protected as the first. Fliss remembers all of this. As she waits. Wait for Lucy. Her child, and his.

Waiting, Brisbane, 1945

IN THE MATERNITY Ward waiting room of the Brisbane Mater Misericordiae Hospital a stout woman sat rigid and alone. Ethel Ennis' dark stockings were askew, dragged on in a hurry.

Wearing a tweed suit, she was ill-prepared for Queensland heat. She flinched at the buzzing of call-bells, metallic clangs and bangs, the sharp tang of Lysol.

The birth interrupted a crackly radio broadcast by Ben Chifley, Prime Minister of Australia. Japan had surrendered. The war was over. Along the corridors, a rolling tide of celebration erupted, a cacophony of sound that jangled Ethel's nerves. For her, war's end brought relief, not jubilation.

The babe cried lustily, a worthy announcement of her entrance to the world. She has been wrenched from the comfort of her mother's body with steel forceps and the considerable strength of a worried midwife.

A tall, veiled Sister nodded approval to enter the room where thin cotton curtains muted the brassy shafts of a Queensland winter sun.

George, wearing a tan cardigan with frayed cuffs curved his lean body into the room, followed by Sylvia, who jettisoned her Land Army hat on the wide window-sill and rushed to her frail sister's side, screeching a chrome chair across the floor.

A first-year nurse stiffened at the sound of newborn mewling—the baby lay naked on the scales, forgotten for the more pressing needs of the mother.

Quickly swaddling the infant, the nurse handed her to George, whose arms reached eagerly. He gazed into her squinting eyes, brushed a caress across her cheek, bruised by the forceps delivery. Pressing his lips to her head, he breathed in the scent of new life. The cries ceased as a tiny pink hand secured his slender forefinger.

IN A CORNER of the room, Ethel confronted Sylvia. 'You know what this means? For you and George. You and George will have to raise the child. No one will question, you've been away six months.'

'We can't just steal motherhood from Fliss.'

'She's had a stroke, Sylvia. If she recovers, we'll talk then. We'll keep it in. Won't tell it out.'

Sylvia looked over at Fliss, her glazed eyes, her limp body. Then, a last protest. 'What about George, Mother?'

Ethel gestured at George, holding the babe and whispering to her, oblivious of the conflict engulfing mother and daughter.

Sylvia sighed. 'He won't think twice.'

THE DOOR was flung open by the maternity ward Sister.

Biting down a retort to the junior nurse, she snatched the infant and headed to the pristine confines of the hospital nursery, where regulations dictate babies may only be adored through glass windows at visiting time.

George stared at his empty arms.

In the corridor, the baby cried.

Answers

Lucy Meredith Carter, Book Of Known Facts, Quirindi, 1955

Dad said it is time for the truth.
Maybe I will understand.
Maybe I won't.
Why does it take so long for the truth?

DAD AND I sit on the bench swing. Dad wants time and privacy for our talk.

'Lucy, now you know that Fliss is your mother. She didn't tell anyone she'd married. It was just after the family had found out that your Uncle David had died in France. I guess she didn't want anything to spoil her wedding. She must've only had a few days. I'm sure she meant to tell everyone. But then...'

'She had the stroke.' I say.

'Yes. That changed things. All we could think about was getting her well. She was pregnant with you at the farm and told no one, not even Sylvia. No one knew until she went into labour. At first the specialists didn't expect her to live, and no one expected the baby, you, to survive. But you did, thank God, you did.' Dad is teary now.

I pat his arm.

'The first time I held you,' he says, and his eyes are all dreamy and bright, 'it was like nothing I'd ever experienced before. It was

266

as if you were mine right from the start. You grabbed my finger and wouldn't let go. You slept on my chest. The family talked of adoption, but no one wanted that. Nanna Ennis wanted to take you, but I fought to keep you. Your mother didn't feel ready, she was only nineteen, she hadn't lived.'

'But Dad, she'd had a job in Sydney. She was in the Land Army...'

'Don't be too hard on your mother. She had a sheltered life. She didn't know what she wanted until, well, she went away.'

'Jerranjerup. That was what she wanted. Jerranjerup and that man. The man who already had a family, the one she met there.'

'How do you know about that?'

I look down. It's my turn to fess up. 'There was a letter...' I begin, and then the story of what I know tumbled out. How it made me feel; lost and alone.

'And now, things are more confusing. I mean, you're my dad, my realest real dad. It's so hard to understand that we're not even related. We don't even share ancestors or ... anything.'

I cry then, and Dad doesn't try to stop me. He cries too, until his nose runs and his eyes were red and swollen.

'I was afraid too,' he whispers. 'So very afraid. I was the only one who had no claim on you. But I couldn't have lived without you. Not for a minute.'

'Is that why, is that why you let Mum stay? Let her come and go when she liked?'

Dad thinks for a bit. 'It might have been like that in the beginning, but then, your mum and I had a friendship of sorts. I knew she wouldn't hurt me, or you. She just belonged in two worlds.'

'With that man. What was his name? The man she loved?'

'Eric.'

'And he had kids?'

267

'Three, two boys and a girl, I think.'

'I'm glad she didn't take me away from you. I'll always be glad about that.'

'She loved you. In her way.'

'Hmm. But … Poor Fliss.'

'Yes, it was hardest on her. Seeing you, not being able to be a mother, not able to hold you. Not for a long time anyway. And then she got pneumonia and we nearly lost her again. That's why it seemed the best thing to live together. We meant to talk about it all with you. We hoped Fliss would be able to come home, to Nanna Ennis's place, to her own home, but she was never well enough. And then your mother started going back to Jerranjerup, to the man she'd met, and it was even harder to talk about.'

'Mum must have loved you once. You know, when you were young, when you helped deliver the milk. Tell me about your wedding, when things were good. Tell me about when you married Mummy. Was it like a wedding for a princess?'

'It was … it was everything a wedding should be … white satin, yards of lace. Your mother could sew anything.' Dad smiles. 'I don't know where she got any of it with rations and all.'

'Did you arrive in the old school bus?' Lucy's voice is sleepy.

'No, don't be daft, Lucy.'

FLISS CRIES and laughs when I see her. I had run straight into her room and kissed her tears. 'You wanted so much to tell me, didn't you?' I say.

Fliss says, 'good, nice' and more. 'Sssorrrr…' She tries to say sorry, but it comes out all funny and I wrap my arms around her neck and say, 'at least we've always had each other'.

FLISS' OFFICIAL papers arrive. The marriage certificate. How strange to see that yellowed paper with two names. Fliss' writing is plain and precise, Felicity Anne Ennis, spinster, 26, nurse, joined in holy matrimony by Reverend J.F Renshaw to H.W. Meredith, Private in the Australian Infantry, vehicle driver, 33, bachelor, who signed his name with cursive flair, a jaunty touch.

H.W. Meredith. Fliss must have loved him very much. She left a note with "Meredith" in her Bible. Dad and Mum thought it was a clue about the name she wanted for her child. Perhaps it was, but it was also the name of the man she loved and grieved.

MOVING IN, MOVING OUT

The Ennis family home, Henry Street, Quirindi

GEORGE AND KATYA are married at Montview.

Maria and Sergei fuss over the food. Sacha is a bridesmaid, and Lucy is a flower-girl.

The nurses have ribbons in their hair and join the celebration even though they have to stop Miss Bertram from collecting slices of wedding cake, and other patients from wandering. Barry James wants to dance with everyone. He even spun around Fliss's chair.

Frank Callaway couldn't come because he was taking Old Pat back with him. Lucy was glad Old Pat was going to have a proper home. He didn't want his swag in the back of the pick-up, so it was squashed in the front seat with him.

Blue Winters is here with his wife and children. Sacha catches the bouquet, pushing the nurses aside roughly.

'What a wedding,' says Alexei. They're nuts! They might as well have been hitched at a zoo.'

Lucy sighs. 'I'm so glad about them. We'll soon be living in Nanna Ennis's house, I think. You can visit us there, Alexei.'

'Not if Katya is cooking,' he says.

THE ENNIS HOUSE buzzes with activity as it becomes the Carter house, getting ready to welcome Lucy, Fliss and Katya, now Mrs Carter.

Harry watches Lucy, happily playing chasing games with Alexei accusing him of cheating.

Will she ever know or understand what George and Sylvia sacrificed? Sylvia's dreams of freedom and love. George, whose love for Lucy brought vulnerability. He had no rights, no familial connection to claim, bound to secrecy by the dictates of a grandmother determined to protect reputations.

Strong brown men carry boxes, pulling grubby handkerchiefs from back pockets to mop up the sweat of their labour.

George supervises the placement of furniture, some old, some new. Alexei loudly instructs Katya on sandwich-making. The boarders are leaving at their leisure. Fliss sits in a rocking chair, humming softly with Lucy at her feet, cuddling her kitten.

Life got in the way of all their plans. Life and death.

Lucy runs to Harry and flops onto the story stool. 'Uncle Harry. Look what I found!'

She holds six war medals with frayed ribbons. 'They were in a wooden chest in Nanna's storeroom. A wooden box, beautifully carved. It has my name on it—"Lucy Meredith" that is, so it's all right, you see. And! Uncle Harry, I know they are for me because the envelope has my name on it too! So that makes them twice mine.'

Her voice is earnest. 'I sleep with them under my pillow,' her voice takes on a conspiratorial tone. 'I think they're my father's. My being-born one.'

There are thumping noises from the house.

'Uncle Harry. The boarders are packing, the factory girls have gone, but, will you leave?' Lucy pleads.

Harry pats her head. 'Not yet.'

NEWS

Cameray, Sydney, 1955

A WOMAN with copper-red hair, and a touch of grey, tamed into elegant submission, bends over a letterbox.

She waves to the mailman as she casually casts an eye over the day's letters.

There's a loud tap on the bay window near where she stands.

Turning, she sees her frail mother's face and the end of her cane tapping on the windowpane.

She holds up a scolding finger, then smiles. Her mother is always impatient for mail. She shakes her head.

The last letter makes her heart race…

THE CARTER HOUSE

Lucy Meredith Carter, Book Of Known Facts, Quirindi, 1955

The cottage rooms echo now, except for Mum's old room.
It is piled high with stuff Dad doesn't want to tackle.
We are shifting into the big house.
It won't be the Ennis House any more.
It will be the Carter House then.

KATYA has taken down the curtains, they smelled of cigarette smoke. It's a dull, cloudy day so even though the windows are bare, there isn't much light.

Alexei is standing by the door, shuffling his feet.

'You can come in,' I say. 'The place isn't haunted.'

'Course it isn't. There's no such thing as gh … is this the room your mother died in?' His voice is a bit squeaky, he's trying to gather some bravado, but it isn't working too well.

'Yes,' I say, 'but it was very peaceful.'

'Were you there when she died?' he asks. I think he's going to be weird about it, but he says, 'I've seen lots of dead people at Montview. They usually just look like they're sleeping, or somethin'. You know.'

I bite my lip. 'I was there … but I was only a kid and I was asleep in the chair when Mum died. She just went deeper and deeper into sleep.'

'It's a wonder anyone let you in. Australians are funny like that, funny about death.'

'Nanna Ennis was really mad at Dad for going to school and bringing me home, to say goodbye. I heard her go on at him. Told him he was irresponsible and thoughtless. I thought at first it was because he came and got me in the school bus...'

'He what?' Drove the school bus to pick you up – just you?'

'Yes, well, we didn't have any other car then. He could hardly dink my on his bike all that way.'

Alexei is laughing so hard I want to slap him.

'What's with you two?' Katya props the door open and stares at us with both hands on her hips. 'Not much is getting done in here.'

'Told you she was bossy,' Alexei says to me, pretending to whisper behind his hand. 'We're talking about death. Lucy's mother died in here.'

Katya doesn't scare that easily. 'Oh well, people die in all sorts of places. She died in bed then, that's good. It's interesting, but it isn't getting anything done, is it?'

'What's all this?' Dad sets down a large tea chest. 'Am I the only one packing things up?'

'We're talking about dying,' Alex says, maybe he thinks Dad will be a better target.

'Crikey,' says Dad. 'Russians, you're such a morbid lot. Come on Alexei, there'll be no tea for you if you don't help me carry these boxes.' Dad points his head in the direction of the hallway where there are piles of boxes. Alexei follows to help.

'Now, my sweet pea, how are you holding up with all the bones falling out of the cupboard?' asks Katya.

'It's "skeletons out of the closet", Katya.'

'Ah, same, *schame*, whatever. How are you?'

'There was always something, you know. Something always felt different, I felt different. There were all those silences and pauses

274

when I came into the room, those looks that connected with my eyes, then skidded away, hiding.'

'You're a smart kid, sweet pea. Were you angry? It's a big secret.'

'At first it burned and stung like raw skin peeled away. I was so angry Dad made me promise I wouldn't run away and make them look for me, like when Mum died. I'm trying to see how good it's been for Fliss for the secret to be out. I can't be angry with her. She wanted me to know, she just couldn't tell me. But, I felt like everyone I love has lied. And now, I'm supposed to act as if all this is normal. I feel like I don't know what normal is anymore.'

'I know, sweet pea, I know.'

'It's funny you know. In the last few weeks I felt like Nanna Ennis wanted to say something. Almost … it was weird really.'

'Maybe she knew her time was near. That it was time to fix the past, bring out the truth.'

'I kind of understand why Dad kept it a secret. He didn't want to lose me. He must have been so scared, especially when Mum kept going away. I can't be angry anymore. He cried so hard when he told me. He must love me a lot. A real real lot.'

Katya's eyes are shiny with tears. She takes a deep breath and hold me close, sobbing. 'So much love he has,' she says. 'So much.'

'He loves you too.'

'And that's okay?'

'Of course,' I say, squeezing her until she squeals. 'I thought I'd have to have Mrs Kingston as a step-mother and those horrible Kingston twins as brothers. Yuk!'

Katya gurgles with laughter. 'Ah yes, but now you have dozens of Barashevs.'

'That's okay,' I say, 'I don't have to live with all of them.'

'You wait and see. They are not so easy to escape.'

'I am glad you are okay, sweet pea. One day you'll understand it was all meant to be, you'll see.'

'But … I don't know who my father is.' My voice is a whisper as if saying it out loud will make things worse.

EVERYTHING has finally been shifted into the big house. I'm learning not to call it "Nanna Ennis's", now that it's our place. I decided to tell Alexei. It's easier telling him. That's one good thing about boys, emotions are a waste of time, especially when they're hungry.

And Alexei is starving, claiming he's shifted tonnes and tonnes of boxes on his own. He is prowling the hallway waiting for food.

'Gee whiz, Lucy! So there really was a mystery with your aunt. Wow!' He says it like it's some sort of adventure, so I frown at him.

'Alexei! Are you upsetting Lucy?' Katya stands in the doorway to the kitchen. She's covered in flour. She's "trying" to make meat pies.

Sacha pops out from behind her. 'I told you to wear an apron Katya. You're hopeless. What's this about Alexei?'

'Women!' says Alexei, shoving his slingshot into his back pocket before his sisters see it. 'Traitors the lot of you. I'm not upsetting you, am I Luce?' He puts his hands up in prayer and I swat them down. 'No more than usual,' I say.

THE FRONT DOOR clicks and Dad walks in carrying a parcel.

'George, what have you got there?' Katya puts her hands on her hips and tries to see.

'Fish and chips,' says Alexei, sniffing the air.

'You didn't! Oh George! Have you no faith in my cooking?' Katya pouts.

'Not really, Katya. Your own mother won't let you in the kitchen.'

Sacha giggles.

'It's true,' says Alexei, getting excited. 'She's useless.' He's pleased to have an ally in Dad, but it doesn't last.

'A woman as wonderful as you doesn't need to cook.' Dad grins.

'Good,' says Katya, dusting the flour off her dress, making me sneeze. 'I'll quit while I'm ahead then.'

'I think you mean while you're behind,' Alexei mutters. 'Can we please eat the fish and chips?'

'Thought you'd never ask.' Dad looks at the kitchen table crowded with bowls and sifters. 'Hmm.'

'What about the pies?' Sacha looks towards the oven, then throw up her hands. 'Oh, all right,' she says, dumping the rolling pin on the bench.

'A zoo, I tell you. It's a zoo.' Alexei grabs a chair and sits, and we all follow his lead.

It's a noisy meal.

'Do you want the last piece of fish, Alexei?' Dad notices Alexei's eyes on the food.

'Don't encourage him, George!' Katya scolds.

I roll my eyes, they're like an old married couple already.

'You want I should discourage the boy, Katya?' Dad wears his innocent face.

'Ah, ha, funny man. Sarcasm.' Katya flips the fish onto Alexei's plate and he makes a grovelling face and thanks her.

Everyone is slower than Alexei. We've hardly made a dent in the chips.

'Did you buy all the chips in the shop, George?' Katya stares at the pile.

'I left half a dozen old dry ones.'

IT'S YOU

Lucy Meredith Carter, Book Of Known Facts, Quirindi, 1955

There are so many new things.

We have all been busy.

I have a whole new family now when it was just Dad and me before.

Katya says I will get used to it.

But I'm worried. So much change.

I am waiting for the war records of my birth father.

I have so many feelings I feel at war with myself.

How will I feel when I read those papers?

THE SOUND of the brass door knocker echoes through the house. It's Frank Galloway. He has a large brown envelope and a serious face.

My tea gets stuck in my throat. My hands sweat.

In the sitting room, Dad accepts the envelope. I can't take my eyes off it. I feel my heart beating like castanets.

Katya moves a little closer to Dad and turns warm brown eyes on me.

Dad stares at the envelope, then hands it to me.

I swallow hard. 'Can I … take it, and read it by myself? I'll be all right. Truly.'

'Sure, Buttons. We'll be here. Waiting.'

THE GLOW of the twilight sky overtakes the attic gloominess. I lean against the box that has been my destination for so many months. My hands tremble as I tear open the envelope.

The last bit sticks. I take a deep breath. The first sheet has a record of my father's AIF Division, the 2/17th Battalion, and the day he enlisted, June 30, 1940 at Ingleburn. The next of kin on his enlistment is Lucinda Meredith, his mother, at 14 Addison Road in Camberay, North Sydney.

On the next sheet I find his handwriting. It's the most real thing I've had of him. I trace the large curved writing. *My father's hand.* Private H. W. Meredith. NX34892. My hands begin to tremble.

I turn the page to read and tears fall silently. It's stamped "DECEASED". Scrawled writing in the last column "killed in action, Borneo, 10 June 1945". Like the next three pages, it's a record of where he served. It's all abbreviated so it's hard to make out.

The last page has his burial details. I cry for the man I never knew. Did he die never knowing about me?

Something slides out of the pages and slides to the floor. It's a small cream card. I turn it over. It's a photograph. All the air in the room seeps out.

It's Uncle Harry. Harry the wounded digger living in the hut; the soldier no one else talks about, who always wears a new uniform, who arrived after Sylvia died. Harry the storyteller.

Harry, my father.

I JUMP UP, and run out the back door, down the timber steps, to the hut, calling, 'Uncle Harry. I know, I know.'

I look around the hut. Uncle Harry has gone. He isn't here. It's just an old shed with boards missing—a place of broken windows, rusty tools, old paint tins and garden pots. Like Alexei said, 'just full of old junk'. The way it was before Mum died. Before Esmeralda, and magic. Before Uncle Harry.

I walk past the chicken coop. Esmeralda is there, pecking at feed pellets and brooding over newly-hatched chicks like the other hens. There is no more magic.

I cry more tears than I ever thought I had.

KATYA finds me curled up on the steps.

She holds me and pats me, murmuring something in Russian. She says there's a bright side to everything. I give her an angry look.

'I wish he'd said goodbye,' I say.

'Goodbye? Wish who said goodbye?'

'Never mind,' I say.

We write a letter. Katya thinks she's helping. But Russian is no use for this letter.

THE OTHER LUCINDA

The Carter House, Henry Street, Quirindi

FLISS is anxious, tsk tsking, tapping and slapping. Grabbing word cards and trying to make sentences. Then throwing them aside in frustration.

Katya, as always, is the cure. 'You'll have to stay at Montview for the day if you don't sort yourself out, Miss Felicity. This visit might be too much for you. And you can't stay here on your own.'

'Not, not,' Felicity stills. 'Good, good.'

George crosses the room to sit beside Felicity, taking her hand. 'It's a big day,' he says. Fliss smiles and relaxes.

'It's been a long time, hasn't it? So many years since you saw Lucinda. How long do you think? Ten years?'

Fliss nods. Katya smiles and fusses in the kitchen. Sacha has made sandwiches and cake.

George thought a longer rest on the way would be a good idea, but when he sees the excitement on the faces of Lucy and Felicity, he wonders if that would only make the apprehension greater.

'We'll take a short break for lunch,' says George. He is pleased to set off early. 6 am seems like the middle of the night, but everyone is up and rushing around anyway.

KATYA carries the picnic basket into the lounge room.

'Are we staying a week, Katya?' George asks, then seeing Fliss tense, he regrets the words. 'Marvellous, Sacha's cooking.' This earns him a sour look from Katya.

'Where's my hat and gloves?' asks Lucy, flying through the room in socked feet.

'We're not going to see the queen, Lucy. And I think shoes will be more important than … Do you even own a hat?' says George.

'Don't be dense, Dad.'

'Where's the lemonade?' Katya yells from the kitchen.

'We can buy lunch.' George wonders how King Solomon coped.

'We have to … Oh don't worry, I've found it,' says Lucy. 'Can Alexei come?' Lucy is struggling to drag a glove on.

'Definitely not,' says Katya, rushing into the room with a bottle of lemonade. Lucy pouts, near to tears.

'Come here, Buttons.' George reaches for Lucy. 'It's okay. Your grandmother will love you. Don't be nervous.'

'But she's a proper English lady, with manners and everything, and we're a bunch of Philistines.'

George's eyebrows fly up. 'Philistines. I'm not sure I like that description. I come from a long line of respectable Irish dissidents.'

He turns to look at Fliss, worried that Lucy's nerves will brush off on her, but Fliss is shaking with laughter.

'Are we Philistines, Fliss?' George asks.

'Tsk, tsk. Not too much.'

'Huh! Thanks a bunch.'

Katya hides a grin.

'Oh blast!' Lucy stomps a foot.

'Are you still waging war on those stupid gloves Lucy?' Katya helps Lucy with the errant gloves and shoves her towards the door. 'At least we won't be late Philistines, sweet pea. Move it!'

The Meredith home, Camberay, 1955

THE COPPER-haired woman reads a worn and crumpled letter to her mother, who rubs rheumy hands together as she listens to the news for the tenth time.

'Now the next one,' says the older woman. After the next one is read, she sighs and rests back in the chair. 'Today? Did you say today, Clarissa?'

A timid knock at the door is answer enough.

Lucy rushes into the room in spite of earlier protestations that she will be on her best behaviour and won't disappoint her posh relatives. 'Oh dear,' she says, stalling inside the door.

The older woman's face lights up. 'So like Harry,' says Lucinda Meredith. 'He was always barging in, asking for biscuits and milk. Do you like biscuits and milk, my little namesake?'

For perhaps the first time in her life Lucy is speechless, merely nodding.

LUCINDA Meredith is charming, and very British. Her skin is a delicate pink, hardly lined for her seventy years. She is visibly moved to see Felicity, and holds her close, patting her back with trembling hands. Lucinda, the elder, introduces her daughter, Clarissa, who graciously greets everyone, then claims Fliss' presence beside her on the sofa, purloining Lucy with her other hand.

'Oh Felicity, I never thought to see you again. I searched and … oh it doesn't matter now, you're here. And bringing me my lovely granddaughter. So like you, Felicity. But she has Harry's smile.'

LUCY STARES in awe at Clarissa. Hair so like her own on another person!

'Wow,' says George. 'Who knew?'

Clarissa bends to kiss Lucy's forehead. She laughs. 'We're quite the twins, aren't we?'

Fliss claps her hands and Lucy wonders if Fliss knew about their likeness all along.

Lucy watches her grandmother closely. She asks if there are any photographs.

'Oh my, yes,' says Lucinda. 'But not many, I'm afraid.'

'One would be wonderful,' Lucy leans towards the old woman and picks up her hand, caressing it. 'If it's not too much trouble.'

The old woman's face lights up. She holds Lucy's hand in both of hers. 'Let me tell you about Harry,' she says.

Clarissa brings a photograph album and hands it to her mother. 'I'll take George and Katya to see the roses,' she says, ushering them to the back garden.

When they return, three heads are bent over the photos, three generations.

Lucy is holding the album as Fliss points and Lucinda weaves the stories that bridge the gaps of the past and enchant Lucy. She stops to pat Lucy's face tenderly. The old woman is tiring.

'Would you like tea anyone?' Clarissa serves tea in an old tea service that has seen better days.

'We left a lot of things behind when we came to Australia, but brought everything of value with us. How lucky we were.' The old woman accepts a cup with one hand, steadying it with the other.

'Mum,' says Clarissa, 'don't we have some of Fliss's things … in a box somewhere?'

'Oh my, yes! There's some clothes, a lace mantilla and a green silk dress.'

After Fliss weeps softly at the sight of the dress, she holds it up to Lucy's face.

'I could remake it for Lucy,' offers Clarissa.

'Oh thank you!' Lucy flies into Katherine's arms. 'Thank you,

Aunt Clarissa.'

After fairy cakes and photo albums, Lucinda, the elder, grows weary, and naps in the chair.

LUCY, pressed by her new aunt, Clarissa, brings out her Book Of Known Facts. Clarissa smiles and rests back in the three-seater lounge covered with English roses. She expects a childish tone and is surprised.

Lucy reads stories of a digger in Tobruk, Mersa Matruh, Deolali, Bombay, and the Nashik district of Maharashtra.

Clarissa startles forward. These moments, these snippets. Like those letters tied with frayed white tape in a drawer in her armoire, but here with more detail, more life. 'Harry,' she whispers, 'oh my. How…?'

At the mention of Harry's name, Lucinda, the elder, rouses from sleep, eyes wistful. 'I saw him, you know, our Harry. He looked so handsome in his uniform. It was just last week, I think.'

FLISS FALLS asleep as soon as she is in the car, but Lucy is full of chatter. 'What lovely people. Grandmother is so delightful, don't you think?'

'Didn't take you long to get a plum in your mouth, Lucy,' Katya says, but Lucy doesn't rise to the bait, she merely scratches her nose inelegantly and pulls off her gloves.

'Gosh darn these things make your hands itchy,' she says.

THaT GOODBYE

Carter family home, Henry Street, Quirindi, 1955

LUCY wanders down to the hut. Perhaps hoping that magic will return to her life. But the hut is just an old shed with boards missing. The way it was before the wake. Before Esmeralda, before magic.

When a man arrived and told her the magic story of Esmeralda, the gypsy girl who gave sanctuary to a misshapen man, while bringing comfort to a grieving child.

The hut is no more than a broken place of cracked windows, rusty tools, old paint tins and garden pots. Bare and stark.

Lucy finds the story stool. There is a leather-bound volume of *The Hunchback of Notre Dame*, autographed *with love* by one Harry W. Meredith.

She sits under the mulberry tree where Harry hung his shaving mirror and she reads.

A shadow passes over the page.

'Oh, Uncle Harry. You're here! I knew you would be, I just knew.' Lucy's hair glows like fire in the early morning sun.

She watches Harry with those green eyes, so like Felicity's, then the words rush out as she scrubs at her eyes to halt the tears.

'Oh Harry! You're my father, Harry William Meredith. I'm named after your mother, Lucinda Meredith—the name on the carved wooden box.' She's breathless from her dash to me. 'When did you know about me? That I'm yours?'

'Forever and never,' Harry says, 'knowing is like that sometimes.'

She looks at Harry's kit bag. 'Oh, your kitbag, you're all packed … and you're wearing your digger's hat. You never wear your hat…' Her voice is flat, she measures the words with meticulous care. 'You're leaving.'

'Yes, Lucy, still we've been lucky to have this little time…' Harry raises his hands, then drops them at my sides.

He sees his medals are pinned awkwardly on her dress with safety pins. She looks down at them. 'The ribbon is torn, but I'll never *ever* fix it … I'll leave them just as they are. I'll wear them,' she says, her voice firmer. 'In the Anzac parade. Every year. I'll wear them for you.'

Harry's smile is wistful.

'Oh Uncle Harry.' She runs to him and hugs his leg. He gathers her into his arms and dries her soft tears.

'Will you…?' Her voice catches, 'will you watch over me?' The words are tentative and low as she looks up at the vast washed-out blue of the sky '…There? Like you have here?'

'I came back for you, didn't I?'

Harry watches Lucy standing under the mulberry tree, poised in the sunset. The medals on her dress glow like gold, new again.

NOT YET

Carter family home, Henry Street, Quirindi, 1955

FLISS is back in the room of her childhood. The same gauze curtains, teased by midnight breezes flutter through the room.

Lucy sleeps on the trundle bed beside her.

Her daughter. The corner of her mouth twitches, like Harry.

Lucy begged George to drag the trundle in, and as always, he was happy to oblige. Fliss smiles in the dark. As long as George Carter lives, Fliss knows her child will be adored.

THE GREEN silk dress hangs on the wardrobe door, draped in the folds of the mantilla, shimmering like pale, still water.

Fliss wills it to enter her dreams. To drift with her, joining her to Harry. Yet sleep slips further and further. Perhaps she will not dream at all. Maybe the gods will never her sleep again, knowing as they do, how much she yearns for it.

Thunder shudders the room.

The tin roof plays the music of the heavens, as raindrops dance down the windowpane. Lightning fills the room, brighter than day.

A dandelion kiss flutters on her lips.

She feels his presence breathes his name. *Harry.*

She asks if he has come to take her away.

He shakes his head sadly, *not yet.*

288

The Lost Stories
Of
Lucy Meredith Carter

& The Book Of Known Facts

EPILOGUE

Lucy Meredith Carter, Book Of Known Facts, Quirindi, 1955

The carved box sits at the end of my bed now.
We found words carved on the bottom.
"Egypt 1942, Harry W. Meredith, for my wife, Felicity."
Frank said Harry made the box at Tobruk.
The answers were here all the time.

ESMERALDA has given up magic and joined the other hens in the pen. She winks when I walk past, as if she's pleased we've shared secrets. She still flies onto my lap when I'm sitting outside, just like before.

I told Katya and Dad I didn't want a fuss for my 11th birthday, but Katya said she wasn't having any of that nonsense so we had a party at Montview. Alexei moaned 'there must be somewhere else to celebrate stuff'. Katya told him it was Montview or her cooking so he kept quiet.

Fliss spends her weekends at home with us, and the rest of the time at Montview. Some of the town folk knew all along Fliss was my mother. Most just don't care, so not as much changed as I thought. Dad said so many families got mixed up in the war that no one will bother about our story.

Old Pat Calloway died in a proper hospital, a home for war veterans. He was surrounded by family. A family he was still confused about, but they didn't mind. Frank drops by, sometimes with his wife and kids. He and Dad have long chats or go fishing.

I start a new year at school in a few weeks. Katya took me to buy my books and helped me cover them with brown paper. When it came time to write my name on them, Katya just looked at me and said, 'Put whatever you like, Lucy', so I wrote Lucy Meredith Carter, because I've always had the right name. My mum, Sylvia, found a note in Fliss's Bible with 'Lucinda Meredith' written on it, so that's what they called me, even though they didn't know about my father, Harry Meredith.

I wore Harry's medals in the Anzac Day Parade, just as I'd promised him. I got all choked up walking with the soldiers with his medals pinned on my right shoulder. The soldiers who've earned the medals wear theirs on the left side, over their hearts. I looked up and blew a kiss to the soft blue sky.

I took the war records and Harry's medals to school the day before the Parade. There was a man from Legacy there talking about how the war affected people. I told my story and the kids were interested. They didn't think it was weird. One of the girls said it was a shame I'd never met my real father. I nearly said, 'Oh but I have!' I stopped myself, because there would be questions, and some questions just don't need answers.

I'm okay about it all now. I guess some things are better than magic.

Image 1: Dancing man[2]

Image 2: The First One Hundred

Ingleburn, NSW. 1940-05-16. A group photograph of the "first hundred" members of the 2/17th Infantry Battalion.

---

[2] Australia Screen, a NFSA website, Movietone Special: Peace: Australia Celebrates https://aso.gov.au/titles/newsreels/movietone-special-peace/clip2/. This clip shows joyous celebrations erupting in Sydney streets at the declaration of peace after the Japanese surrender. Footage includes enormous crowds crammed shoulder to shoulder in the city. A tracking shot from a moving vehicle shows the famous image of the dancing man who does a pirouette and doffs his hat for the camera.

Image 3: Australian soldiers on shore leave, Bombay

Bombay, India. 1942-03-26. Australian troops returning from The
Middle East, take advantage of shore leave to stretch their legs and to see
the sights.

*Image 4: 2/17ᵗʰ Battalion soldiers attending to sore feet in
Tripoli*

Tripoli, Syria. 1942-04-21. Members of the 2/17th Infantry Battalion
nursing sore feet at their bivouac on the aerodrome after the 100 mile
route march from Latakia to Tripoli.

Image 5: Smoke break, Tobruk

Members of the 2/17 Infantry Battalion are enjoying a smoke while they scan the horizon for signs of enemy activity. They are part of the 'Bush Artillery' and are operating a captured Italian 75/27 model 06 field gun.

Image 6: 2/17ᵗʰ at Tobruk, camouflage

Tobruk, Libya. 1941-08-27. Advanced headquarters for 2/17ᵗʰ Infantry Battalion looking north-west toward The Derna Road. Camouflage played an important part in the Western Desert Campaign.

Image 7: 2/17ᵗʰ Intelligence Section

Men of the Intelligence Section, 2/17th Australian Infantry Battalion,
digging a new home.

Image 8: Tobruk, 2/17ᵗʰ at underground El Adem Aid Post

Tobruk, Libya. 1941-09-30. 2/17th Infantry Battalion's Regimental Aid
Post in the El Adem Sector.

Image 9: Meal preparation in dugout at El Alamein

AUSTRALIAN WAR MEMORIAL 025051

A Member of the 2/17th Australian Infantry Battalion, preparing a meal from the entrance to his dugout in the forward area on the El Alamein Front.

Image 10: 2/17ᵗʰ Mail delivery

AUSTRALIAN WAR MEMORIAL 059138

Private C.G. Bailey of the 2/17th Australian Infantry Battalion collects his armful of mail

Image 11: 2/17ᵗʰ with Dyak guides at Borneo

Kuala Belait, Borneo. 27 June 1945. Members of a patrol of 2/17ᵗʰ in a native canoe on a river patrol. The Dyaks with them act as guides.

Image 12: 'Land Girls'[3]

Australian Women's Land Army members working on Fowler's Farm at Home Hill in the Burdekin district during WW2.

[3] Dunn, P 2015, Australian Women's Land Army in Australia During WW2, *Oz at War*, online blog, https://www.ozatwar.com/ausarmy/wla.htm

www.ingramcontent.com/pod-product-compliance
Lightning Source LLC
Chambersburg PA
CBHW010259100726
47904CB00011B/2662